Praise for the Burton & Lamb series

The Burton & Lamb series always provid~   nts
and a thoughtful exploration o̶f̶   ly
to make a big difference in ˎ
Crime Review

Intelligently conceived and cleˑ   ˑievant and
engaging
Ted Childs, creator of *Kavanagh QC*

An evocative and gripping thriller, where the present day meets the technology of the near future. Abi Silver raises startling questions about the dependence and interdependence of technology in our lives in this pacy courtroom drama
Maha Khan Phillips, author of *The Curse of Mohenjodaro*

A refreshing debut from a former lawyer – a first-rate courtroom drama
Daily Mail

Abi Silver has carved a niche exploring the moral and practical issues thrown up by technology, and how the law responds. She is adept at turning complex legal debate into compelling legal thrillers... If *The Cinderella Plan* finds its way onto your holiday reading list, expect to deliver a favourable verdict
Jewish Chronicle

You may not have heard of Abi Silver, but if her new book, *The Pinocchio Brief,* is anything to go by, you soon will have done
Jewish News

A quirky and charming debut novel that combines modern technology with a good old-fashioned courtroom drama
Irish Independent

Was the man in the driving seat or the car itself responsible for the fatal accident? And is it the AI or the flaws of the humans involved in creating it that poses the greater danger? Tense thriller wrought from a cutting-edge subject
Times Crime Club

An enjoyably elaborate and distinctive variation on the courtroom thriller
Martin Edwards, author of *Gallows Court* and the Lake District Mysteries

Raymond Maynard, a precocious 15-year-old schoolboy, is accused of the brutal murder of one of his teachers. Silver, a former solicitor, conjures up a shock for his defence team: the boy's testimony will be judged by a machine. If this sounds far-fetched, it's not. Swingeing cuts to legal aid budgets around the world are resulting in ever increasing digitalisation. Silver's taut thriller provides ample food for thought as the defence team confront the implications of machines dispensing justice
The Times

Like a chess grandmaster, Silver expertly manoeuvres the pieces of her plot to craft a tense, intelligent mystery
Chris Simms

Pinocchio is the name of a newly developed device that detects lies and which the government has decided to use in law courts. It is supposed to perceive and interpret facial expression and body language, its conclusions providing more accurate judgements than any jury could reach. Regarding this machine as infallible is a dangerous and plausible idea that is central to this fascinating tale... This is a good read and an excellent first novel
Literary Review

An intense and compelling legal drama – quite wonderful
Geoffrey Wansell

A legal thriller with a neat angle and loads of twists: I cannot tell a lie, this is an excellent read
Sunday Sport

An ingenious and compelling whodunnit
The Times

A sparklingly clever and entertaining mystery with a juicy helping of courtroom drama
Daily Telegraph

It is Abi Silver's imaginative touches as well as her thorough legal knowledge that make her courtroom thrillers stand out
Jake Kerridge

Rumpole of the Bailey, Kavanagh QC, Perry Mason – now joining their ranks is Judith Burton
Jewish Chronicle

More a whatdunnit than a whodunnit...it is a good story which discusses factual issues society will have to tackle. Previous books by the author have won well-deserved praise
Law Society Gazette

Also by Abi Silver in the Burton & Lamb series:

The Pinocchio Brief
The Aladdin Trial
The Cinderella Plan
The Rapunzel Act

THE
MIDAS GAME

ABI SILVER

Published in 2021
by Lightning Books Ltd
Imprint of Eye Books Ltd
29A Barrow Street
Much Wenlock
Shropshire
TF13 6EN

www.lightning-books.com

ISBN: 9781785632426

Cover by Nell Wood
Typeset in Minion Pro and Brandon Grotesque

British Library Cataloguing in Publication Data
A catalogue record for this book is available from the British Library.

Printed by CPI Group (UK) Ltd, Croydon CR0 4YY

For Nao and Jen

Sisters, sisters
There were never such devoted sisters

Irving Berlin
(and frequently sung to me by my Grandma Kitty)

'Words can't even explain it right now, I'm just so happy'

Kyle 'Bugha' Giersdorf,
on winning the Fortnite World Cup Finals, in July 2019

PART ONE

LONDON, NOVEMBER 2019

1

Steady, steady, keep my hands steady. Forward, forward, ease my way forward.

Which way now? Straight ahead, I'm exposed. Left or right, I'm a sitting duck. Stay here? Not an option.

Need a strategy.

Stay alive, that's a strategy. Ha! But how?

Keep moving to stay alive. That sounds better.

Heart rate's up. Take a breath. Look around. I'm going out there, across that wasteland.

So, here goes.

Moving fast, cover the distance in double time.

I'm fast, but they are too. Need to get to the higher ground. If I'm stuck down here, I'm a goner.

How far to the big hill? Read the map. Breathe.

Not too far. Pace myself. Take it in stages.

Almost at the first buildings, check they're empty. Check.

Take refuge inside. Check.

Mission accomplished. Easy peasy.

Refill ammo. Clip it on, turnaround. Check location.

How'm I doing?

Eighty-seven left and I'm closing in. Seems quiet for now. Oh God.

One to my left. Bam! Got him. Ew. One more behind that pillar. He's a crafty one. No rush. Wait for him to poke his head out and then blow him away.

How's my ammo? Needs refreshing. Not till I get him though.

Come on baby, rise and shine. Come on! My finger's itchy on this trigger.

There he is. Bam! Bam! Bam! Yesss!

Feeling good. Blood pumping.

Took a while for him to die. Pity, he had a cool bandana.

Take a look around. All alone. Then, I'll have it. Anything else? His ammo too, and that nice little customised knife. Talk about grave-robbing.

How'm I doing? Eighty-one still standing. I'm doing my bit for the numbers. Where's everyone else? Come on, if you're hard enough [laughs].

Hey buddies, there's a storm coming. Better get moving. Back to that plan. Move on up.

Check my health. I'm going to drop some cash and grab some armour.

Hm, mmmmmm [hums through teeth].

Moving forwards. Where's that hill? Head for the higher ground.

Come on! Get those toned limbs moving. What's the point of cardio, if you can't get going when the going gets tough. Ha!

Tricky bit here. Like a rat run. Mustn't get caught.

There's someone behind that wall. If I wanted to hide, that's where I would be. I was wrong. I'm slipping. Take a moment. Breathe.

Check the location monitor. Someone coming in fast from the left, again. Is that my weak side? Where are they, where are they, where are they? Bam! That's where they were. Yeuch.

Time to use my grenade. Three of them ahead in that barn. Just pull the pin and toss it in. Whoosh. Wow. Look at those guys burn. Char-grilled. Sixty-three left. And I'm coming to terminate them all.

Taking stock. What did I forget? Bounty? I could try that. Why not?

Jump in the truck. Oops, my steering's not the best. Which way? Good job I can use a compass.

Where are they? Over there, I think, behind the aircraft hanger. Out I get, running forward. My feet are pounding; thud, thud, thud. Feel the vibration all through my body. Ready for a fight. Breathe.

First one's close now, I can smell him. There? No, false alarm. There? Missed him. There? Bam, bam, bam. Gone, obliterated. Bounty cashed. Kerching!

Feeling good. Everything's pumping.

Seconds ticking down. Buy another grenade and something to boost my health to survive that storm. Not a second too late. Here it comes, from the East, destroying everything, bending low. Wait it out. Fifty-two left.

Taking stock. Slow my breathing. Where was I before all this? The bounty, the storm. The hills. That was it. Run for the hills, the higher ground. That's what they said. That's where I'm going.

Getting hot. Really hot. Should've opened a window. Too late now.

Focus, focus. Hot, hot, hot. All that blood making me hot.

Can't have sweat rolling into my eyes. Flick my head back, just for a second and it should splash off. Don't take my eyes off that doorway. There's sure to be someone behind it.

Oh God, oh God, I need to speed up. They're catching up on me. Higher ground. Need to get to that higher ground. How to get there faster? Come on, come on. Use my brain. Think. No time to think. Breathe. No time to breathe. There, over there. A microlight. Can I fly it? Let's have a go.

Side to side, wobble, wobble, pull back on the joystick, harder. Now I'm getting the hang of it. I'll need to rise quickly. Shots coming from the ground. What was that? Too close for comfort. Check location. I'm getting away. Yay. You can't catch me. Five hundred, 1,000, rising still. At 2,000 feet I'm safe.

This is crazy. Fly like a bird. I could get used to this.

Whoa. Don't look down. Gun battles galore, blood and guts spewed over the corpse-strewn ground. Take my time. Still my pulse. Exhale.

Only twenty-two left. I'm doing pretty well for a rookie. I should buy a life. That's what they said, but nowhere to cash in, not up here. But where to come down? Can't stay up here for ever.

Time to land then. Those rocks should give me cover.

Grenade from the right. Shakes the ground. Shakes the world. A flash and another. And now, my legs won't move. I'm down in the dirt, horizontal, prone, prostrate. Down but not out.

Get up! Get up! Get up!

Rushing, pounding, thudding.

Hot, hot, hot.

I'm fading fast. Was I hit? Don't think I was hit.

There's no blood. It's in my ears, in my head; bumping, pumping, thumping.

It's getting dark. Two more hours of daylight, but it's getting dark.

No air. I'm outside but there's no air. Breathe. I can't breathe. I can breathe but I can't breathe.

Am I alive or am I dead?

I just need to get to the higher ground.

2

CONSTANCE LAMB STOOD opposite Hackney police station, shifting her weight from one foot to the other, her breath freezing in the cold November air. She hadn't been told much about why she'd been summoned: another youth in trouble, eighteen years old, burglary, they'd said and she'd considered staying home and letting the job pass to the next in line. But then she'd heard her own voice, detached, some distance away, agreeing to take this one, even as her outstretched hand drew back the curtain and she saw the frost glistening on the pavement outside.

Cross with herself, confused as to the precise mechanism by which her mouth had said *yes* when her brain had said *no*, she had zipped up her boots, thrown on her thick coat, turned off the oven – her dinner would have to wait – and walked briskly to her destination. Except now she hesitated, on the threshold, taking a moment to gather her strength. Not her physical strength; it was less than half a mile's walk from her flat, although she'd moved quickly to keep warm, tucking her scarf in tight, her hands thrust deep into her pockets, and she was hardly bothered by the distance.

No, it was inner strength, resolve, determination that was required on these occasions; assimilating information calmly, efficiently and from disparate sources, the need to act professionally, the requirement to gain and maintain the trust of a total stranger and the necessity to make the right decision about next steps, when so much depended on it.

She made a tunnel with her mouth and blew out three short breaths, tipping her head back and watching the white plumes stretch forwards and up. Then she crossed the road and went inside.

The policewoman on duty – uniform too tight, hair scraped back in a high ponytail – nodded to Constance and waved her off down the corridor.

'Number five,' she said.

'I don't have any details yet,' Constance called out, over her shoulder.

'You do now.'

Constance turned at Chief Inspector Dawson's voice. He was thinner than the last time they had met. Was it a deliberate health drive or had he been unwell? His eyes were fine points of light, his cheeks were sunken and his hair, cut short at the sides, was greyer than she remembered. And it had only been a matter of weeks.

He handed her a wedge of papers and accompanied her to the interview room. Constance sat down without removing her coat, and her eyes skimmed over them, the words 'murder' and 'robbery' shouting out to her from the page, before settling on the name of the victim.

'They told me burglary,' she said, knowing, as she spoke that her complaint was meaningless.

So what if she'd expected some trumped-up petty theft, which would occupy her for half an hour? She was here now and she would have taken the murder charge anyway; she always did. Dawson shrugged and she noticed him wincing at the involuntary movement; the tiniest twitch of one corner of his mouth giving him away.

'What's the connection? Between my client and the victim?' Constance asked.

'That's what I'm hoping he's going to tell us.'

'I mean, what evidence have you got?'

Dawson sat back and his eyes found hers. 'We've got fingerprints, his prints in her apartment.'

'Anything else?'

'We'll have the post-mortem results shortly.'

'What makes you think she was murdered? Two days ago, you thought it was natural causes. I saw the headline. *Eminent psychiatrist slips away in her sleep.*'

'You noticed it was her.' Dawson's tone was conciliatory.

'Elizabeth Sullivan. There can't be two of them, both dying on the same day, on the same street. I do keep up.'

Dawson smiled. 'That's why we have post-mortems, isn't it?' he said.

'And the burglary?'

'Her handbag was stolen. There may be other items too. We've yet to locate any family who can verify what's missing.'

'You've found the bag since?'

'Not yet.'

'All right. And my client – Jaden Dodds?'

'We picked him up this afternoon. Like I said, his prints match. He's a neighbour.'

'Cause of death?'

'We don't know yet.'

'But no signs of violence.'

'I can't say.'

'Was the news report wrong then?' Constance suddenly felt tired and hungry and conscious that her need for sleep and food were unlikely to be satisfied for some time.

'I can't disclose anything. But I'll let you know what I can, when I can.' Dawson stood up.

Constance tutted. This was useless.

'Can I see Jaden now, please?' she said.

'Sure. I'll have him brought in.'

***

Jaden Dodds entered the room and sat down opposite Constance. He was wearing an expensive-looking bomber jacket, with an orange camouflage pattern, a crisp, white t-shirt with 'King' printed on it and a beanie hat. On his feet, he wore striking canary-yellow trainers; the right one had the word 'human' written on it in black lettering and the left, the word 'race'. He crossed one foot over the other and rested his hands on the table. He had a cut above his right eyebrow, just starting to crust.

Constance waited till the police officer had gone, then picked up her chair and moved it around, tucking it in at the table end, so she was seated to his left side.

'Hello Jaden.'

Jaden didn't respond. Constance also leaned forward, her fingers almost reaching his.

'My name's Constance Lamb. I'm a solicitor. You spoke to someone at my office earlier, Julie, I think it was. I'm here to advise you.'

Jaden shifted his hands from the table top to his lap and blinked lazily.

'I didn't do nothing,' he said, staring straight ahead.

'Did you know Dr Sullivan?'

'Who?'

'Dr Elizabeth Sullivan. The lady who's been killed.'

'I don't know no Dr Sullivan.'

'Dr Elizabeth Sullivan of 38 Dunloe Close, E2, found dead on Saturday morning, at her apartment. You don't know her?' Constance took out her phone. 'It was in the papers. OK, not the top story and more local. Here's a photo. Why don't you take a look?' She held her phone out to him. He turned his head, scanned the image and then he focused on Constance for the first time.

'She told me her name was Liz. I didn't know she was no doctor,' he said. And, for a second, the mask of bravado slipped, his voice quivering as it tapered off. Constance allowed him to recover his composure before pressing on. Exposing him too soon would not help build his trust.

'You knew her well?' she continued.

Jaden didn't reply.

'How did you get the cut over your eye?'

Jaden shrugged.

'All right. I'll tell you what I know and you join in when you can. Two days ago, this lady, Dr Elizabeth Sullivan, was found dead at home, in bed. You live directly opposite at Montagu Court, flat 31. The police believed she had died in her sleep and that's how it was first reported. Like I said, more local interest than national. Now they're looking at it again, thinking she might have been killed and your fingerprints are inside her flat. That's why you're here. What were you doing in her flat?'

Jaden shrugged again.

'What were you doing there?'

'I just helped her with some shopping.'

'You helped her with some shopping?'

'Yeah.' The bluster had returned, but that was all right. At least he was talking.

'Did you know her?' Constance asked.

'To say hello to, that's all. She had some shopping in the car. I was walking past. I asked if she wanted help.'

'And you took the shopping into her apartment?'

'Yeah.'

'Can you remember what was in the shopping?'

'Nar. Just shopping. Tins and stuff.'

'What supermarket was it from?'

'I don't know.' He looked at her again, this time for longer, his mouth closed tight to emphasise the finality of that response, his eyes challenging her to contradict him, goading her on. Constance chose, instead, to take a step to the side, rather than engage in full-on combat.

'Was that the only time you've been in her apartment?' she asked. Jaden registered the shift away from a full confrontation. His shoulders relaxed.

'Yeah,' he said.

'How long did you stay?'

'I just dropped the shopping and that was it.'

'You were there, what, one, two minutes?'

'That's it, yeah.'

'But you didn't know she was a doctor, a psychiatrist?'

'Why would I know that? Why would I care?'

'She might have told you.'

'Nar.'

'What did you do after you helped her with her shopping?'

'I went home.'

'And then?'

'I was home all night.'

'Can anyone confirm that?'

'Yeah. Nathaniel can.'

'He's a friend of yours?'

'We live together.'

'Where can I find him?'

'He'll be at home.'

Constance made a note. 'What do you do for a living?'

'I'm a gamer.'

'What does that mean?'

'Gamer, gaming, online gaming. I have a live stream on Twitch and a YouTube channel.'

'That's what you do for work?'

'Something wrong with that?' Jaden uncrossed and then re-crossed his legs, the word 'human' now taking a solid stance on the floor and 'race' nodding agreeably at Constance.

'How would I find you on Twitch?' she said.

'JD & Nath. Take a look. We have 120K followers. It's totally legit. We did a live show that night. Lots of people tuned in. Maybe you want to talk to them all, too, to…corroborate my alibi.'

Constance sat back. She was the one who had shifted her chair close to Jaden in the first place, to be friendly, to gain his confidence. That was one of her usual tactics, but it was having no noticeable impact on him. The story he was telling, whether it was true or not, was not recounted especially for her. The same words, the same gestures would have been churned out for anyone occupying her role.

Now she wished she had remained more distant, asserted some authority. That might have worked better, might have paved the way for Jaden to confide later on, when it finally dawned on him that he needed her help. It was like those mothers who constantly told their kids they were their 'best friend'. Didn't they realise that was not what kids needed from a parent?

'How did you get the cut above your eye?' Constance asked again, trying to harden her tone.

'I cut myself shaving,' he said.

'Would you like me to tell any family you're here?'

Jaden shook his head. 'No one to tell, thanks. Just Nath. And he knows where I'm at.'

***

'You haven't got anything on him,' Constance tapped on the window of Dawson's office. He was sitting staring at the screen of his PC. He beckoned her in.

'What was that you said? He's ready to sign a full confession?'

Constance sat down and scrutinised Dawson. In the artificial light of his room, his skin had taken on a sallow hue.

'Hardly,' she replied. 'He lives locally. He helped her with some shopping, end of.'

'He has a record.'

'Possession, I've seen. It's nothing.'

'We've got neighbours saying there are lots of young people hanging around the flat. He's probably been dealing.'

'Probably? You know that means nothing, either. He's a celebrity, that's why kids hang around him.'

'A celebrity?'

'YouTube. Twitch. He has lots of followers.'

'Blimey, he's pulled one over on you, all right. In how long? Twenty minutes.' Dawson stretched his arms up above his head, exposing two dark patches beneath his arms. Constance looked away. 'There was also a caution for theft. Did he mention that one?' he said.

Constance was silent.

'And did you ask him whether he carried the shopping into her bedroom?' Dawson tried again.

'What?'

Dawson smiled and lowered his arms and, for the first time that day, he resembled the Dawson she knew.

'Dr Elizabeth Sullivan, found dead in bed, bag stolen; money, keys, mobile phone. Your client was seen with her, chatting, going into her flat. No *shopping* was mentioned. And his fingerprints were everywhere, including in her bedroom...all over her bedroom. I think you need another word with Mr YouTube Celebrity Jaden Dodds,' he said. 'And once the post-mortem is complete, I think we'll all be sitting down together for a nice group chat.'

3

THOMAS SULLIVAN SAT in his room, his window open, the last scrap of a cigarette hanging from his fingers. Normally, they wouldn't let him smoke; no one was allowed – not even teachers – but they were hardly going to argue today, two days after his mother's death.

He took a final puff and then stubbed the cigarette out on his history book. It left a brown hollow in the cover and gave him a momentary pang at his unnecessary act of vandalism. Then he sank his finger into the dip and allowed it to rest there. He looked across to the two beds, one neatly made, the other a testament to his disrupted night, its covers flung back, exposing his flamingo-patterned pyjama bottoms.

The pristine bed belonged to David, his best friend, but David had been evicted, temporarily, on the basis that Tom might want his own space for a few days. He shook his head. They really hadn't a clue. Granted, they probably didn't have a dedicated 'how to deal with traumatised orphans' policy, but he would have expected some common sense. Anyone with an ounce of empathy would not have left him alone for hours on end.

As he turned away, he caught a fleeting glimpse of his mother's face, smiling at him in that wistful way of hers. Sometimes, he wondered if it was regret for all the things she'd lost; a husband, those early milestones of his, her youth. Catching her in one of those moments, he'd asked her once, 'Why do you look so sad?' But she had shaken her head and held him close. 'I'm not sad,' she'd whispered, her fingers tangled through his hair, pressing his face against her neck. 'I'm never sad. Not when you're here.'

Tom reached for the cigarette packet; only two left. It hardly mattered. There'd be more if he wanted them. You could get most things you wanted, most of the time, and no one would deny him now, in his hour of need.

'Pleased to see you're awake and up. How are you today?'

If Mr Jenkins had knocked, Tom hadn't heard him. But then all sounds were muffled to him, as if he was hearing underwater or through dodgy headphones, the rise and fall of familiar voices all siphoned into a monotone of sameness.

'Will you come down for breakfast?' Mr Jenkins enquired.

Tom wondered if his headmaster really was relieved to see him alive and dressed, or if he would have preferred to find the room empty; Tom run away to join the circus or splattered on the ground immediately below his second-floor window. Maybe that was the real reason he had declared Tom should be left alone; to allow him to do 'the honourable thing', so as not to be a burden to anyone.

That made Tom think of the poem they had studied in English on Friday, before he heard the news, about Liz, his mother, before his world turned upside down and inside out and topsy-turvy.

'Kamikaze' it was called, all about a Japanese man in the 1940s, who had so loved life, that he had aborted his wartime suicide mission, only to return to shame and ostracism. Mr Docherty had asked Tom to read it aloud to the class. The last line, the one where the man wonders whether his heroic soldier's death would, ultimately, have been preferable to his 'dishonourable', miserable life – that had caught in Tom's throat.

If Mr Docherty had noticed, he hadn't said, the class had continued with their analysis and comment: *simile, metaphor, alliteration*. Mr Docherty had told them that the word 'kamikaze' translated as 'divine wind', that, in the thirteenth century, Japan had been saved from invasion by a typhoon and that its soldiers engaging in their gruesome assignments, in more recent times, had claimed the romantic title. David had piped up then, said he thought it was ironic, that 'wind' was usually associated with life, not death. Stephen Wilson, sitting behind him, disagreed. 'Wind', he said, 'often brought destruction' and whipped up fire too. Mr Docherty, pleased with the lively discussion, added that wind often moved at great speed; 'Ride like the wind', 'fly like the wind'.

All Tom could think then, was that it was easy for these boys, his friends, his companions to talk glibly; to speak, with apparent inside knowledge, about the quality of the returning soldier's life, to shake their heads and sanctimoniously judge him: 'deserter', 'double-crosser', 'traitor' even. Tom understood everything about the Japanese man, that he'd gazed down at the shimmering sea, reflected on the life he loved and vowed to cling on to it for as long as he humanly could. For his family and community to fail to understand that, to place so little value on his life and the meaning it gave them, to reject him – that was the real disgrace.

But today, this morning, this minute, he was no longer sure of the feelings which had swelled inside him on Friday. Perhaps he had been too idealistic, perhaps there could be honour in death, especially when the alternative was a truly empty life.

'If you're not feeling up to it, I can get David to bring something up for you. Would you like that better?' Mr Jenkins said.

Tom dug at the hole in the cover of his book, pressing his thumb into the groove and gouging at the fleshy paper beneath with his nail.

'I'll ask him to do that, anyway; keep your strength up. Then, maybe after breakfast, you'll come down. We could have a walk. Fresh air is always welcome.' Mr Jenkins wrinkled his nose. Evidently the smell of Tom's cigarette, lingering in the air, prompted his invitation. 'Is there anything I can get you in the meantime?' he offered.

Tom heard Mr Jenkins clearly this time and a shiver travelled through his body from his head to his toes. He had dreamed of those words on Jenkins' lips, but had never thought he would hear them in real life. *Every cloud has a silver lining, so they said.*

He turned towards the jittery man and their eyes met for the first time. Tom thought Jenkins appeared genuinely concerned. Whether it was for Tom or for himself he couldn't tell. So it would be good to ask for something, wouldn't it? He'd read a bit of psychology and wasn't that right? That you should take people up on offers of help; it made them feel good about themselves. If you just said *no thanks* or *I'm fine*, as so many stoic people did, then the person offering felt deflated. He should do this for Mr Jenkins, as well as for himself.

'I'd like my laptop please,' he said. 'Not the spare one, *my* laptop.'

Mr Jenkins hesitated a moment, then he nodded. 'Of course,'

he said. 'I'll get David to bring it up to you, with your breakfast.'

And just like that, Mr Jenkins was gone, obligation fulfilled, back to the day job of presiding over meals and assemblies and, no doubt, endless planning meetings. They said he used to teach, that he'd been a pretty good teacher. Geography was his subject or was it maths? Tom couldn't remember.

He pulled another cigarette from the box and held it to his lips, hunting around for his lighter. None of it really mattered now: geography, maths, any subjects he'd been forced to study these past eleven years. None of them any use to you. Who needed to know the names for all the different ways the Earth's plates moved? Either you were at the other side of the world, in which case it was a total irrelevance. Or, you were there at the epicentre, and you would get the hell out, rather than be occupied with the appropriate terminology for what was happening hundreds of miles below your feet.

And maths? Who needed a graph to show how an object was accelerating as it fell to Earth? If it was large, like a meteor, surely what was important was that it would make a great big hole and you'd better get out of its way. If it was small, then you were probably OK.

Locating the lighter in his desk drawer, he lit the cigarette and drew its smoke deep into his lungs. He visualised the cloudy vapour rolling through his body like tumbleweed, unfurling its fronds like a fern in time-lapse, extending deep inside him. He coughed once, deliberately, to close his internal passageways, before the fog reached the pain which consumed him and sought to salve it.

He exhaled and flicked his ash onto his desktop and remembered what Mr Jenkins had just promised him. A frisson of excitement sparked his fingertips. Soon he would be out of here and this tired little room, this stale environment would be a distant memory. He, 'Sully', was going places. If David would just hurry up and bring him his laptop, then the fun could begin.

4

'YOU WANTED TO SEE ME?' Luke Smith tapped at Eric Daniels'
office window and hovered on the threshold. Eric waved him
in and pointed at the chair opposite his desk, shifting his own
chair away from his laptop and his four extra-large screens to face
Luke. He smiled, but only with his teeth. Then he picked up one
of the miniatures which adorned his desk and stared at it, before
replacing it exactly where it had been.

'Do you remember when you joined us here at Valiant, eight
months ago, I made you sit through a film with key messages?'
Eric said, his eyebrows rising and falling as he spoke.

'I remember, yes.' Luke sat himself down and shifted his weight
from side to side. It sounded like his newest design idea might not
have hit the spot.

'And there were some real "no nos", do you recall? Things you
absolutely must not do, in a Valiant game. Do you remember
that?' Eric's index finger poked at the model again. Luke noticed
it was the earliest iteration of Major Valiant, their namesake and

champion of Valiant's first successful online game. He'd changed since then, but Eric often talked about the need to keep sight of their 'humble beginnings'.

'No nos,' he tested the words on the inside of his head. '*No nos*', '*mangos*', '*yoyos*'. Was Eric trying to patronise him? 'Yeah, sure I remember.' Perspiration broke out on Luke's top lip. He didn't want to look at the all-conquering Major Valiant. Instead, he focused on the Bruce Lee poster behind Eric's head. Bruce Lee? Who had a poster of Bruce Lee on their wall these days?

'Can you tell me what any of those were, those "no nos", those bridges you mustn't cross, commandments you mustn't break, on pain of death?'

Luke's throat was dry. He'd been warned that Eric could be like this, pushy, aggressive, dictatorial, but he had thought the others were pulling his leg. He hadn't seen signs of it himself, before now. And he did recall the introductory film, but not verbatim. '*No nos*', '*avocados*', '*peccadillos*'.

'Hm… No padding,' he said.

'Absolutely. No padding. That's right. Why not?' Luke focused on Eric now, his anxiety levels still rising. Eric was half out of his seat, his eyes large, one arm waving in Luke's face.

'Players lose interest in aimless tasks,' Luke said.

'Yes. Players like clear objectives. If we only have five minutes of purposeful play, we can't set them a forty-hour game. What else?'

'No repetition.'

'Why not?'

'It's boring.'

'Yes, but sometimes humans like boring. When's that?' Eric's eyes were as wide as saucers.

'When they choose it.'

'You're good at this. You did listen. That's why I don't understand how you've fucked up so monumentally on this one.' Eric's fist came down onto his desk with a thud, on top of the drawings Luke had placed there early this morning.

Luke swallowed. For a second, he had wallowed in his boss's praise, but it had been short-lived. Now he was in virgin territory.

'OK, I'll give you a clue, what we're talking 'bout here,' Eric was speaking again. 'What's the sixth commandment, in the Bible? Any idea?'

Luke was flailing around a bit. Religious studies wasn't his thing and he had only been in a church twice – his brother's wedding and nephew's christening – and the Ten Commandments had not been mentioned on either occasion.

'Numbers one to five – no interest for us. All that shit about "I am the Lord, your God" and "keep the sabbath day". That's not important. Although don't tell my mother I said that. Number six, however, is key, crucial, fundamental. *Numero Uno*. Well, it's not, cos it's number six, like I said. But *numero uno* in significance. No? You give up?'

Luke still didn't speak. But if it was number six, it couldn't be that important. It could be the adultery one. He knew that was in the Bible somewhere and it was forbidden. That was why Jesus had to step in to save the prostitute. '*Numero uno*', '*gigolo*', '*flamenco*'. He almost giggled.

'Thou shalt not murder. Do you remember now?' Eric answered for him.

'Yes.' Luke could hardly make the shape with his mouth.

'But what's Valiant's take on that? What's our take on that?' Eric prodded Major Valiant Numero Uno, one last time.

'I don't remember.'

'You don't remember.' Eric prowled around the desk and stood over Luke, his hands making fists, his eyes as enormous as dinner plates. 'After we've finished here, I want you to go back to your desk and watch that video again, the beginners' video. I want you to watch it as many times as it takes for you to learn those commandments, Valiant's commandments and you're fucking lucky I'm not taking a knife, Aldo Raine-style, and carving this one across your fucking face. *Make killing fun.*'

He tapped Luke on the forehead with his finger at each word. '*Aggro*', '*lay low*', '*let go*'.

'I remember now,' Luke said.

'Too fucking late. If you're gonna kill someone in a Valiant game, we don't want nondescript, grey, tiny, scrabbling rodents to exterminate and, when we've done it, hundreds more just pop up in their place, zombie-style. Where's the pleasure in that?

'Or to be handed a bullshit weapon; no one defends their country with a monkey wrench, when they could have a Samurai sword or an AK47. And, even worse breach of the rules, when you use that weapon, it has to have impact; blood spray, limbs spurting, heads rolling. You can't slash a guy across the face and he looks like Captain America straight after.'

Eric picked up an empty glass bottle from his desk and waved it over Luke's head.

'What are you feeling now, tell me?'

'Scared,' Luke mumbled, cowering back into the chair.

'Good. And if I were to smash this bottle over your head, it would hurt, there'd be blood, you might lose an eye. Right? That's impact. That's what gives players satisfaction. If there's nothing, you just carry on sitting there and everything's just fine, shirt tucked in, hair neatly combed – well, yours isn't, but you get my drift – then what's the fucking point? Give the players the pleasure of killing with style, with flair, with panache!'

'I was just trying to start slow, build up gradually.'

'No! No! No! No!' Eric returned the bottle to the table. 'Is my message clear?'

'Torpedo', *'staccato'*, *'gung-ho'*, *'psycho,'* Luke thought. 'Yes,' he said.

'Look, there's loads of good stuff in your proposal; loads. Some of your characters are awesome and I love the backstory. But what you gave me; it needs a major re-think. Talk to Mikey, he's a great researcher. Talk to Bill about the artwork, but until then, you know what? Let's do this the old-fashioned way.'

He grabbed a piece of paper from his desk drawer and took out a marker pen and some Sellotape. In large, uneven letters he wrote 'Make Killing Fun!' and taped the message around Luke's head. 'You wear that all day, until it's sunk in. Now get out.'

5

CONSTANCE SAT IN Judith Burton's flat, her laptop open on the table. Judith was an eminent criminal barrister and Constance had instructed her on a number of cases over the last few years. Even when they weren't actively working together, she valued Judith's views and advice. And, partly because Judith didn't have to work – she had been left a significant sum by her husband on his sudden death eight years ago – she was generous with her time and tended to be an objective sounding board for most tricky issues.

Judith brought over two large glasses of white wine and Constance pressed *play* on her laptop. Immediately, a whirring noise and repetitive thudding began and the screen filled with a stylised desert scene, the camera flitting at speed over its undulating landscape. Then, the barrel of a gun appeared in the centre, moving from side to side. The soundtrack was still punctuated by those gunshots, now with the overplay of breathing and a male voice talking. Judith watched for a while without speaking.

'Let me get this straight,' she said, eventually. 'This is the boy, Jaden,' Judith pointed to a figure, wearing headphones, in the bottom left corner of the screen. Constance paused the action.

'Yes. This is a year or so back, when he was still filming from the family home.'

'And now?'

'He has his own place, well, shares with a friend, Nathaniel, another YouTuber.'

'And what's the rest of the screen?'

'So, although you can't see his hands in the shot, Jaden is actually playing the game. And the rifle moving around – he's controlling it. This is a version of a game called *Call of Duty*, a kind of army mission with lots of shooting. What you see in the main picture is what Jaden can see himself and he's talking you through his moves as he completes them: what he's doing and why, everything he's anticipating, what his aim is. This number, at the top, is his score, going up.'

Judith took a sip of her wine. 'And what is this moving feed, here, down the side,' she asked, 'in all these different colours?'

'Ah, so that's the chat. This is where people who are watching, the "subscribers" – they pay to subscribe – they are all talking. The colours... I don't know. They just make it look nice. If you watch carefully, you'll see some of the same names coming up more than once.'

'But it moves so fast. Do they talk to each other?'

'Sometimes it's slower. And you'll see, every now and again, Jaden will read and register something from the chat and he'll answer. See, a minute ago, someone said "I love that gun" and, just now, he said "it's a custom skin", so he's replying. "Skins" are coverings you can buy online to customise your weapons or your characters.'

'And this?'

'Subscribers also make donations. This person "GentlMan" flashed up a couple of minutes ago, as a new subscriber and now this message is telling Jaden he's donated a hundred pounds. Jaden should say something to acknowledge that, any second.' Constance pressed play again.

As they watched, Jaden grinned, looked out to his viewing public and said 'Hey man... Mister Gentle Man. That's so appreciated. Tell me, which is your favourite game and I'll be giving you some tips later on.'

'And how long does this go on for?'

'Jaden has a show, most nights, at 9.30, for an hour, together with Nathaniel, but he also has other slots online, for example, if he was playing in a particular game, it could be scheduled any time, night or day. And on top of this live stream, he records some of his show, usually the best bits and posts it on YouTube, where he has more followers.'

'And how do they pay the rent, Jaden and Nathaniel?'

'They get a good income from their subscribers and, when he uploads material to YouTube, he gets advertising revenue as well, sometimes even more than he makes from the original streaming, if he gets enough views.'

'So he doesn't have a job?'

'This is his job.'

'This is the full extent of what he does, play a video game, while everyone watches?'

'Pretty much.'

'And this makes him rich and famous?'

'Jaden is just starting out, but he's hoping to emulate some of the others who've gone on to huge success – become major celebrities. Some of them move into music videos or sport, depending on their talents.'

'Turn it off, will you? It's hurting my eyes and my ears.'

Judith sat back and Constance laughed, as she paused the recording again.

'Am I the only one in the world who didn't know any of this existed until now?' Judith said.

'It's an enormous industry, worth billions. *Fortnite*, that was one of the biggest games of 2018, made its manufacturers four billion dollars. At one point, they said seventy-eight million people were playing the game at any one time, all over the world.'

Judith took a larger gulp of wine. 'And what do the players get out of it?'

'The satisfaction of winning. And they don't play alone, like a few years back. They interact with loads of other players, compete against them, so it becomes a community.'

'A community of people you've never met, who are all trying to kill you in horrible ways.'

'It's just another form of leisure. I mean, you might choose to go to the theatre for your night out. That might set you back, what, £100? Even going for a drink can be expensive. Or you could stay in and play this game with your friends, for a few pounds. In fact, most of the games are free; it's the extras that cost, like the customised items, special clothes for your avatar or the subscriptions to people like Jaden.'

Judith played the video again for a few minutes more, without the sound, her eyes darting around the screen, before finally switching it off, with a shrug.

'Perhaps I can understand the game, the competitive element,' she said, 'but why spend real money on a costume for your character, if you don't need it? I assume they don't come cheap.'

'Because if this is how you like to spend your time, in this virtual world, then you want to make your characters look good. It gives them status and that gives you status among other players. And I don't blame kids like Jaden for wanting to cash in on what's popular, make an income from it. They have to plan their show, make it entertaining enough, or the viewers go elsewhere.'

Judith sighed and finished her wine. She worked her fingers up and down the stem of her glass.

'What've they got on him?' she asked.

'Fingerprints, including in Elizabeth Sullivan's bedroom. He says he "carried her shopping" into the flat, but there must be more. Her bag was stolen, containing purse and mobile phone and it hasn't been found, so that's why they're suspicious that someone else was involved. And they're waiting for the post-mortem.'

'And what's he like?'

'Jaden?' Constance found herself smiling, as she recalled her interaction with him. Judith tutted loudly. 'What?' Constance was immediately defensive.

'I think your response speaks for itself.'

'It's not like that,' Constance recovered her composure. 'He's just not like most of the others I see. He's… What's the word for when you're older than your years?'

'Precocious?'

'No, that's not Jaden. Not if it's a criticism. He just has an inner confidence, but not brash, a quiet confidence in himself. Then his clothes are the opposite, really loud and…expressive. He has these designer yellow shoes…'

'Business must be good.'

'I suppose it must be.'

'He'll be a good witness, then? I mean, if we get that far.'

Constance was silent. She wasn't sure that Jaden's assured manner would generate credibility. It was as if he was so certain he had done nothing wrong that he expected everyone to just believe it, without him having to say anything.

On top of that, Jaden had already encroached on Constance's private thoughts, on her own time and that was even less usual. Last night, after their short meeting and her follow-up with Dawson, she had dreamed of him. She had been navigating her way through some dusty, subterranean tunnel leading to a cavernous chamber. At the far side, among the intricate rock formations, Jaden was sitting on an ornate throne, a garland of roses around his head, his feet swinging manically, those distinctive, yellow shoes blaring out their message.

As she approached him, the throne had changed to the electric chair and Jaden was screaming 'Help me! Get me out of here!' Flames were leaping all around him. And a paralysed Constance had stood and watched, powerless to help, as they engulfed him, until only the shoes were left.

Constance took a sip of wine and swallowed it slowly, trying to force the unsettling image down and away, at the same time. Fortunately, Judith was moving on.

'What about her – Dr Sullivan?' Judith said.

'Consultant psychiatrist at Hackney Hospital, also ran a private clinic once a week, specialised in addictive behaviour.'

'And Jaden accepts he knew her.'

'He says he didn't know she was a doctor, just a friendly neighbour.'

'Her family?'

'One son at boarding school. Her husband died some years back. A sister travelling in Nepal. The police are trying to get hold of her. Parents dead. That's it.'

'When are you going back there?'

'Dawson's asked me to go over at four; thinks he'll have everything from the pathologist by then. After that, if they're charging Jaden and I can't persuade them otherwise, I'll head to the hospital, speak to one or more of her colleagues. See where that leads.'

Judith stood up and headed for the kitchen, returning with the half-full bottle of wine and filling her own glass for a second time.

'Have you heard from Greg at all lately?' Constance asked, taking advantage of the break in the conversation.

They had been together, Judith and Greg Winter, for six months or so. He had even moved in for a while, though they had never called it 'living together'. But he'd resurfaced in the last case she'd worked on with Judith. He'd helped unlock a secret folder on the victim's laptop – the kind of work on which Greg thrived – and Constance had let on that she'd been out with him, that he'd assisted more than Judith had appreciated, that he'd frequently asked Constance how Judith was. Of course, Judith was grateful for Greg's expertise, but what Constance really wanted to know, was whether he and Judith had resurrected their relationship.

'The odd message,' Judith deliberately kept her response casual.

'I thought you were going to catch up, after Debbie's trial?'

'I've been so busy,' Judith waved her hand in the air and then motioned to Constance to drink up, but Constance pushed her glass to one side. It was too early in the day to risk a fuzzy head.

'That's just not true,' Constance said.

'All right. I couldn't face it.'

'He cares about you, a lot.'

'And my feelings don't come into this? Anyway, you can talk.'

'What?'

'Have you even been out with anyone since you broke up with Mike, the actor?'

'Why are you making this about me?'

'Have you?'

'I've been…too busy,' Constance giggled now and she reclaimed her glass, tapped it gently against Judith's and took a sip.

'What a pair we are,' Judith joked. 'We always find time for this stuff though, the Elizabeth Sullivans and Jaden Dodds of this world. It's funny, isn't it?' she said. 'Part of me, the inquisitive, constantly dissatisfied part, is hoping it was a murder. I mean, I know it's only been a few months since our last double act, but there are only so many times I can read *Wolf Hall* or grate beetroot. And the other part, the more content part, admittedly frequently overshadowed, wishes the poor woman had met a peaceful end.

'I can tell *you* that's how I feel,' Judith added, 'without feeling ashamed or without you judging me. Anyone else would call me heartless, don't you think?'

6

Tom sat with his fingers resting lightly on his laptop, his chest rising and falling. He reached for a glass of water and drank it down in one go. Then, tentatively, he sought out the site forbidden to him for a while now. He knew the exact date and time of his last visit: Sunday April 21st, 6.02pm.

It was funny; at first his fingers were stiff, reluctant, holding him back. Then, as he began to navigate the familiar pathways, his joints began to ease, to loosen up, his digits finding their own way to his destination. He gasped. He was there. So easy. 201 days since he had last set eyes on the sweeping backdrop, populated by garish characters with expressive faces, but the intervening time dissolved away as if it had been only 201 seconds. He switched to full-screen mode and the glory of *World of Warcraft* was spread out before him. Who to choose? Titan or Elf, Goblin or Orc?

His eyes darted quickly around, drinking in every aspect, firing up the frontal lobes of his brain, releasing the dopamine and oxytocin into his blood, activating the body's pleasure circuits.

'Welcome Back Sully!' flashed across his screen. 'We've missed you!' His own cry of excitement rang out and the sound pulled him back from the brink.

Tom closed his eyes and tried to still his breathing. He forced his hands off the keyboard and onto his knees, where he dug his nails into the skin. 'You don't want to do this,' his mother's voice whispered in his ear. 'You have so many other ways to occupy yourself, so many talents.' She was persuasive, even now she was dead. 'You can't risk it, not even one time.'

Shutting his eyes had not kept her out. Tom could see her inside his head, just in front of him, blocking the doorway to his room. She was wearing her favourite olive green t-shirt with 'Merci Beaucoup' written across it and her hair was wet from the shower. 'Listen to me, Tom. You are so much better than this.'

Tom opened his eyes and his mother's face disappeared. All he saw was the screen looming, gigantic and alluring, the characters beckoning him in. 'You don't want to do this,' his mother's voice remained, but her tone was pleading, her strength was waning.

'I do,' he muttered. 'I do want to do this.'

For a brief moment, the word 'sorry' formed in his head, but he didn't articulate it. He couldn't risk being distracted again by the sounds of the real world, the tug of human obligations. He pushed it away almost as soon as it came to him. Because he wasn't sorry. Not now, and he wasn't sure he had ever been sorry for playing. The only thing he had been sorry for was any hurt he caused her; nothing else. And now she was gone, there was no one left to hurt.

He inhaled deeply through his nose and exhaled through his mouth, feeling the power which came from preparing his body for battle. He placed his fingers on the keyboard and then he began to play.

7

'INTERVIEW WITH JADEN DODDS, solicitor present, starting tape at 4.06pm, Tuesday 5th November. Hello Jaden. How did you sleep?'

Jaden sat next to Constance in the subterranean police interview room, their shoulders almost touching. It was chilly and she pulled her jacket tight around her. Jaden was surprisingly well-groomed, given a night spent in the cells, and he was wearing the change of clothes which his flatmate, Nathaniel, had sent in, another pristine white t-shirt and joggers. His eye was almost healed.

In contrast, Dawson looked a mess, his shirt hanging loose around his newly scrawny neck. Whatever had caused his dramatic loss of bulk, he hadn't followed it up with a wardrobe update. Dawson felt the heat of Constance's gaze and fiddled with his collar. Jaden ignored Dawson's question.

'All right. Let's get started,' Dawson continued. 'You are here as part of the investigation into the murder of Dr Elizabeth Sullivan, who lived right across the street from you. You raped her, killed her, robbed her and then left her to be found the next morning, hoping that we'd all think she died in her sleep.'

'Rape?' Constance asked, managing to control her voice, given her heart had just leapt into her mouth. 'That's new.'

'You're right. It is.'

Jaden's eyes shifted a fraction towards Constance. 'You can't try to scare my client like that,' she said, touching one hand to her throat, to help calm herself. 'You have no evidence of any of this,' she said.

Dawson passed some papers to Constance. 'Post-mortem shows a few things of interest,' he said. 'First, faint marks on each of Dr Sullivan's wrists. One of my lads picked them up and it's been confirmed, by the pathologist, on close examination, that her wrists were bound, only loosely, but they're definitely rope marks. Do you know anything about that, Jaden?'

'No.'

'You didn't tie her up then?'

'No.'

'Are you sure?'

'Yes.'

'But you did have sex with her?'

Constance shook her head.

'No comment,' Jaden said.

Dawson pointed to the papers he had handed Constance. 'Elizabeth Sullivan had sex in the hours before her death,' he said, 'without protection, with…guess who? Jaden, you may as well admit it; the science doesn't lie.'

'No comment.'

'What happened? You tied her up, raped her, but she wouldn't keep quiet, said she would tell on you, so you had to kill her?'

'No comment.'

'What's the cause of death then?' Constance asked, both surprised and relieved that her client, the subject of Dawson's barrage, had retained his composure. 'Originally, you said heart attack, said, what was it? That she had a family history. Is that no longer the right diagnosis?'

'Still a heart attack,' Dawson said, 'but brought on by being terrorised in her own home. You'll have time to read all the gory details the pathologist has discovered. Plenty of time in your case, Jaden. Who says "dead men tell no tales"? Not me, that's for sure.'

'Why is my client supposed to have killed Dr Sullivan?'

'To stop her talking, like I said. Is that what happened, Jaden? You had to shut her up. Or maybe you just meant to scare her, but you didn't realise your own strength. Lift weights do you? In your spare time, you and Nathaniel? I've been doing this for fifteen years, so you can't surprise me any more.'

Jaden closed his mouth and folded his arms.

'And robbery,' Dawson continued. 'You know her bag was taken. We've since discovered her credit card was used the following day, to run up bills on various sites. You must have thought you were so clever. The police there, searching her flat, looking for the killer, you were out spending her money. You knew you had – what? – forty-eight hours at most before all the cards were stopped, so you wanted to ensure you made the most of your spree.'

'No,' Jaden said.

'So, just in case it isn't clear, we have a warrant and my team are searching your flat, ooh...' he looked at his watch, 'right now, in fact. Maybe we'll find a few more clues, while we're at it. If you've nothing else to say for now, you can come back here in a couple of hours, when we've seen what else we can find. Interview terminated at 4.11pm.'

Dawson nodded to each of them, rose stiffly and exited the room.

***

'How can I help you if you lie to me?' Constance berated Jaden, once Dawson had gone and the door was firmly closed behind him.

Jaden had lowered his head into his hands and was sitting so motionless that Constance wondered if he was still breathing.

'You don't have to tell me your life story, you don't have to volunteer information. You don't even have to pay me, but if I ask you a direct question, you don't lie to me. That's not how it works.'

She was surprised at the sharpness of her own voice, how wound up she was. Her clients were often economical with the truth and it didn't touch her. But, as she'd try to articulate to Judith, she had sensed something different with Jaden in their first, short meeting. He had seemed more refined, more modest. And with that reserve had come a natural reluctance to explain himself. Why, then, had his failure to tell all, to share all the details of his evening with Dr Sullivan, bothered her to this degree?

'Did you think they wouldn't find out about you and Dr Sullivan?' she said. 'You know about DNA, don't you? Now I'll ask you again. What was your relationship with Elizabeth Sullivan?'

Jaden lifted his head and tapped his hands together lightly, one, two, three times.

'It's like I said,' he said. 'She was a neighbour. Look. I've lived there nearly a year and I never noticed her. Then, about ten days ago, she knocked at the door, asked if I could jump-start her car. We got talking and then...'

He covered his face with both hands for a few seconds, before dropping them down to his sides. 'She asked me why people were often around, outside. Sometimes, me and Nathaniel, we have special guests on the show, to lift the ratings, and kids come and hang out, so they can get to see them. So, I told her. She seemed interested.'

'And then?'

'Nothing for a couple of days. Then she baked us a cake. Brought it round. Said it was a thank you for the car. And then...' Jaden shrugged.

'You had sex. Just like that?' Constance said, completing his sentence, her contempt barely hidden.

'What are you? My mother? She wanted to and...I couldn't see no problem.'

'At her flat?'

'Yeah.'

'Anywhere else?'

'No.'

'How many times?'

'Twice. The first time was the day she brought the cake over, around a week ago. Then nothing. Then, she came around that night, said she'd made too much dinner, did I want to come over and share it with her. I wasn't doing nothing, so I did.'

'What happened?'

'It was really nice. We had dinner together, lots of wine. I don't normally drink wine. It made my head spin. We went to the bedroom. I left around nine. Then I saw the police there next day. I asked someone what was going on and they said she was dead.'

'You didn't think, then, to tell the police that you knew Dr Sullivan?'

'Are you kidding? Why would I do that? Look, I didn't kill her. I did nothing wrong, except feel a bit sorry for her. She told me she was on her own, no husband, her son was away. She did seem like a really clever lady, but she never said she was no doctor. She told me she was in HR. I didn't ask anything else.'

'You didn't steal from her?'

'I can't believe you're asking me. No, I didn't steal from her and I didn't use her credit card.'

'And what about the ropes? Tell me the truth now.' Constance knew she was pushing him, but she had to know what he would say, not only for his defence, but to judge, for herself, if she believed him.

'No ropes!' he shouted. 'I ain't into that stuff. And it's crap what the police said. I mean, why would I tie her up? Unless she was struggling. And if she was struggling, I'd've thought she would've had big marks on her wrists, not something that's only uncovered under some microscope or whatever the pathologist does, but that's just my opinion. And, if I'd tied her up, what was my plan? To wait around till she was asleep and then untie her? It's bullshit, total bullshit. We had sex. It was nice. She was nice. She said nice things to me. Then I went home and me and Nath, we did the show.'

8

CONSTANCE HEADED STRAIGHT to Hackney Hospital from the police station. It was only a few streets away, but the clouds, which had persisted throughout most of the day, had cleared and it was bitterly cold. She crossed to the sunny side of the street, to try to soak up any vestiges of warmth, but her breath appeared in great white clouds, and she increased her pace and shifted her scarf further up her neck.

'Dr Williams, I'm Constance Lamb. Thanks so much for agreeing to see me.' She extended a gloved hand to the doctor and he led her down the stairs the way she had come and back towards the entrance, to the hospital café.

'You're looking into Liz's death, is that right? But you're not the police.' Dr Williams sat down at a corner table, folding his arms and his legs simultaneously. Given his informal dress – blue jeans and a Fair Isle jumper – she would not have taken him for a doctor, had she passed him in the street, perhaps even in the corridors of the hospital. But, once he began to speak, she appreciated, at once, the extent of his powers. Although quite a large man, his voice was soft and lilting and he inclined his head as he engaged with her, to emphasise his capacity for listening.

'I'm a lawyer, representing the young man accused of her murder,' Constance said, unbuttoning her coat, then deftly extracting her tablet from her bag and powering it up.

'And I'm happy to speak to you, like I said on the phone, but I have told the police all I know. I can't imagine hearing it all again is a very worthwhile use of your time…or mine for that matter.'

'Sometimes the police don't ask the right questions or make notes of the right answers. I'm sure anything you tell me will be valuable. You were one of her colleagues?'

'We worked together on various research projects over the last eight years, although we've known each other much longer. We did our first placement together back in the early noughties.' Dr Williams glanced at his phone before stuffing it back into his pocket.

'What kind of work did she do?'

'She was a psychiatrist, as you know. She had a daily clinic here and, on Wednesday evenings, she saw private patients in the City, near Liverpool Street.'

'Did she have a speciality? The papers talked about addictive behaviour.'

'Most of Liz's patients were fighting addiction of one kind or another: alcohol, gambling, pornography. She was an expert in the control of impulsive behaviour, with a particular interest in the impact on young men. We were working together on a research project when she died.'

'And did you know her personally?'

'Of course. We spent so much time together and she was a

lovely person to be around; great fun, with a wonderful, dry sense of humour. Sadly, she'd been alone for almost ten years. I don't know how she didn't meet anyone else.'

'Her husband died?'

'In his early thirties, an aggressive cancer. I don't think she was short of offers, but she couldn't replace him.'

'She has a son?'

'Thomas, yes, but he's away at boarding school. After Will died, she decided it was the best thing. She was travelling a lot with work, conferences in the States, China. She didn't want to leave Tom alone or with carers.'

'Do you know which school he attends?'

'It's fairly near. I'll remember what it's called in a second. It's named after some do-gooder. She didn't want him far away, so they could spend weekends together whenever possible. If you're going to see him, you should know he's not the easiest boy – although who am I to judge? The boy's father died when he was six years old.'

An elderly man wearing faded pyjamas brushed Constance's arm on his way to sit down at a neighbouring table. He chewed on a stray thread from one of his buttons while he turned his eyes to the heavens and the dusty skylight, and then slumped down into his chair. His face was an intricate web of red lines, radiating out from his purple-tinged nose. Behind him, he dragged a bag of fluid, connected at one end to a mobile stand and, at the other, it disappeared into his sleeve.

'Do you know anyone who might have wanted to hurt Dr Sullivan?' Constance continued.

'No, of course not.' Dr Williams checked his phone again, this time leaving it on the table, face down.

'No patients who were unhappy with their treatment?'

'No one she mentioned, although we are sometimes threatened by patients. But we're very careful to keep home addresses private, that kind of thing. If you work in crime, it may be hard for you to believe, but medicine, on the whole, it's a pretty safe profession.'

'No rival doctors or disputes with drug companies, then?' Constance attempted a smile.

'You've been watching too much TV,' he said, rewarding her with a smile in return. 'We do work with drug companies – of course we do. Both Liz and I believe in a combination of medicine and therapy to treat our patients. But none of them killed Liz. I'm telling you that for a fact.'

The old man was now joined by a skeletal woman, carrying a tray bearing two scones, a pot of jam and a second pot overflowing with grey-tinged cream. She walked slowly and deliberately, like she was navigating a tightrope; heel, toe, heel, toe, with the occasional wobble, her hospital gown gaping at the back, to reveal a pale and saggy buttock. Constance almost reached out to tug at the loose straps, but then the woman sat herself down and the chair back covered her modesty.

'That still leaves a lot of other potential suspects, though. I am also interested in understanding a bit more about Dr Sullivan's research.'

Dr Williams picked up his phone again and checked his screen. 'I'm afraid I don't have time to talk about that now. If you can imagine, Liz built up a fair body of work.'

'I understand. I've arrived in the middle of your day and you have patients to see. Is there any way I could take a look myself? Is her work…accessible to the general public?'

'I can provide you with copies of the papers she wrote and we co-authored a book. You could have that too, if you like. Hardly a bestseller, but that wasn't the point.'

'Thank you. And I heard what you said, but also the names of any partners on your research projects please, for completeness.'

'They're usually disclosed in the papers themselves, but I'll double-check.'

'I'm very grateful.'

'No problem. It's always nice to have someone taking an interest in your work, even if it is for such a macabre reason.' Dr Williams' mouth turned down at the edges for a second, before he brightened up again. 'I'll be off then,' he said.

'Just one more thing, I forgot to ask. When was the last time you saw Dr Sullivan?'

'Oh, gosh. Whenever her last clinic was. It must have been Friday, the day she was killed. She probably left here around five.'

'How was she getting home?'

'She usually walked, although there is a bus.'

'Was there anything different about her, that day? Anything she was worried about?'

'Nothing. Same old happy-go-lucky Liz.' He sniffed and his mouth drooped a second time.

'And what did you do once she left?' Constance asked.

'I finished up and went home.'

Constance tucked her tablet into her bag. Dr Williams was already weaving his way between the chairs and tables, occupied by patients and visitors and the occasional member of staff by the time she looked up. Then he turned around.

'Mill Hill. That's where Tom's at school,' he called out. 'He boards. But I'm damned if I can remember the name.'

'Don't worry. That's enough for me to find it.' Constance

nodded her thanks.

The old woman was tucking heartily into her scone now, a blob of jam lingering at the corner of her mouth. The old man reached across and wiped it for her, with a folded paper triangle, scrunching it between his fingers and laying it tenderly on the table by her plate.

Constance slipped her scarf into the front of her jacket and buttoned it up, ready to face the elements as she headed back to her office.

9

LUKE WAS WORKING LATE. If he was to meet Eric's deadline for revisions to his new game, there wasn't a moment to be lost. He couldn't afford to sleep more than the absolute minimum. If it hadn't been for the short deadline, he might have rather enjoyed the experience. He had to admit that there was something satisfying about ending characters' lives with a bang, rather than a whimper.

He had decided to extend Eric's instructions to injuries too. He'd taken his inspiration from those old comics, the ones where every contact was marked with a 'bam', 'kerpow' or 'thwack'. Now, every time any of his characters sustained an injury, there would be a suitable noise, and visuals too – anything from a dribble to a river of blood, as appropriate. But he kept it mock, unreal, fantastic. It was satisfying but not sadistic. 'Make killing fun.'

Luke was so engrossed in his work that he hadn't noticed everyone leave until the lights began to dim and he had to fling his arms around like some demented scarecrow to reinstate them.

He sat back and rubbed at his eyes. He really did need a break, even if it was only for a few minutes. Sometimes, that was all it took to recharge his creative cells. He began to pace around the office, stretching from side to side.

It was funny how things seemed different at night. The room had grown to twice its daytime size, the monitors lined up like battalions of menacing marauders, the chairs positioned strategically to help launch an attack. That gave him another idea: 'The Office; a game of urban survival!' he whispered in a deep-toned, American accent, 'featuring Gillian, the efficient receptionist and Luke, the intrepid designer.' And then he heard it – a rhythmic thud, interspersed with less regular grunting noises – and it appeared to be coming from Eric's office.

Cautiously, he approached, inching his way along the darkened corridor. Someone was making quite a commotion in Eric's room. He sidled over to peer through the vertical pane and had to stuff his fist in his mouth to prevent himself from laughing out loud. Eric, stripped to his boxers – black silk with 'Kick Ass' emblazoned across the front – and with his t-shirt knotted around his head, was repeatedly kicking at a large, freestanding punchbag, situated in the centre of his room. Every few kicks, he would spin around, thump his chest, shout out some encouragement to himself and then bow to an imaginary opponent. The presence of the punchbag answered Luke's question about the enormous parcel delivered that afternoon, which two men had struggled to carry through the office.

Luke was about to withdraw, considering it might be career-limiting to be found spying on his boss in his underwear, after-hours, whatever his motivation, when Eric suddenly ceased his cavorting and reached for his mobile phone. He pressed some keys, raised it to his ear and then Luke heard him swearing loudly: 'Stupid, crazy bitch, pick up, will you?' He shook his phone from side to side, then pressed some keys again, more profanities escaping his lips when his call remained unanswered. Then Eric raised the phone above his head and flung it across the room.

Luke gasped. *'No!'*

He didn't wait to witness the aftermath. He scuttled back to his desk and grabbed his bag. *'Macho', 'dojo', 'loco'.* The finishing touches to his storyboard could wait till the morning. He was going home right now.

10

'HI NATHANIEL. I'M CONSTANCE, Jaden's lawyer. I left you a message, but I didn't hear back. Have you got a minute?'

Constance stepped forward so that Nathaniel Brooks had little choice but to let her in to the flat he shared with Jaden. Either that or risk injuring her if he closed the door in her face. She had, in fact, left three messages and she was not going to allow him to evade her any longer, having gone to the trouble of making a house call.

Nathaniel was still in his pyjamas and the flat smelled of pizza. He shuffled into the living room and removed the offending box, carrying it out into the hallway and adding it to two more. Then he opened the curtains halfway, covering his eyes as the light flooded in.

'Did I wake you up?' she asked.

'Late night,' he said.

'Online?'

'Nar, a party. How's JD?'

'That's what you call Jaden?'

'It's what everyone calls him. He didn't do nothing, you know that?' He sat down on the window ledge and Constance perched opposite, on the edge of the sofa.

'Did you know Dr Sullivan, the lady at number 38?' she asked.

'She had some trouble with her car. JD helped her. Next thing she brought us a chocolate cake, with icing on the top, real professional, like you get in a shop. I didn't know nothing was going on between them. Then, last Friday, he went out for a few hours, to her place; got back just in time for the show. That's all I know.'

'What time was that?'

'Around nine. We went live at 9.30. We had to make stuff up a bit, 'cos usually we do some planning just before, but we had a really good show, in the end. JD was buzzing.'

'Buzzing?'

'I don't mean really – not like he'd taken nothing – but he was on fire. We got five hundred more than the usual subs that night.'

'Did he tell you he had been visiting Dr Sullivan?'

'Nar. But I knew. I saw him coming out of her place. I wasn't spying or nothing but, when it got near nine, I was getting a bit edgy.'

'You didn't ask him?'

'It wasn't like that between us. He'd tell me if he wanted.'

'And the next morning?'

'We heard police, maybe around ten. JD went out to ask some kids outside what was wrong and they told him. He came back in and he was in a state.'

'In a state?'

'You keep on repeating what I'm saying. He was shaking his

head from side to side. I asked him what was up and he told me that her – he called her "Liz" – he said Liz was dead, police said she'd been found dead in her flat. I said that was a real shame, as she'd seemed such a nice lady. And he said yes she was.'

'Then what?'

'He went out for a coupla hours. For a run. Said he wanted to clear his head. That was it. We did our show as usual. Next day, the police knocked at the door and hauled him off.'

'Did you ever go into Dr Sullivan's flat?'

'No.'

'She had a handbag stolen, quite distinctive, bright red one side, zebra stripes down the other.'

'Never seen it.'

'With all her things inside: purse, mobile phone, car keys.'

Nathaniel shook his head. 'They think that's why he killed her, to steal her money?'

Constance shrugged. 'What do you think?' she asked.

'No way!'

'Are you sure about that?'

'Course, I'm sure. I've known JD a long time. We was at primary school together. He don't take no shit from no one, that's true, but he don't steal and he don't beat no women neither.'

'Does he have a girlfriend?'

'He used to a year back, but she went off with another guy. He was a bit cut-up and since then, nobody special.'

'Can I speak to her? JD's ex-girlfriend?'

'I can give you her number, but I'm not sure she'll talk to you.'

'What family does he have?'

'Me. I'm his family.'

'No parents?'

'He never knew his dad and his mum died last year. They were talking about putting him in care, but things got dragged out till he was eighteen, so we moved in together.'

'What did his mother do?'

'She was a nurse. Really good lady, well respected.'

'And JD's phone, laptop?'

'The police took them all, and some clothes, and the other clothes I sent for him.'

'If this case comes to trial, would you be willing to come to court to say the things you just told me?'

Nathaniel stood up and wiggled his head from side to side, visibly weighing up his answer.

'I'm not sure,' he said. 'It's one thing saying stuff to you, here. It's another standing up and saying it all in a court.'

'Have you been in a court before?'

Nathaniel looked at his feet and Constance cursed herself for the insensitivity of her question.

'I meant I could show you what it's like, being a witness,' she said. 'I could take you into another trial. Then you'd know what to expect.'

'Look, I want to help. JD's the reason I'm alive and not fucked up in the head, like some kids wanted me to be, or under the ground. He saved my ass over and over. But you need to know I've been inside – just youth stuff – nothing big. I didn't hurt no one; nothing like that. Just, will they know that? 'Cos, if so, I'm not sure they're gonna believe me over some doctor or lawyer, you know what I mean?'

***

Judith sat at home observing a recording of Jaden on her laptop. She'd been watching for three hours now, trying to get the hang of the game he was playing. She believed she had mastered the basic elements of the story and its aim and had toyed with downloading the app herself, albeit the free version, purely from a research perspective. But she couldn't quite bring herself to do it. It felt like a step too far, some kind of endorsement that the game had value, which she wasn't yet prepared to accept. Instead, she focused on Jaden.

It was quite remarkable that he could perform at such a high level and, simultaneously, chat with his fans, moving seamlessly from one to the other. And the chemistry between Jaden and Nathaniel was palpable. They sparred with each other good-humouredly, they teased each other mercilessly, but it was never mean-spirited. And over the course of a few shows, they even swapped clothes. Nathaniel was good, Judith could see that, but Jaden was better, not just with his results but with his rapport with his audience. He was more self-assured, more stylish. Even when he wasn't playing, when he was easing back in his chair, laughing at his own jokes, he was immensely likeable.

She paused the stream of play and crossed the room to press her hand against the radiator, which was peaking at lukewarm. Her boiler needed an overhaul, but she'd put it off and now she had to wait another week for a plumber. She hoped the system would last that long; otherwise she'd be digging out her old hot-water bottle and fluffy bed socks.

She entered her bedroom and sat down at her dressing table. She'd torn an article from today's *Evening Standard* about exercises you could do to keep your face looking young and she smoothed it out in front of her. Now she was reading it closely, it only provided scant instructions on what was required. Anyone seriously interested was supposed to sign up for one-to-one sessions, at a private clinic, undoubtedly at great expense. Even so, she would try anything once. She leaned forwards, stroked her fingers across her forehead in sharp, downward motions, while sticking out her bottom lip. Then she pinched each side of her nose hard and blinked over and again. Finally, she slapped the back of her hand against the bottom of her chin.

Her phone rang and she dragged it towards her. Greg, again. Second time this week. He was certainly persistent. She let it ring out.

Now her phone pinged a message from Greg. She perched her glasses on the end of her nose and viewed it.

Dinner tomorrow night, Delomino, 7.30 prompt, it read. No enquiry as to her health or whether she was free, not even a question mark. She should write back and condemn his audacity. Her fingers hovered over her screen. And, now she read the message again, she could see that he'd spelt the name of the restaurant wrong. That had to be corrected. Then she paused and laughed. The absence of polite introduction, the order to attend, the mis-spelling, it was all calculated to generate a response from her. And once she responded, she would meet him. He knew that. He knew her too well.

Judith sighed. Did she love Greg? She wasn't sure. After her late husband Martin's betrayal, she had forced that part of her heart to shut down, but she had certainly enjoyed having a companion again for a few short months, even one who insisted on wearing polo shirts and blow-drying his hair. But having gathered the courage to ask him to leave, she didn't want him to inveigle his way back into her life. She didn't need a soul mate, even one with a generous nature and a tendency to call out her prejudices. She really didn't. She didn't need anyone at all.

***

Constance stood in the street, outside Dr Sullivan's flat. It was still marked with police tape, but Dawson had said she could visit. Now she just needed PC Thomas to come and let her in.

The street was quiet, a mix of modern, low-rise red-brick buildings and one 1970s high-rise monstrosity on the corner. Jaden and Nathaniel's flat was on the first floor of 'Montagu House' – one of the low blocks – and it looked out over the street. Just in front, there was a concrete yard, with the faded lines of what was once a basketball court. There were few cars. She stood outside Dr Sullivan's window. The boys would have had a perfect view of anyone entering or leaving her apartment, had they been looking that way.

She shivered. They had predicted an Arctic winter so many times in the last decade, but this seemed to be the year they had got it right. And the clocks had only just changed. She shuffled from one foot to the other.

Suddenly, Constance had the sensation she was not alone. She didn't quite hear someone behind her as much as sense it; a change in the light, or the temperature or the breeze. She wheeled around but no one was there. Still, she was sure of it. One minute she had known she was the only one standing outside on the freezing afternoon and the next, someone else was sharing that space, somewhere close by, watching and waiting.

She shifted back towards the door of Nathaniel's block. At least she knew he was home, if she needed him, although she'd have to make it up the stairs and, if Nathaniel stuck on those noise-cancelling headphones she'd spied by the TV, he wouldn't notice if the space shuttle landed in his bedroom.

Then she heard it; a branch snapping underfoot and an intake of breath. She sank further into the doorway, her finger hovering over the buzzer, her eyes sweeping the street. A low scuffling sound followed, which could have been a squirrel or a rat, except she knew it wasn't.

The overdue police car turned into the street, switched its beam up full to illuminate its destination and pulled up outside Dr Sullivan's flat. Constance thought, for a second, that she saw a figure, silhouetted through its back window, before she was dazzled by the lights and turned away. When she looked back, it was just her and PC Thomas on the well-worn street.

11

TOM'S SCORE WAS INCREASING even faster than his pulse rate. If he could keep going at this pace, he could easily defeat the opposition, or at least most of them. There were one or two tricky opponents he could see, performing at a similar level to him. But that was what made it so much fun. 'Battle of the equals', maintaining standards.

Anyway, no one wants to win from the front. He'd argued with his mum about that very concept. She was all for steady progress, keeping up, even getting ahead by doing work before it was due. Tom couldn't see the point in that. Far better to do only what was necessary and bide your time and then turn the taps on full, when the pressure was on, like right now.

How long had he been playing? He'd lost track of time. He had humoured Mr Jenkins by going down for breakfast and even walking around the playing fields once, to tick the 'fresh air' box to which Jenkins had constantly alluded over the last few days. But he'd refused lunch, so a few hours at least. He could check the time, but that would involve looking away from the screen. He needed the toilet; he should never have had orange juice to drink, but he'd have to wait a bit longer. Just one more game and he could quit. That would be pretty good for his ranking. Although there was a battle at 8pm where he could win double points.

Someone was coming up behind him at tremendous speed. He wheeled around and caught the guy in the eye with his pickaxe, the satisfying crunch of metal against bone and a cascade of blood soaking the soil, before the next assailant was on him, launched from the side, feet first. But he was prepared for the twin-pronged attack. This time he used his butcher's knife to disembowel his young opponent, before gathering up his weapons and running on. He blinked heavily to help himself focus. Now he was really motoring.

He was suddenly aware of someone speaking to him – someone outside the game – and David was there in the room.

'What're you playing?' David asked.

Tom grunted in response. Anything more and he would lose his concentration.

'Wow, is that your score?'

Tom increased the tension in his right index finger and blew up a wagon load of enemy elves, together with their hoard of gunpowder. He ignored David.

'It's stifling in here.' David crossed the room and opened the window, a gust of wind streaking in, lifting a flurry of papers from Tom's desk. One of them floated over his keyboard and he batted it away with his nose, growling as he did so.

David stood behind him, bending over to watch the action, his breath close to Tom's ear. Tom felt the warmth and weight of human contact, but blocked it in favour of the sensations he was experiencing in the game.

'Just one more...' he said, hoping David would take the hint and back off. He was nearly there. There were only six of them left now; six from a starting line-up of over a hundred.

David leaned in closer. Tom's eyes flickered for one millisecond away from his screen and towards his friend and, in that moment, he missed the mace spinning towards him from a great height. It smashed into the side of his head, the spikes embedding themselves in his face. He squealed at the pain, as if it were real and then, just like that, his character had gone, crumbling until only a pile of dust remained, the game rushing on, unsympathetically, without him.

'Agh!' Tom banged his fist down onto his desk and his empty glass rolled over, off the table and on to the floor. David stooped to retrieve it.

Tom sat back in his chair, then leaped up, bolted out of the room and down the corridor to the bathroom. He returned with wet hair, grabbed the glass and filled it with water from the wash basin in the corner, then poured it down his throat. Then, finally, he looked at David.

'Are you OK?' David asked, his face serious.

'I just got a bit excited,' Tom replied. 'But I did pretty good. Did you see?'

David nodded. Tom sat down on his bed and smiled at him.

'You won't tell Mr Jenkins, will you?'

David shook his head.

'Thanks,' Tom said. 'I know *you* help me, talking to me and stuff. You're awesome, but this helps me too. It helps me forget. If you tell Mr Jenkins, he'll take it away from me and I couldn't bear it. Right now, more than anything else, this is what I need.'

12

AT HACKNEY POLICE STATION, Constance was on her way in to pick up some papers for a case she was appearing in later that day, when Dawson called her into his office.

'Two things you should know about your client, Dodds,' he said, pointing his finger at her. She noticed he looked better today, a healthier complexion, less saggy around the eyes too. Maybe he'd had a heavy night last time she'd been in.

'Go ahead,' she said, waiting in the doorway.

'We've found Liz Sullivan's handbag.'

'Where?'

'In a park, other side of London. Someone handed it in, after our appeal.'

'And?'

'It was empty, nothing left inside.'

'How do you even know it was hers, then? Surely, there's more than one out there.'

'We're checking, but it's hers.'

'And the other thing?'

'One of the recent purchases on her credit card was for "Adidas Yeezys Boost, V2, size 11."' He read from a Post-it note stuck to the side of his PC. 'Before you ask, they're trainers.'

'So?' Even as Constance asked the question, she knew what was coming.

'Dr Sullivan's feet were a size 6,' Dawson said.

'She has a teenage son.'

'Good try.' He reached into a bag at his feet and placed a pair of soft-top black trainers, with red lettering down the side, on the desk. 'Look what we found at your client's flat, at the back of the cupboard under the kitchen sink. Unworn. And, in case you're not as familiar as I am with branded footwear, these match that description.'

'They must produce hundreds of those trainers every day.'

'I've never believed in fairy tales. Don't pretend you do. We'll be charging him now, just so you know. And then you can go for bail, but you won't get it.'

Constance was halfway out of the door. She wanted all the information on the credit card statement, but she could ask for it later. And she wanted to see Jaden, to put the latest revelation to him, to listen to and assess his response, but there was no time. She had to be in court in only an hour.

'This is a straightforward case, cut and dried,' Dawson called from his chair. 'I don't want you and Judith trying your tricks in court. I know about his background, that he hasn't had a lot of breaks, but he's a bad 'un. Not worth breaking your balls over, if you excuse the expression.'

Constance bit her lip and hurried back along the corridor towards the exit and the papers she needed. It seemed that, with each day that passed, another piece of evidence emerged, linking Jaden to the crime. She had felt so positive after the session with Nathaniel, that it was all circumstantial. Now, here was something tangible, really tangible; black and red and in a hefty size 11.

And she knew Dawson wasn't deliberately trying to irritate her, that he was doing his job, and he was friendlier than many of the other officers she dealt with, but she also knew his 'advice' wasn't objective. He didn't have the best track record for convictions where she and Judith were concerned and that must be a factor influencing him, even if he didn't appreciate it himself.

13

LUKE HAD ALMOST FINISHED his presentation to the whole Valiant team. He knew he looked a wreck, his hair was matted close to his head, his left eyelid was twitching with various degrees of intensity and he sported a prominent, pus-filled spot immediately to the side of the bulb of his nose, which he had squeezed dry last night, but which had filled up with green-tinged liquid again by the morning.

Normally, he wouldn't have been quite so nervous but, after he had been chewed up and spat out by Eric only seven days before, and Eric had insisted on going straight to this semi-public demonstration, rather than allow him another private audience, the pressure was really on. Luke could count on the fingers of one hand the hours of sleep he had had over the past three days.

On the screen, the last player stood, arms out, victorious, in the centre of the rainforest, sweat pouring down his face, an armadillo-like creature yapping at his heels. Luke turned up the lights.

'So, that's the idea for the new game. I'd be happy to answer questions, now,' he said, struggling to control his breathing.

Eric was stalking him, around the perimeter of the room. Now he eased his way forwards through his team, parting them like a herd of zebras, looking over each of their shoulders as he moved, to view the scores they had awarded for features of Luke's latest efforts.

'There is only one thing I can say to that,' Eric said, his face inscrutable, his eyes suddenly jumping to fix themselves, limpet-like, on Luke.

Luke gulped. If Eric didn't like it, that was it. He would be out on his ear and in front of all his colleagues. He might never work in the industry again. '*No nos*', '*burrows*', '*shadows*'.

Eric hesitated, still giving nothing away. Then his mouth broke into a broad smile, which gradually took over the rest of his face.

'Unbe-fucking-lievable,' he pronounced, clapping his hands wildly, until the rest of the room followed suit. Reaching the front, he grabbed Luke by the shoulders and kissed him on the top of the head. Everyone cheered. Luke's knees just managed to keep him upright.

'What can I say?' Eric began. 'The onboarding mock-up was a masterclass in holding players' interest; teasing them with tasters of things to come, while developing their skills one step at a time. I love what you've done with the HUD – just the right combination of information – and your sketches – I know Bill helped but they're your ideas – so polished, so clear; the weapons, the ammo, the health score. Like Peppa Pig on acid.

'The music you brought in to accompany the harvesting; superlative. Of course, we'll have to ask if we can use it, but it's perfect. No player will ever want to stop hacking away at that rockface, while that anthem is blaring out. I love the animation. You've got balls, I'll give you that. K9 and PikNik are pushing towards lifelike, but I go with your caricatures every time. Human enough for the kids to engage, cartoonish enough to stop the parents – and the authorities – complaining we're encouraging real-life violence when they're splattered across the screen.

'And use of colour, so clever – sometimes subtle, sometimes sharp. You've kept the red for danger, as ever, but the combinations are masterful. As long as Pete can reproduce it in the game.' He spun around and pointed both index fingers, pistol-style at Pete, Valiant's developer, who returned the gesture. 'Of course, we may need a bit of adjustment for those colour-challenged individuals among us.' He spun through 360 degrees on one foot and pointed at his FD's t-shirt and short combination and everyone laughed, 'but it's still brilliant. I'm not totally sure about the pangolin, but, hey, they are the most trafficked animals ever, so why not?

'Let's talk numbers for a second. Mikey, what do you think?' Eric settled himself at the front now and sought out Valiant's researcher and numbers man.

'The game itself has to be free. That's what everyone's doing now and there's no going back.'

'Agreed, go on.'

'The way I see it, after the initial launch, we issue regular updates and we have a cycle of eight to ten weeks, to keep the players interested. At the end of each cycle, points get re-set, but we can give the highest scorers something; not a boost next time, we have to keep a level playing field, but maybe a certificate. Or, how about a hall of fame?'

'Yep. that would work, some kind of recognition for all that hard work. Keep them hooked. What else?'

'Entry to a live event?'

'Bingo, yes. The top twenty players, every, say, ten cycles, get a wildcard entry to our live event, where they can compete with the top teams, have a chance to get picked themselves and we can do a feature on each of them; kinda giving something back to loyal followers. I love it. But we need stuff to keep all of them playing in the short term – even the losers.'

'Daily challenges.'

'Great. Work with Luke to put those in. PikNik gives double points at weekends. We could do that too. But where do we make our money?'

'I'm still working on the shop,' Luke's chin sagged down into his neck. 'It's not quite ready yet and I want it to be perfect before I show you.'

Eric smiled again. 'No worries, if this is what you can do with the game, the shop will be awesome. We customise everything?'

'Pretty much; costumes, skins. I found these amazing Native American Indian designs we can use on the boots and some brilliant masks too; keep things current.'

Eric laughed aloud and beat his chest. 'Bravo! What do I pay you?' he asked.

'Oh man.' At this point, Luke's legs really did fail him and he slumped down into the nearest chair. 'It works out around £3K a month, after tax.'

'Is that all? That's not enough for this creative genius. Come by my office tomorrow and we'll talk pay rise.'

'Thank you. I'm so pleased you like it.'

'Go get some sleep till then. Take the rest of the day off. You look like shit.'

Luke thought he really should collect up his things and make a deliberate and triumphant exit, but, now the adrenalin had stopped pumping, he could not be certain he would manage, without one or other part of his body giving way again. He was saved by his colleagues, filing out one by one, most of them preceding their departure with shaking his hand, high-fiving him or slapping some exposed part of his upper torso. Eric had called the meeting at lunchtime and they were all hungry or keen not to lose more of their break than was absolutely necessary. Eric was last to go, throwing Luke an all-encompassing smile, which warmed his body from top to toe. 'Bravo,' Eric had said. Luke wouldn't forget that. Not ever. '*Bravo*', '*virtuoso*', '*superhero*'.

14

CONSTANCE AND JUDITH RODE the northern line to Mill Hill and
took a short taxi ride to The Wilberforce School, where Thomas
Sullivan was a pupil. Judith had expressly asked to be included in
this visit. Constance wasn't sure if it was nostalgia for their first
case together, in which they had represented a boy on trial for
murdering his teacher, or whether she had a particular interest
in Tom or what he might volunteer. Although now she thought
about it, she was amazed that Judith allowed her to conduct any
enquiries herself. It wasn't that Judith was a control freak, or that
Judith didn't trust her; more that Judith had an endless thirst for
knowledge, which she preferred to consume first-hand.

'I'd like to see some of Dr Sullivan's research papers,' Judith
spoke, as she paid the taxi driver and they hovered outside the
impressive building. 'Has Dr Williams sent them over to you yet?'

'A few, and I've found some online, but I'm still waiting for the
book they wrote together. I'll send you on the best ones.'

'All right, but can you still catalogue them all? Then, if there's something interesting I don't have, I'll still know it exists.'

'Sure,' Constance smiled to herself. True to form, Judith didn't want to miss out on anything. 'You saw the email I sent you, from the post-mortem, about the tablets she was taking, anti-depressants?' she asked.

'Yes. You said Dr Williams said she was *great fun*.'

'He did, although he also called her *happy-go-lucky*, which isn't quite the same.'

'No, it certainly isn't. Hm. Let's see what Tom says about his mother, although, he's unlikely to be objective, is he?'

***

'Thomas. These ladies are both lawyers and they are here to ask you a few questions about your mum. You don't have to see them, as I explained. It's up to you.' Mr Jenkins introduced them to Tom in his office, an airy double-aspect room with a leafy outlook and a portrait of its namesake, William Wilberforce, hanging behind the desk. Constance thought that a rather unhelpful introduction, but she couldn't see Judith giving up easily, if Tom tried to turn them away now.

Tom was seated on one of two sofas. He was wearing his school uniform – white shirt, grey trousers, burgundy blazer – and there was a pot of tea on the table in front of him, next to a plate of shortbread biscuits. His fair hair was sticking up on one side and his neat, compact face was riven with worry lines.

'You're defending him, aren't you? The boy they say killed mum.' He looked from Constance to Judith and back to Constance.

'Yes,' Judith began. 'I expect the police have already asked you some questions. But we don't believe he killed your mum and we want to help the police find the real killer.'

'I don't know anything. I'm not going to be much help.'

'There might be something you know, something that seems really unimportant, but ends up being just what we're looking for. Sometimes it happens that way.'

Judith sat down opposite and Constance settled herself next to Tom. Mr Jenkins leaned back against the window ledge.

'Who were your mum's friends? Can you tell us that?' Constance took over.

'She has a good friend called Sandy; her real name's Cassandra Bell. They've known each other since university and, I suppose, Bev, another doctor. Bev Reed. They're her best friends.'

'What about male friends?'

The corner of Tom's top lip curled up and then uncurled.

'Other doctors I suppose.'

'Do you know Dr Williams?'

'Tony Williams. Mum wrote a book with him. That's all I know.'

'She didn't have a boyfriend?'

Tom shrugged.

'What about hobbies?'

'You mean like going to the gym?'

'Yes, like that.'

'She was always working. She tried to take days off in the holidays, or if I was back for a weekend, but her patients were always doing stupid things; "unreliable" she called them. She'd get a call and she'd have to go and section them or else calm them down. She talked someone off a roof only last month, over the phone, while we were making pasta. He called her, said he was going to jump off a multi-storey car park in Wembley.'

'I think you're saying she had little time for hobbies,' Judith chipped in.

Tom nodded.

'But she must have had some time for relaxation. Did she go to the cinema, out for dinner or drinks, listen to music?' Constance continued.

'We did stuff like that together. I don't know what she does… did when I'm here. Work mostly.'

'The post-mortem, it showed that your mum had a problem with her heart.'

'I know. The policeman said.'

'Did you know about that?'

'No, but Mum always liked to protect me from things. Which is stupid, isn't it? 'Cos she also said, it's good to know what's around the corner.'

'I agree, it's always good to be prepared,' Judith interrupted again and gestured to Constance to allow her to take over the interview. 'But sometimes that just isn't possible, whatever our intentions.'

'Yeah. If you say so.'

Judith's eyes flickered up to the wall portrait for a moment and Constance knew she was gearing herself up for a difficult question, weighing up the harm it might do to ask it, versus the possibility of something useful being gleaned by way of an answer. It was funny how they knew each other's body language now, the non-verbal cues which ruled them. If she told Judith she could read her though, she could imagine the curt response.

'Was your mum a happy person, do you think?' Judith began gently.

'What do you mean?' Tom fidgeted on his cushion.

'I mean that some things might have made her feel unhappy.'

'You mean, like when Dad died.'

Judith took a breath. 'Yes,' she said. 'Like that.'

Tom's body tensed and he chewed at his bottom lip. He didn't respond.

Judith tried again. 'Do you know what depression is?' she asked.

Tom nodded. 'I think so.'

'I'm not talking about being a bit sad, when something doesn't go exactly to plan. That's very understandable. I mean more than that. Being sad for days or even weeks and nothing really cheers you up.'

'OK?' Tom's eyes were narrow now. Was he scared of what was coming next?

'Do you think your mother ever felt like that?'

'No!' Tom shouted, wiping the back of his hand across his eyes. 'She had *me*, you see,' he said. 'She had me and she didn't need anyone else.'

He leaped up, ran out of the room and they heard the clatter of his feet on the stairs, followed by a door slamming, somewhere above their heads.

***

'Was it really necessary for you to ask the boy about his *father's* death, on top of everything else?' Mr Jenkins chastised Judith, after all sounds associated with Tom's exit had faded.

Judith's stare would have frozen the sun. 'I am not in the habit of causing unnecessary distress to anyone, I can assure you,' she replied.

Mr Jenkins met her gaze and then lowered his head. 'Yes, of

course. I am sure you are only doing what you need to do.'

'Thank you. That's very gracious of you. Is Tom a good student, can I ask?'

'He's above average, certainly, but not very engaged. His teachers all think he could do better, but he maintains he's working flat out. And his mother, well, she would never push him. She always backed him up.'

Constance marvelled at Judith's skill. In the space of a few words, she had shifted Mr Jenkins from moral outrage to compliant lapdog and, at the same time, she had complimented him for his past behaviour.

'And, in the circumstances, you didn't press too hard?'

'That's right. We hoped that, as things got more serious, academically, he would step up.'

'And he hasn't?'

'Not really. It's a shame. A real shame. I mean, I worry what he'll do when he leaves here. He doesn't seem to have any interest in university or college or any of the apprenticeships we promote.'

'I'm sure you'll do all you can to motivate him, at the right time.' Judith smiled warmly.

'Can I just ask if *you* ever saw or heard anything – maybe the boys talk among themselves – anything that might point to Dr Sullivan having an enemy?'

'We're a long way removed from the boys' private lives here. Parents visit for events but, generally, they arrive to take the boys home and we don't interact much. Dr Sullivan was very local, of course. Some families aren't.' Mr Jenkins had now unfolded his arms and was speaking freely for the first time.

'And when was Tom last home?'

'We don't have a half-term break, but he had a weekend at

home at the beginning of October. It was his birthday, so I made a special exception.'

'And Dr Sullivan picked him up and drove him back?'

'I think so. I doubt we have any way of checking.'

'Was Tom in regular contact with his mum?'

'I don't know.'

'They don't receive letters?'

'The boys mostly communicate by phone or online.'

'And you don't monitor that?'

'We don't listen in on their personal interactions, no.'

'So, what, they have access 24/7 to their phones and the internet?'

'They are not allowed phones during the school day, but there are no limits at other times for Tom's year group. We trust the boys to be sensible, but we do keep an eye on them, even so. Occasionally, there are problems which arise and then we have to act.'

'What kind of problems?'

Mr Jenkins suddenly stiffened up. 'We seem to have strayed from your original area of interest which, as I recall, was Dr Sullivan,' he said. 'And I think I answered all your questions in that regard.'

'Yes, you did. You've been very helpful. Just one more thing, just in case we need to speak to Tom again, it occurred to me when you were talking about his future, will he stay here at school, now? I mean, presumably a place here is, understandably, costly.'

'We're not sure,' Mr Jenkins said, after a short pause. 'Like I said, I certainly hope so, but it may be out of my hands.'

***

'He didn't seem difficult to me.' Constance and Judith stood outside the entrance, after saying their goodbyes.

'What's that?'

'Dr Williams, Dr Sullivan's colleague. He said Tom was a difficult boy; to be prepared.'

'He flounced out of the room when the questions got the tiniest bit uncomfortable.'

'That's unfair. You told him his mother had depression and, like the headmaster said, you talked about his father too. That would be difficult for anyone to cope with, let alone a boy who's grieving. I knew you were going to ask him something awkward. You looked up at the painting. I could tell.'

'Actually, I was thinking how incongruous it was that a man who abhorred slavery, our illustrious school patron, Mr Wilberforce, was being exposed every day, from his vantage point, to the machinations of a modern-day slaver, in the form of Mr Jenkins and his rigorous school regime.'

'You just thought of that now, but you don't want to be caught out.'

Judith grinned. 'You're probably right...about me and about Tom's exit. It was certainly within the bounds of normal responses. His hands were shaking though, even when we first arrived. Did you see?'

'Yes. Poor thing.'

'I do wonder that she sent him away.'

'Dr Williams said she was lecturing around the world, was worried she couldn't look after him properly. Said they spent a lot of weekends together to make up for it.'

'Jenkins didn't say that, did he? Suggested Tom was only

allowed home for holidays or "special exceptions". That's why I took against Jenkins, by the way, in case you think I had no justification. What do I know? I imagine Elizabeth Sullivan was just trying to do what was best for Tom. And if he knew his mum was on anti-depressants, he did a tremendous job at covering up.'

'Why would he know?'

'I think it must be hard to keep secret, if you live together, even if it's only weekends and holidays. Pills in the cabinet, pills by the bed, take after food, with water. Maybe that's another reason she sent him away. Mr Jenkins was defensive though, wasn't he?'

'You think?'

'I can't believe they don't have more control over what the boys are accessing online. Teenage boys! What do the parents think of that?'

'And I can't believe you asked him if the kids write letters to their parents. When did you last receive a letter from anyone under the age of twenty-one?'

Judith smiled.

'How many minutes till our Uber?' she asked.

'Four.'

'Let's meet it by the road. It was warm in there, wasn't it? Although I appreciate it's all relative. I am currently residing in the foothills of the Himalayas.'

'What?'

'My boiler's on the blink. Anything vaguely temperate feels like the Costa del Sol.'

As they approached the gates, they heard a rustle and a cough and then a tall boy, in matching school uniform to Tom, stepped out in front of them.

'Hi,' he said, waving one hand at them.

'Hello,' Judith answered.

'You've been to see Tom?' he said.

'Yes,' Judith said. 'Are you one of his friends?'

'I'm David. We share a room.' The boy peered over his shoulder towards the school and stepped back into the bushes, out of sight of the entrance. Constance and Judith followed suit.

'Was there something you wanted to tell us?' Judith said.

'It's about Tom. I don't know what to do.'

'We're not...'Constance began, but Judith drowned her out. 'Tell us what's bothering you?' she said.

David bit his lip, wrung his hands together and gazed again at the school façade, before speaking. 'I think Tom has a problem,' he said.

'What kind of problem?'

'Gaming. Online games. Mr Jenkins gave him his laptop, kind of, to cheer him up, I s'pose. But he's playing all the time, getting all wound up. Forgetting to eat or drink, just wanting to win. He says it helps him. I promised I wouldn't tell Mr Jenkins.'

'I see,' Judith said, catching Constance's questioning eye.

'Do you think I *should* tell him? Mr Jenkins.' David was shifting from one leg to the other, as he simultaneously weighed up his loyalties. 'I don't want Tom to get ill or anything.'

'A promise is a promise,' Judith said. 'And I think it's important that Tom has a good friend he can trust right now.' She smiled at David and he smiled in return. 'Leave this with us,' she said, turning around and heading out of the gates. 'We'll see what we can do.'

***

'Well, that may explain the hands shaking,' Judith commented, half to herself, as she and Constance stood on the platform at Mill Hill station, waiting for their train.

'You mean Tom?'

'Yes. And the poor academic performance. Any ideas on what we could do for him, given that, officially, it isn't any of our business and we probably have a fairly good idea what response we'll get from Mr Jenkins, should we choose to interfere?'

'There's supposed to be a sister. I'll check with Dawson if she's been found yet. We could talk to her.'

'Good idea. And those medical papers Liz wrote, do they explain how to stop teenage boys playing games?'

'Not the ones I've read so far. I could ask Dr Williams. I could do it without mentioning Tom?'

'Good idea number two. Was there anything Tom told us we could use? Maybe find those friends of Liz's. Dawson may already have their details.'

'I doubt it. He made it pretty clear he stopped investigating when he found Jaden.'

'Not that surprising, I suppose. All right. Let's take stock of where we are with the industrious Jaden.'

'Sure.'

'Is he still impressing you with his wisdom?'

'I don't know,' Constance said.

'What do you mean, you don't know?'

Constance sighed deeply. 'He's been more cooperative, actually – opened up a bit more. And his answers with Dawson were calm. He didn't lose the plot when he could have done, when Dawson pressed him. It's just…I don't know…the rape charge.'

'What? It's made you feel uncomfortable?'

'I don't get it. I was happy to pull my chair up close and play his buddy when he was accused of murder, of taking someone's life, but when Dawson accused him of rape and, just like that, matter-of-fact, afterwards, he admitted the sex – he says consensual – something changed in me. I…I just wanted to get out of there.'

'Look. I don't know why you felt like that. I suppose this murder, if it even was a murder, was so clean, no blood, no bruises. It was easy to accept Jaden's explanation, albeit it had to be wheedled out of him. Now, we're all suspicious that there's more to come.'

'I'm not suspicious, though; not yet, anyway. And, although I told him off for keeping it to himself, I can see why he wouldn't own up, in the circumstances. I suppose it was two things that bothered me; he was so casual and relaxed about the sex, and that…offended me, somehow. And then he made me doubt everything I had believed about the case up till then. I had thought I knew him, but I realised, in that second, that I didn't know a thing about him.'

'Don't beat yourself up over it. We have to make judgment calls all the time and we can't even begin to know the half of our client's lives. It's better if you're more…distant. That way you'll be more objective. Did he accept he used ropes? I saw the report about marks on her arms.'

'He says that's rubbish. He seemed quite…insulted.'

'But you believed him, that it wasn't rape?'

'Yes. I really did. I believed him, but the uneasiness remained.'

'All right. We'll need to get the rape stuff out there, right at the beginning then. No light touch. The jury will need to feel that distaste you experienced at the outset, and then get over it, before they judge him. What about the trainers, bought with Liz Sullivan's credit card? Have you asked him about that yet?'

'It's next on my list.'

'Keep me posted on his response. What else?'

'No history of violence, caution in 2018 for possession of marijuana, another before that, for theft of a wallet from a teacher. Lives with a school friend, Nathaniel Brooks, who spent a year in a young offenders' institution.'

'Ah. Do we know why?'

'I'm working on it.'

'You've been to see him?'

'He's nervous about being a witness. But I think, with help, he'll come good. His evidence supports JD – especially the timing. He says JD was back in time for their show, that he wasn't upset or agitated.'

'That's good. We shouldn't underestimate the importance of having that confirmed by someone else, even a close friend. And their show was live, wasn't it?'

'Yes.'

'So, maybe we find one or two *fans* who can say they watched all night, that kind of thing. Was JD on screen throughout the show?'

'I haven't checked.'

'You need to, although of course it's all irrelevant if Elizabeth Sullivan was already dead. Back to Jaden then. No other family, you've said. Makes a good income from his gaming, money in the bank, pays rent on time. There's no motive, is there? Let's say he did steal her credit card and he bought the trainers. What did they cost? A hundred pounds?'

'More like two hundred.'

Judith raised her eyebrows. 'Even then. He's going to kill her for a pair of trainers?'

'Maybe.'

'Listen. For a second, let's just assume he did it, test out that motive. It was an accident. He misread the signs. He said he wasn't used to drinking wine and they had a bottle between them. He thought Liz fancied him. She was just being friendly, returning a favour. He pressed her for sex. She resisted, he persisted and her heart gave out. He panicked. On his way out, he picked up her bag. Maybe there was something identifying him on her phone? The invitation to come over or a photo? He took the bag to cover his tracks.'

'OK.'

'But couldn't resist using the credit card?' Judith pressed her fingers against her lips. 'It doesn't stack up,' she said. 'If he wanted to conceal his involvement, he would have chucked the bag and all its contents; not allowed an easy connection straight back to him.'

'Unless he was super-confident no one would make the link. I think we need more on the cause of death.'

'I absolutely agree. Not many forty-year-old women die of previously undiagnosed heart conditions. I'm going to talk to a pathologist I know, see if he can make some sense of it. Maybe that's our best defence.'

'What?'

'That the police got it right at the start. It was natural causes. Tragic as it is, Elizabeth Sullivan just died in her sleep and it was nothing to do with her encounter with Jaden.'

'OK. If your pathologist will support that, it might work.'

'But we'd have to persuade him to admit to the theft. Maybe, we could even get Dawson to do a deal. Jaden pleads guilty to the theft, gets a suspended sentence and the rest is dropped.'

Constance shrugged.

'What?'

'Sounds like you've given up before we've even started,' she said.

'That's unfair. If this was only about me, I'd be happy to fight every time, you know that. But it's not. I'm thinking about the boy, Jaden, how it will play out in court. On his own evidence, he was there with her, just before she died. And, despite my strategy for dealing with the rape allegation, the jury will hate the sex thing. You hate it and you're defending him and, on top of their revulsion, they'll have Thomas Sullivan sitting in the courtroom, virtually the same age as Jaden. Even if they believe Jaden, they'll feel uncomfortable with it, that it shouldn't have happened. Add in the trainers and the lies he told when he was picked up...'

'OK. I'll talk to Jaden about the theft. But you'll talk to your pathologist friend?'

'I will. And those research papers. I want to see them too, remember.'

The train pulled into the station and they stepped inside the carriage and sat down. Two minutes into their journey, Judith stood up, grabbed the overhead strap. Then she gravitated to the vertical bar nearest the door and allowed herself to be thrown around, anchored by the wrist, as the train bumped its way along to the next station. Constance couldn't work out why Judith would wish to stand, when there were seats free, but she knew better than to question her when she had that serious 'thinking' look on her face. Not long after, Judith reclaimed her seat, as jerkily as she had left it. For the rest of the journey, they each sat in silence, reflecting on the day's events.

15

CONSTANCE STOOD OUTSIDE the interview room for a few seconds longer than usual, trying to work out the best way to approach things with Jaden, without it appearing like a total betrayal. She knew Judith was right, though. Although the evidence was circumstantial, it didn't leave him in a strong position, unless something else turned up to point to another culprit. Taking a deep breath and smoothing down her hair, she pushed the door open.

Jaden was sitting slumped in his chair, his back to the door. Today he was in more modest clothing; grey tracksuit bottoms and a blue top, but without seeing his face, she couldn't begin to assess how he was feeling.

'Hi, Jaden.'

'Hi.' He hardly moved.

'Would you rather I call you JD? That's what you like people to call you, isn't it?'

A shrug.

'I talked to Nathaniel. He seems like a good friend.' She sat down and waited, but he didn't respond. 'Look. There's been a couple of developments. The police have Liz's handbag, but it was empty, found in a place called Golders Hill Park, near Golders Green, North West London. Do you know it?'

'No.'

'And there's something else. They found a pair of trainers – these ones – at your flat.' Constance walked around to stand in front of him and showed him a photo on her screen. 'Do you recognise them?'

He lifted his head to look at the screen and then he looked directly into Constance's eyes.

'I didn't do it,' he said.

Constance took a deep breath. This was going to be even harder than she had envisaged. 'I didn't ask that,' she said. 'I asked if you recognised these shoes. Are they yours?'

'Maybe.'

'Maybe?'

'I got lots of trainers. I get sent trainers to wear, for the show. I can't be expected to remember them all.'

'Do you often put them in the cupboard under the kitchen sink?'

'Tcha… Maybe.'

'What? You ran out of space in your wardrobe… A pair of these same trainers, in a size 11, were bought using Elizabeth Sullivan's credit card, from a website called Yeezy UK.'

'So? I can't help it if she had crap taste.'

'They were bought five hours *after* she died!'

Jaden closed his eyes tightly, then opened them wide and rolled them to heaven.

'I don't know nothing about that. When am I getting out of here?' he asked.

'I can try for bail, but I doubt you'll get it. You want me to try?'

'I don't want to be in here. I shouldn't be in here.'

'OK. Listen, I will level with you. At the moment, things are not looking great. I'll follow up the trainers the police found in your kitchen, see if we can show they weren't the ones Liz bought. And Judith – she's your barrister, so she's the one who'll stand up and talk in court for you, if we get that far – she's speaking to a pathologist she knows. We may be able to show that Liz just had a heart attack, after all, that it was nothing to do with you. Did she say she felt ill when you were there?'

'What kind of ill?'

'I don't know. Short of breath, chest pains.'

'Is that what you want me to say?'

'No. I want you to think back and tell me what you remember.'

'I don't remember no chest pains or nothing. She was just fine.'

Constance took a deep breath and then sat back in her chair.

'I read a book last year; it was a bestseller; "true crime". You know what that is?' she asked.

'Like Ted Bundy shit; I know.'

'This book was about a man convicted of murdering an old man – a musician; a horrible, brutal murder and the only thing connecting him to the killing was that he had used the man's credit card after his death. He couldn't deny he took the card; he was caught on CCTV at a cashpoint machine using it; he even changed the PIN on the card over the phone and there was a recording of his voice. His lawyers tried to persuade him to plead guilty to the theft and use of the card. Said it would save him, but he refused and the jury convicted him of everything, including the murder. He was sentenced to life with a minimum of fifteen years. He's inside now, still maintaining how innocent he is.'

'Why are you telling me this? You think I want to borrow the book?'

'I think you know why. I don't want you to tell me what you think you should say. Of course not. But you should try very hard to remember everything you can about Liz's bag and her phone and her credit card and see if anything comes to mind. And, if so, you tell me.'

'Am I allowed visitors?'

'What?'

'If I'm not getting out, I'd like to see Nathaniel.'

'It's usually just family.'

'He's the closest I have to family.'

'I'll see what I can do.'

16

'Hey, Tom?'

Tom heard the words through a haze. His head hurt and his eyelids were heavy, when he tried to prise them open. Then his world shifted sideways, as David threw himself down on the next bed and leaned his weight back against the headboard. Tom rolled over and raised himself up on one elbow. Thankfully, David had left the curtains closed.

'Hey, Dave,' he managed. He rubbed at his eyes and sniffed the air, then pulled at the sleeve of his t-shirt. 'I need a shower,' he said.

'I think you probably do,' David replied.

The boys sat together in silence, only broken by Tom scratching at his head and yawning widely.

'Why do you do it?' David asked, after a while.

'What?'

'The gaming. Why do you do it?'

'I like it.'

'Do you?'

'Nothing compares. Not for me, anyway. You must know. It's not as if you've never played. I mean, who doesn't want to be the last man standing, or save the planet from alien invasion or score the best goal ever with an overhead kick from fifteen metres? Here, in the real world, what am I? A nobody. I'm rubbish at sport, OK at English and maths, but I'm never gonna win any prizes.'

'You play for so long, though. It's like nothing else matters.'

'That's right,' Tom said. 'There, in there,' he pointed at his laptop, sitting open on the desk, 'when I'm playing, I'm a hero, people depending on me, putting their trust in me. I'm Archimonde, Wrathion and Brann all rolled into one.'

'But don't you get fed up doing it all the time?'

'Never. That's why it's so awesome. The more I play, the better I feel and the stronger I get. It's like anything you train for. You have to have the talent to start with, and I do. I know I do. You know, before…before I had to stop, I'd been accepted by The Wanderers.'

'Who are The Wanderers?'

'A new team being put together by K9 Games. They picked me, out of more than a thousand, but I had to say no. So I know I have the talent. But then, you have to be committed to operate at that level. You think Roger Federer got to be the best tennis player in the world, by just playing a couple of times a week? Or KSI could knock down Logan Paul, if he didn't train?'

'But it isn't real, like you said. You're not winning a real battle, are you?'

'Good thing it isn't, or I'd have a lot of deaths on my conscience.' David laughed and Tom managed a smile.

'Aren't you lonely sitting in here playing on your own?'

'Lonely? This is what people don't understand, what Mum

never understood.' He swallowed hard. 'I have friends, loads of them, and from all over the world. We speak, we compete together, we support each other and this is what we have in common. I'm never alone when I'm playing.'

'What about other stuff; you know, exams?'

'I don't need them where I'm going. I'm going to play professionally. Listen, can you keep a secret?'

David squirmed on the bed and his cheeks flushed red, but Tom had already taken his silence for acquiescence and he was speaking again.

'I wrote to them yesterday, to The Wanderers. They're moving up the league and they're looking for new blood. I told them I was playing again and they're watching my progress.'

'Wow.'

'Yeah, I know. I reckon, two or three more big wins and I'm in with a chance. I got a wild card entry to the *Fortnite* tournament last year, which I had to give up. I didn't tell anyone about that. That would have been epic. Ha! Well, really epic, seeing as it was organised by Epic! I told him – the scout from The Wanderers – and he was really impressed. You saw what happened there, at the tournament?'

'No.'

'Bugha won the $3million prize.'

'Bugha?'

'Yeah, a kid just like me, aged sixteen, not in any of the big teams, walked away with first prize – and his mum had always nagged him to stop, just like mine did. He said she even threw his console out of the window and stopped all his allowance. But now she understands how skilful her son really is – how this is what he wants to do – and he's made shedloads of money.'

'Your mum didn't want you to play, then?' David fiddled with one corner of his duvet.

'No,' Tom said. 'She said I was *addicted*. She took everything away from me, so I couldn't play. That's because that's what she does...did; treat these hopeless addicts who were sick, because they couldn't do anything except gaming. And none of them were any good – all losers. That's not me. I'm not an addict. I could stop, if I wanted. See, I'm not playing now, am I? Anyway, she's gone now, so I can do what I like.'

He pushed himself up from the bed and stretched his arms above his head – then wrinkled his nose. 'Ew!' he waved his hand in front of his face. 'I really stink.' He grabbed a towel from behind his door.

'I'm going for a shower,' he said. 'There's a tournament beginning at 11, which I don't want to miss. You can stay if you like, and watch me play, as long as you keep really quiet this time.'

17

ERIC HAD BEEN IN A terrible mood all day. He had arrived late, marched past everyone without speaking and slammed his door so hard that his collection of Mr Valiant-through-the-ages had fallen over, each one knocking into its neighbour, setting them all off domino-style. This had resulted in a run of expletives and a request for Gillian to come in, urgently, and stand them all up again.

After that, he appeared to spend much of the day on his phone, striding up and down his office and tearing at his hair. No one knew what the problem was.

'Maybe it's his ex-wife?' Gillian suggested. 'He hates her. He always said she bled him dry on their divorce – even took his Spotify account.'

'I hope it's not the accountant,' Bill, the artist, said. 'Last year, when we heard that the profit figures weren't looking so great, Eric threatened to *cut Gerry's heart out with a spoon*. Do you remember that?'

Gillian nodded solemnly.

'And what happened?' Luke almost spilled his mochaccino.

'Gerry admitted he'd made a mistake and we met our target. I'm sure it was around this time. Maybe you should take Eric in some coffee, Gill? See if that helps.'

'I'm not going in without being asked. Remember when he had that new dartboard put up and didn't tell us. He only just missed my eye. Anyway, I was in there this morning. He'll think it's strange if I go in again.'

'You go then, Luke. You're golden boy at the moment. Take him a coffee and see if you can find out what's got him so wound-up.'

Luke sauntered down to the coffee kiosk at the foot of the building, deep in thought. If Eric was stressed, then he assessed that machine-manufactured coffee, of the type the office had to offer, may only enrage him more. It also put off the moment at which he would have to go in and face Eric. He only realised once he was in the queue that he had no idea how Eric took his coffee: straight up, black, white, with sprinkles? He should have been more observant; everyone knew how their boss liked their coffee, didn't they? In the end, he decided that a double espresso suited Eric's image, so that even if he didn't like it, he wouldn't want to admit he didn't.

Eric surprised him by smiling broadly, as Luke tapped at the door.

'Luke. Hurray. Just the man I wanted to see. Come and sit down. You're not too busy for a chat, are you?'

Everything appeared to be in order, Luke thought, the punch bag neatly tucked in the far corner, no missiles flying around. He staggered forward.

'Now's good, thanks. I thought you might like a coffee.'

Eric grinned again and reached out to take the cup from Luke's hand, sitting it snugly on a coaster. Luke sat down, as instructed, shocked by the warmth of his welcome.

'Oh, do I need to make notes? I didn't bring…'

'No notes. Just your ears. For now, anyway.'

'Sure.'

'Have you ever been to Nice?'

'Nice? I don't think so.'

'It's a beautiful city, in the south of France.'

'I've never been.'

'How'd you like to come with me, to Nice?'

'I'd love to, I think. Is there something…'

'The conference. You know, the big one.'

'Oh. *The conference.* I knew it was in France...'

'Trust me. Nice is a great choice for a venue. And it's going to be the biggest and best Esports conference yet. Everyone will be there, and we heard, today, that the Olympic Games selection panel finally accepted their invitation. They needed a bit of arm-twisting, a few favours being called in, but they're coming. It's just the first step, but let's not underestimate its importance.'

'No, it sounds…amazing. What…why?'

'I've been asked to speak. And, if I remember correctly, you have English 'A' level. Am I right?'

Luke nodded, his face flushing.

'A wordsmith, as well as a master craftsman. So, you'll help, with my speech. But first thing's first. Do you watch the Olympics?'

'Sure. Doesn't everyone?'

'I don't know they do. I think some young people, these days, they might prefer to be doing other things; the Olympics may not be quite so…relevant to them as it was for, say, their parents. And do you know why that is?'

Luke hesitated. He could hazard a guess, but he really didn't want a repeat of the paper around the forehead incident, if he selected the wrong answer. It had been painful enough, last time, peeling off the tape, without simultaneously removing clumps of hair. Fortunately, Eric had decided to answer his question himself.

'It's because they haven't accepted gaming as a participating sport. But Esports – it's the way of the future. It's the way to get young people engaged in the Olympics. We help them more than they help us, and that is the message we're going to deliver to them, right between the eyes, in Nice.'

'OK.' Luke was beginning to share Eric's excitement.

'That's why we need to talk about the new game.'

'You still like it?'

'Oh I like it. But, you see, if we get the green light for the Olympics, they're going to want a game. They're bound to, they have to choose one. When NBC started showing Esports, they partnered with Psyonix and used *Rocket League*. The Olympics is no different. They can't just say "We accept Esports", they'll want to be able to show everyone what the players will be playing.'

'OK.'

'So…I love your new game. I *love* your new game. And I know, as a designer, you probably think it's perfect and you don't want to change any aspect of it.'

'Well, I…'

'I know I wouldn't, if it was my game.'

'OK.' Luke knew he kept repeating himself – he was too scared to say anything more until he knew where the conversation was going. But now Eric was finally getting to what he really wanted to discuss.

'What if your game – the game you imagined, sweated over, brought to market. What if your game was the first game *ever* to be played in the Olympic Games?' Eric said. 'Wouldn't that be the most awesome achievement?'

Luke couldn't help but agree with Eric. It would be a pretty huge head rush, if your game was selected like that.

'We've got a chance, you see.'

'We do?'

'They don't want a big manufacturer. Most of the big guys already have tie-ups with news stations and big corporations and it makes it difficult for the Olympics' standards guys. You know – it's for amateur sport and all that, and no politics. They've whispered, unofficially of course, that they want an indie. And, like I said, they're going to be there, in Nice. And we're going to sell your game to them.'

Luke suddenly felt nauseous. Eric was right. This was the most fantastic, once-in-a-lifetime opportunity he was being offered. He couldn't begin to imagine the impact it would have on Valiant's business and his own career, even to be considered for an international event, let alone one on the scale of the Olympics. But to fail? That would be unbearable, wouldn't it?

'You know what I said about your game?' Eric was speaking again.

'That you loved it.'

'And I do. We are going to have to make a few modifications, though. It's not too late, is it?'

'Bill was going to start the artwork on Monday and Pete is just beginning his work...'

'Not too late then.'

'What kind of modifications were you thinking of?'

'No killing.' Eric enunciated each word slowly and deliberately, his eyes gleaming.

'No killing? But you said "make killing fun".' Luke was now confused as well as queasy, and his hand found its way, involuntarily, to his forehead.

'I know, I know. But that's when you have killing in a game. *If* you have killing, it has to be fun. But in this game, your modified game, we're not going to have any killing at all. We just can't. You must see that. They'll never accept it – well, not at first. The first Olympics Esports tournament will have to take place without a single drop of blood being spilt. After that, once they see how amazing it is, how it will drag those dusty old men into the twenty-first century, when they see how many more viewers they get, the extra advertising revenue, then they'll come cap in hand to us and we can give them anything: hanging, burning, decapitation, suicide bombings. But this time, the first time, we need a game without killing. Can you do that, do you think?'

'You want me to…modify my game, to take out the killing?'

'Yes.'

'How long do I have?'

'The conference is in early February. We'd only need a trailer by then, not the whole thing. Can you do it?'

Luke's pulse was beating in his temple. He hadn't even realised he had a pulse there, but it was definitely throbbing away.

'Yes,' he said. 'I can.'

'Great!' Eric slapped him hard across the shoulder blades. Then he picked up the espresso Luke had brought him and drank it down in one mouthful.

Luke waited, but Eric sat back down and began scrolling

through his phone messages. He saw that as his signal that the session was over. He headed for the door.

'There is one more thing,' Eric stopped him in mid-tracks.

'There is?'

'The name…of the game.'

'I had one or two in mind, but now we're changing it…'

'Midas,' Eric said.

'Midas?'

'We should call it Midas.'

'But the name has to suit the game. If it's called Midas, doesn't it have to be all about, well, gold?'

'It has to be called Midas, because it's a brilliant name – I can hear them chanting it now, across the Olympic stadium, can't you? Mi-das, Mi-das, Mi-das – and it's going to make us all very, very rich, but that's just for us to know. It's up to you if you make the game about gold or not. I doubt anyone'll notice, once they start to play.'

18

CONSTANCE MET SANDY (Cassandra) Bell in a café in Covent Garden. She'd forgotten what a melting pot the area was, the crush in the lift to escape the underground, surrounded by all the languages of Europe, plus a few more for good measure. The melee just outside, as countless couples and groups reunited to head for shops or theatre or restaurant land. They sat by the window and Constance ordered a sandwich to eat with her coffee.

'I still can't believe Liz's gone,' Sandy said, tucking her hair behind her ears and sipping from a mug of camomile tea. 'We used to meet here, once a month, if she was in the UK. She liked it because it was so different from the world she operated in.'

'What was she like?'

'Warm, funny, very serious about her work. She felt there was a real gap there, helping young people, mostly young men, with their addictions.'

'She worked very hard on her studies, as well as with patients, didn't she?'

'She did.'

'Did she prefer the academic side then?'

'No, never. She saw it as a way to get people to take notice of what she was doing and to get funding for research. I think she hated the fact it took time away from treating patients, but she felt she had no choice.'

'Did she ever seem…depressed?'

'Why do you ask?'

'Her post-mortem showed she was taking anti-depressants.'

'Oh,' Sandy lowered her mug to the table and smiled a sad smile. 'That doesn't surprise me. She never said. But she hadn't had much luck in life. Will, her husband – they'd been together since university. You know he died.'

'Was he a doctor too?'

'Noooo. He was a musician. He used to compose for radio and tv. That was what was so wonderful about the two of them. She gave him stability and determination, he gave her…music and frivolity. They couldn't have children at first. Had a few false starts. She tried to keep positive, but I know it was difficult for her. They looked into adoption but that was a disaster. The social workers hated her, because she travelled so much. They told her she wasn't good mother material.'

'That must have been hard.'

'Then along came Tom and they both adored him, so things were good for a few years. Then Will was sick, and he died so young. Less than three months from diagnosis. And, of course, Liz knew how ill he was, but she didn't say – not to us anyway. Just bottled it all up. She kept all his music and all his instruments and then, one year to the day after he died, she gave it all away.

'So, yes. With us she was always cheerful, never complained, but I knew that, underneath, she was sad.'

'Was she in a relationship with anyone, do you know?'

'I don't think so, but it's almost exactly a month since we last met. And she kept a lot of things to herself, like I said. '

'And what about Tom?'

'Ah, Tom. You've met him?'

'I went to visit him at school.'

'He was a gorgeous little boy, with all this blond, spiky hair. And then, well, he grew up. You know about the gaming?'

'Yes.'

'Liz blamed herself. She couldn't believe it. She was out consoling parents of these kids who didn't wash any more, because all they could do was play video games and, suddenly, she was one of those parents too. That's why she sent him away, where they could keep a closer eye on him than she could. It was a terrible wrench, as he was all she had. But she thought it was the only way to stop him. At least she got that bit right.'

Constance had suddenly lost interest in her sandwich. 'Was there anyone she was scared of? A patient? A former boyfriend? A colleague?' she asked.

'I'm not sure Liz was scared of anyone. She was one of those people who just got on with things and I think, after Will, she thought she'd had her share of bad luck. When her book was published, I know that caused some problems, though.'

'What kind of problems?'

'Ask Tony Williams, but all sorts of things, even from doctors. Telling them they were backward and against anything new, saying their testing wasn't rigorous, complaining they were scaremongering and Liz said she had to talk to some government committee about it all.'

'Why was the government interested?'

'I don't know exactly, but there was a big meeting three or four months back. When we met here previously, she was fussing about all the preparation she had to do. She was quite stressed about it.'

'What about her family?'

'Her dad died when she was little. She didn't remember him. Talk about history repeating itself. And she has a sister: Eve.'

'Are they close?'

'They get on, but they don't see each other much. Last I remember was Liz said that Eve was on some round-the-world trip. I would have expected her to call me, if she was back, but I haven't heard anything.'

Constance finished her sandwich and drank down her coffee. Then she checked her watch.

'Thanks so much. You've been really helpful. Is it all right if I call you again, if I have any more questions?'

'No problem. I'm here. There is one thing, I was just thinking. You asking about whether Liz was seeing anyone.'

'Yes.'

'So, once, a couple of months back, I called her in the evening and I could hear noise in the background, you know, voices, low music, like she was in a bar or a restaurant. She denied it later, when we met, said she'd had the radio on. But she had this look on her face, when she said it. You know, like when you remember something enjoyable. I thought, at the time, that she'd probably been out with someone, but she didn't want to say.'

***

Judith sat at her PC. She had moved on from watching Jaden to actively participating in a game. She had told herself it was the only way to even begin to understand her client. But the truth was that she was curious. If Constance was right about the number of people playing these games, then either they were all misguided wastrels who would never be attracted to culture or beauty, or there was truly something appealing in them for everyone.

After considerable vacillation, she had downloaded a free one and played it for the last hour and a half, and how the time had flown. It had tempted her, at first, because of its potential to educate – it was set in the eighth and ninth centuries and focused on Viking settlements – but it was the battles with their thunderous music and palpable tension that had held her attention far more than the authentic 3D communes.

She walked around the room and stared out of her window. The condensation dribbling down her streamed-up pane told the story for her, even before she touched the ailing radiator. She grabbed another jumper from her bedroom, together with her phone, which she powered up and checked for messages.

Spare ticket for Miss Saigon, dress circle, Sat night 8pm. What d'you say? G.

Judith sighed. 'You know I don't like musicals,' she muttered to herself. Then she returned to her PC and searched Google, before laughing out loud. 'It's not even on any more!' she admonished her phone.

She had to hand it to Greg. He was tenacious and he knew her well. She almost replied – almost, but not quite. Anyway, there was always a risk that if she replied, the messages would stop and she was beginning to look forward to them, their spontaneity, their thoughtfulness.

Then she admonished herself for her weakness, and that led her to be cross with Greg. Why was he pursuing her like this? Why couldn't he just leave her alone? Had he thought her ending the relationship was not really the end, just some kind of test of his resolve?

Perhaps she shouldn't be surprised. It was in Greg's character not to give up. He had told her as much on many occasions. Judith was different. She couldn't see any point in flogging a dead horse. But then Greg had consistently challenged her to change her perspective on life. She remembered the time he had dragged her to the latest *Mission Impossible* film, replete with Butterkist popcorn, an experience she would never have undertaken on her own, but found she thoroughly enjoyed. Not that she had let on, at the time.

She pushed her phone away and minimised the Viking game. It surprised and irritated her that she could so easily have continued to play, that she wanted to re-build the chief's house and compound, to shore up its defences, and from there, move on to the thick of the next epic battle. Did that mean she had the potential to become an addict? Was this how Tom Sullivan had started out? Greg would definitely have found her confusion amusing. In any event, she was stopping the game now. Instead, she would devote a few minutes to Elizabeth Sullivan.

She searched the Hackney Hospital website and Liz's smiling face appeared, together with her credentials; educated in Bristol, then university in London and most of her career in Hackney. All those letters after her name.

Some people loved to laud their qualifications to high heaven, when they were meaningless drivel – the odd open-book online test passed without turning a hair, a diploma achieved for daily attendance at some nondescript facility. But with a doctor, Judith knew what sacrifice each of those letters represented. Not hours or days but weeks, months and years of eye-strainingly, back-breakingly difficult, committed graft. She ran her fingers over the image of Liz's face. 'Poor Liz!' she said. Then she closed the page with a sniff. Context and background were important. But she needed to remember whose side she was on.

19

'Miss Lamb, how nice to meet you.'

Constance was taken aback by the warmth of the welcome she received from Ian Mason, principal of Hackney School. It was in stark contrast to Mr Jenkins' more circumspect reception, and particularly surprising given the context of her enquiry, although she had provided only scant details over the phone. She returned his greeting and joined him on a quick walk around the playground, before decamping to his office.

'You wanted to talk about Jaden Dodds, you said.' Mr Mason ushered her into his sparsely-furnished room and closed the door. But the lack of equipment was more than compensated for by the jam-packed walls, covered with pictures; class photos, sports teams, pupils waving awards aloft. Constance even spotted Prince Charles in one of them.

'And Nathaniel Brooks,' she said. 'They were both your pupils, weren't they?'

'They were. Thick as thieves those two; no pun intended, I

assure you. Yes, I was their form teacher in year 11, their last year at the school, and before I was made principal. In fact, if you give me a moment, I can probably find them for you here somewhere.' He spent a few seconds searching the walls, before pointing to one of the more formal, posed images. Constance followed his directions and two shorter and slightly smaller-featured versions of JD and Nath stared back at her. 'What are they up to, then?' Mr Mason asked jovially.

'It's actually quite serious, I'm afraid.' Constance hated to disappoint him. 'Jaden has been accused of a rape and murder. You may have seen it in the papers, the local doctor who died, Elizabeth Sullivan. They were neighbours.'

Mr Mason frowned, his shoulders drooped and he shook his head violently from side to side. Then he slapped his cheek with the flat of his hand.

'As you can probably tell, I'm incredibly shocked to hear that. And sorry, too. Jaden was a good boy. Sure he was a bit of a charmer and not the hardest worker, but with a good heart. I can always tell. And the way he looked after Nathaniel. That showed me what a really generous person he was.'

'I'm his defence lawyer, so anything you can tell me which might help – perhaps some background on Jaden and his family – that would be really great.'

'Let me think back. So many pupils. From what I remember, Jaden was an only child. His mother was a nurse. A very gracious lady, but she was ill for most of the time he was in my class. I heard she died the following year. He looked after her, as best he could. There was no other family around, as far as I could tell. He was bright, articulate, had that kind of sparkle in his eye when he spoke to you, but he wasn't really interested in academic work.

'We persuaded him, once, to audition for the school play. Mr Timpson, our drama teacher, said he was wonderful, but he wouldn't take the part, said it was too many evenings away from his mother. He absolutely left here with all good wishes and the respect of everyone. He was very popular. I felt certain he would make something of himself.'

'And Nathaniel?'

'Ah. Nathaniel was a sad boy. Sweet and gentle but always sad, and he was bullied, in the lower years. I don't know why. He was quiet and kept himself to himself, had this fragile quality, that other kids sometimes take advantage of. Then he met Jaden and they clicked. Best of mates, they were. And from then on, no one messed with him, because if you messed with Nathaniel, you had to deal with Jaden. And they didn't want that. Is he involved too, in this horrible crime?'

'I don't think so, although the two of them live together, not far from here. They run a website for gamers. They've become quite popular, locally.'

'That doesn't surprise me. It's big money, I heard, if you make it.'

'I've been told that Nathaniel spent some time in a young offenders' institute. Do you know anything about that?'

'I do, but I'm surprised you do. It was when he was much younger. I thought these things got written off. Maybe nothing's written off any more? Look, it was related to what I said, about when he was first at the school. He got into trouble for selling drugs. I thought he was put under pressure to do it and he was the one who got caught. There wasn't much support at home, so they put him away for six months. He came back to school afterwards and that's when he and Jaden got close. There were no problems after that.'

'But Jaden also got into trouble, once, didn't he? He stole from one of your teachers.'

Now Mr Mason's face hardened. 'You're reminding me of all these things I had forgotten. That should never have even been reported and, if I had been principal, I would have stopped it.'

'Are you saying it didn't happen?'

'We had a new teacher – a student; young and timid. I had to…bail her out a few times when some of the classes got too rowdy. But she was doing OK, gaining in confidence. And then she claimed that some items had gone missing from her handbag: some keys and money. She'd left it in class when there was a disturbance in the corridor. '

'And she suspected Jaden?'

'Not immediately. But he was caught the next day, hanging around the staff room. He refused to say what he had in his pocket, the police were called, they searched him and there was Miss Stevens' keys and £20. We all got the impression he was trying to put them back, without anyone seeing. But Jaden wouldn't say anything, so he got stuck with the theft. Like I say, I would never have called the police.'

'Thank you. You've been very helpful. If I asked you to give evidence, on Jaden's behalf, would you be prepared to do that?'

Mr Mason looked again at the photograph of the two boys he had taught and then he allowed his eyes to travel around the room and out through the window to the playground, until they fixed themselves on the sign declaring 'Hackney School. Leading by example.' 'I'm not sure,' he said. 'I'd have to ask the governors. You know what it's like, these days. And given the seriousness of the charges…'

'I understand.'

'And would they be able to ask me about the things you asked me? Maybe I wouldn't be so useful?'

'No, maybe not.' Constance swallowed her disappointment.

'Give him my best – well, to both of them – Jaden and Nathaniel,' Mr Mason said. 'And I hope you're right and the police find the real culprit. It's never nice to hear that any of our pupils have got into trouble. Or to admit to myself that I might have been wrong to believe in them.'

Constance forced a smile. Why were things never straightforward?

'Now, there is one favour I'd like to ask of you, if I may,' he stopped her, as she rose to leave.

'Go ahead,' she said.

'I'd love you to come back and talk to the children in one of our careers assemblies. It's always inspiring for them to hear directly from people with interesting jobs, especially someone local like you.'

Now Constance's smile was genuine. 'I'd be happy to do that,' she said, 'although I'm sure I could find someone more…eminent than me, if you prefer.'

'I think you'd be perfect. I'll email you across some possible dates.'

20

Judith and Constance sat in the prison interview room, waiting for Jaden's arrival, Constance mulling over her discussion with Mr Mason even as they heard Jaden's step in the corridor. Jaden slouched into the room, gave Judith a sulky glance and then sat down, folding his arms and legs tightly around his body. Constance was disappointed. She had hoped he would make an effort to impress Judith, to illustrate, with his attitude and behaviour, why Constance believed in him. Instead, with his brooding entrance, he appeared no different from most of the others she represented, day in day out, on a variety of more tedious charges, of which they were invariably guilty.

Maybe it was the days of incarceration taking their toll on him. If he really was innocent – and Constance's belief in him had been reinforced by her conversation with Mr Mason – then it must be difficult for him to maintain his composure, under constant challenge. In any event, if Judith was bothered by his petulance, she didn't show it.

'Hello Jaden. I'm Judith Burton.' She stuck her hand out, her fingertips almost touching his chest and he was forced to take it, giving it a perfunctory shake. 'It's very nice to meet you, after I've heard so much about you and, of course, after watching your show.'

Jaden didn't respond but Judith continued, undeterred.

'We wanted to talk to you about the trial, how it will work and who may be witnesses for you and against you. Has Nathaniel been in to see you yet?'

Jaden nodded.

'Good. He's agreed to give evidence and he will be an important witness for you. But, first of all, have you thought, again, about the theft of Elizabeth Sullivan's credit card? Is there anything else you remember now, that you could share with us?'

Jaden took a deep breath and looked up at Constance. Then he shifted his gaze to Judith.

'They were a present,' he said, 'the trainers.'

'A present?'

'Yeah. Like you get on your birthday.'

'Was it your birthday?'

He shook his head, then jumped to his feet. 'I'm not a thief,' he shouted, the words echoing around the walls, before dying down.

Judith appeared unfazed by his outburst. She waited. Jaden bit his lip and then returned to his seat.

'Look,' he continued. 'She was being nice to me, said her son was away, asked me what kind of shoes I liked and, before I knew it, she'd gone online and bought them for me. I wasn't going to say no, was I?'

'When did she buy them for you?' Judith asked.

'That night, when I went over.'

'Was this before or after you went into the bedroom?'

'Before.'

'And, what about dinner?'

'Um, after I think.'

'What kind of time are we talking about?'

'Around seven-thirty. And I know what you're gonna say. The policeman's already said the shoes were bought after she died. When you buy stuff at the weekend or in the evening, it doesn't show up till the next day. That must've happened this time; that's all.'

'Thank you for explaining that to me. And you…what? Just forgot she'd bought them for you, when you were first questioned?'

'There was a lot going on. I wasn't thinking straight.'

'I see. That clears that one up then. That only leaves the rape and murder charge.' Judith was cross now. Constance could tell. Her lips had turned white and almost disappeared into the rest of her face. Didn't Jaden realise this was his chance to convince her of his innocence? That histrionics and surliness, quite apart from this improbable explanation about the trainers, were not advancing his case? But Judith's brusque manner had the effect of eliciting a spirited but controlled response.

'Look. I didn't rape no one and I didn't kill no one,' he said. 'That's it, nothing more to tell.'

'We'll have a very short trial then, won't we? You'll stand up and say that and we'll all be home by lunch time.'

Jaden sat himself up straight and focused on Judith, but he remained silent. She took that as her cue to continue.

'All right. I'm pleased you've got all that off your chest,' Judith said. 'Now let's get down to business, shall we? I understand you feel strongly about all of this. I would too if I was wrongly accused.

But we are spending a lot of time, Constance and I, pulling the threads of your defence together, to get you out of here. And we need your cooperation to do so.'

She paused to allow her words to sink in. Constance breathed again. Judith was definitely becoming more conciliatory in her old age.

'I know you've talked to Constance about this before,' Judith said, 'but the post-mortem mentions marks on Liz Sullivan's arms. Inspector Dawson thinks that means you tied Liz to the bed.'

'I already said. I never.' Jaden's eyes flashed with the indignity of the accusation, but his voice remained calm.

'You didn't see any ropes in her bedroom?'

'No.'

'She didn't...suggest to you that you tie her up. I need you not to be embarrassed about any of this, Jaden. I know it's hard; probably doesn't help that we're women asking you these things.'

'She didn't ask me to tie her up, I didn't tie her up. I didn't see no ropes. I don't have no problem with you being women. Is that clear enough for you?'

'Very clear. There was a chair in Liz's bedroom. Do you remember it?'

'No. I mean, maybe there was, maybe there wasn't.'

'Did either of you sit down on that chair?'

Jaden shook his head. 'No. We went in the room and we went straight to the bed.'

'And, after you had sex?'

'I put my clothes on. I went to the bathroom. When I came back, she was getting dressed too. I collected my stuff and I left. Why is that so hard for everyone to believe?' His voice cracked around the edges and he looked away again.

'Because you were the last person to see Liz alive and, if you didn't kill her, it's hard to explain her death. And humans like explanations for things. They don't like random or sudden. They like cause and effect. Without you, we're just left with her suddenly up and dying. Now she did have a serious and probably undetected heart condition and it is possible her heart just gave up, on its own. It's just that people usually need to believe there was a catalyst. Do you understand what I mean?'

'Sure, I understand. You mean something made it happen. I've been thinking about that too and I don't remember her saying nothing about feeling ill. She was laughing and we ate dinner and, when she said goodbye, she was just fine.'

'OK. Let's focus on that for a moment. When she said goodbye to you, what exactly did she say?'

'What do you mean?'

'Did she, for example, arrange to see you again?'

Jaden sat up even straighter, nodded to indicate he had registered the question and then he closed his eyes tight for a few seconds. Then he shook his head slowly. 'I don't remember exactly,' he said. 'It was something like "I'll see you this week, sometime", very casual. But she also…she was kind of in a hurry to get me to go. She was checking her watch and her phone. So I made this joke that maybe she had another guy waiting and she was going to make him dinner too.' He laughed at the memory. 'She just said no, she liked to get an early night, but then I saw her light was on later, after my show, so she probably just said that – you know – so as not to hurt my feelings.'

'Did she kiss you, before you left?'

Jaden stared at his feet. Then he looked at Constance. 'Yes,' he said.

'Why do feel bad about that?' Judith asked, registering his embarrassment.

'I feel bad because, I mean, I liked her and all that, but, I don't know, when she kissed me, I got worried that maybe she was more into me than I was into her. I think she saw it, that I was not… comfortable with it and that's why she got all casual and said "see you later" kind of thing, like it wasn't important to her neither.'

'Thank you, Jaden. That's very good.' And Judith meant those words. Of course, she might be being fooled – it wouldn't be the first time – but Jaden's level of engagement and whole demeanour shouted out to her that the exchange he described with Liz had really happened. But he misinterpreted her silence as disapproval again.

'You don't believe me?' he said.

'On the contrary, I absolutely believe you. My job, however, is to work out the best way to present all of this, so that the jury believes you too. One more confusing thing. It's a detail and it may mean nothing, but I need to ask.'

'Go ahead.'

'There were some photos taken of Liz, shortly after she was found, lying on her back in bed. I'm going to share them with you.'

Constance called them up on her laptop. Jaden looked closely for a few seconds, then he looked away.

'What am I supposed to be looking at?' he said.

'Like I said, it may be nothing. If you look at Liz's forehead, there are some marks on her skin. Can you see them?'

Jaden looked again and held the screen up close.

'You mean here. Yeah. I see them.'

'She wasn't wearing a hat, a baseball cap, a headband, anything like that?'

'Nope. It was a cold night, but it was really toasty in her flat. A bit too toasty, in fact. She had her hair loose, like in the photo, and no hat.'

'OK. It was worth an ask. There's no mention of those marks in the pathologist's report. And in the photographs from the post-mortem, presumably later that day or the next, they seem to have disappeared. Probably nothing important.'

Constance reclaimed her laptop and moved to a new screen.

'All right. You already have Nathaniel in your corner. Let's spend a few minutes talking about other people who could potentially give evidence, to help you. Constance, why don't you run through your list?'

21

Luke sat in his bedroom, laptop before him, trying to brainstorm some additional ideas for his revised game. But first he had to calm himself down. '*Blow*', '*flow*', '*go slow*'.

He didn't like having the goalposts moved – and not once but twice. Didn't Eric realise that each time Luke sat down to design a game he threw everything into it, every ounce of his strength and creativity? That when Eric had set out the original brief, Luke had stayed up day and night, living and breathing his prototype? That when Eric had scolded him and taped the sign around his head, he had gone for broke, unleashed his inner assassin with the game he had shown the team? And all the pieces had to fit together: story; characters; background; aim; even music. If you changed one of them, they all had to change. Eric talked glibly about 'modification'; he might as well have said 'obliteration'.

But now Luke was calm, he told himself not to ruminate. There was no point. It was destructive. Eric couldn't have known, until today, about the opportunity to pitch to the Olympic selectors.

And Eric was right. They had to have a go; another opportunity like this may never come along. They had to embrace it. He had to adapt his game. And, the more Luke thought about it, the more he realised that, perhaps, a lot of his work so far, could be retained, after all.

He could certainly live with 'Midas' as a theme; kings were always good in games, the bold colours they delivered, the plush materials which surrounded them, the possibility of designing elaborate kingdoms and the creation of strutting, conniving pretenders to the throne. And, despite Eric's comments about the dispensability of the gold, Luke knew he would use it, and pots of it, everywhere. Midas' kingdom would be dripping with it.

Then, he could still utilise his rainforest setting and collection of interesting creatures. After all, the Mayan culture had their temples in the middle of the jungle. Granted, his monarchs were not going to be loin-cloth-clad, but this was a fictional creation and he knew he could make it all fit together.

And, given his new potential global audience, he wanted to develop the sustainability angles of the game too. He had already given Eric palm-oil plantations, logging and oil exploration companies, belonging to a series of dastardly villains. Now he was going to create a local army of resistance fighters, building their own weapons using wholly natural materials. And the source of their wealth? You got it: gold. He would construct a secret gold mine, replete with intricate tunnels and a hierarchy of workers, to work the rich underground seams.

After an hour of sketching out his ideas and scribbling down more, he took a break. He was feeling more positive than ever about the game. The trip with Eric to the South of France, however, worried him on a number of levels. First of all, would they have to share a room? Money was tight – he knew that, despite Eric's relative largesse regarding his potential pay rise. Then there was Eric's temper, or rather, 'volatile nature': the bear hugs and kisses, the foul mouth and physical threats. Eric was the closest Luke had ever met to a schizophrenic, his personality straining towards the furthest boundaries of the thermometer of human nature; one moment dazzling charm and warmth, the next menacing chill, morphing into the blazing heat of an uncontainable rage. Would Eric display any of this contradictory behaviour on their trip and, if so, how would he cope?

Luke thought back to the night he had, unwittingly, spied on Eric after hours; how Eric had flung his phone across the room, screaming at some unsuspecting and absent female companion. He didn't envy the intended recipient of Eric's call that night. It was lucky he hadn't managed to get connected.

Perhaps it was all bluster, he mused. After all, even when Luke had disappointed Eric bitterly, with his first tentative steps into the design of the new game, Eric hadn't actually hurt him. Terrified him, yes, and embarrassed him, but the combination of those emotions had led him to produce his best work yet, led to this moment when he was poised to take the top prize. And one thing he would say in Eric's favour – he was not selfish. He was willing to share the glory with Luke, to allow Luke to rise up with him. And for that Luke would be eternally grateful.

22

Tom was at his desk again, laptop open, index finger switching around with tremendous speed and skill. He had searched online, only that morning, whether there were particular exercises you could undertake to strengthen your fingers. Someone had told him, some years back, that piano lessons were good; all those scales and arpeggios forcing your digits to hammer up and down the keyboard. He had almost asked his mum to find him a teacher.

Then someone else had argued that was rubbish and that piano lessons were dull and he had assessed his chances of getting out of them within six months, if the dissenter was correct, as almost zero. That wasn't his mother's style. She made you stick at things once you'd started. Today, he was a tiny bit cross he hadn't taken the pain of the lessons. Anything to give him a competitive edge would have been worth an hour a week of discomfort.

Tom allowed his eyes to flick up and register his score. He was really motoring. Everything about today's game had gone well, from his choice of character, with the word 'Sully' tattooed across his back, to his sublime, customised hunting knife, to the extra ammo he had collected from the first man he killed. There were only three of them left now, all racing at full speed to the top of the hill. His flag, with its falcon insignia, was tucked in his back pocket. He could see opponent two over to the East, closing in fast and contestant three was almost certainly directly ahead of him, masked by the rising ground. If he could keep his cool and avoid the various hazards the game designers would send his way, then he was on track for his best performance yet.

Suddenly, number two had gone – not his doing: he had been surprised by some marauding robot buffalo and trampled underfoot. Ew! What a way to go! But number three was still in there and the dot representing him on the map, showed they were almost exactly equidistant from their goal. Tom began to scale the hill, leaping boulders, when he could, flinging ropes ahead and levering himself up on the trickier terrain. But unseen competitor three, his nemesis, must be progressing similarly quickly, as they remained neck and neck.

Tom progressed swiftly to the top, to stand on the plateau, the entire universe spread out before him, the cross on the ground, where his flag must be placed to win overall, only a few steps away. As he advanced and reached back to draw it from his pocket, a curious, ragged man, with a wide-brimmed hat, clambered over the precipice, directly ahead of him. His opponent stood up tall and wide, a cross between a pirate and the Incredible Hulk. Then, sword in hand, he charged at Tom.

Tom kept his cool. He knew it was risky, but he calculated that the other character's bulk would make it difficult for him to stop when moving at full tilt, and the summit on which they were standing was little more than the size of a heliport. He waited, brandishing his own favoured weapon of the day, a pair of nun-chucks and then, at the last second, he stepped back. The other man's momentum carried him onwards and right to the edge. For a second, Tom thought he had fallen over, but the pirate giant had checked himself just in time and now he clung, by his prehensile toes, to the rim, arms flailing, staring down at the valley floor, trying desperately to reverse his direction of travel and right himself.

Without wasting any more precious time, Tom flung his nun-chucks and they wrapped themselves around the man's ankles. The man gave him a regretful, over-the-shoulder, last glance, before tipping over and swan-diving to the ground, fifty feet below. Tom leaped forward and planted his flag.

Party poppers exploded everywhere, the world was covered with their multi-coloured streamers and a crown came floating down from heaven to hang in the air above Tom's avatar. First place after two seconds and a third. He had done it.

Tom slid his hands along his thighs to his knees, soaking up their heat and absorbing the sweat from his palms. Then he rose to his feet, turned around and went over to the window. It was dry outside and sunny, despite the persistent cold spell. He opened the window as wide as it would go and felt the icy blast caress his face. He spun his wrists through 180 degrees to ease the tension. Then he climbed up and surveyed the school grounds from his window ledge.

He could see the trees around the school perimeter, the gate – currently open, the rugby pitch, on which Year 8 were slogging away – even from here he could see their red noses and dirty shins. Beyond that, the residential streets of normal life and the sign for the underground station, which had so often transported him home, except there wasn't any home, any more.

What a feeling! To be on top of the world in the game and to reproduce it in real life. He spread his arms and legs across the frame, making a perfect 'X' with his body. Then he heard a shout from below. It took him a moment to register the source of the noise. Two boys, walking between the science and language blocks, had noticed him and were shouting up to him. He couldn't tell if they were being friendly or sounding anxious. He withdrew. He didn't want to draw unwanted attention to himself or to push his luck with Mr Jenkins. Not now, not when he was on the verge of something tumultuous.

23

CONSTANCE AND JUDITH were seated at the table in a small meeting room at Constance's office. Constance was reviewing the notes she had taken of their interview with Jaden, while they revived themselves with coffee and digestive biscuits.

'What did you think?' Constance asked.

'Of Jaden?'

'Yes.'

'I think we need to do what we can, to keep him positive.'

'How do we do that?'

'Work on Nathaniel. Get him to talk to Jaden about things they can do when he gets out, maybe planning some shows. And find out how he's spending his days, see if there's something he can do to occupy himself. I think he's in danger of losing faith and that won't serve him well in court.'

Constance was reassured. If Judith was maintaining this stance, she must believe in Jaden.

'All right,' she said. 'I'll try. I didn't have time to tell you earlier,

I spoke to Sandy Bell, Liz's friend.'

'And?'

'Nothing much, just reinforced a lot of things Dr Williams said. But she mentioned Liz giving evidence to a government committee a few months back and I had a look into it.'

'Oh.'

'The government commissioned an enquiry, last year, into mental health and online gaming. They bowed to pressure from a charity set up by parents of problem gamers. Lots of people from different professions spoke to them and it's recorded online, all the questions and answers.'

'Including Liz's contribution?'

'Yes.'

'What was their conclusion?'

'It's not been published yet, but the introduction is also available, setting out the history to the enquiry and it was really interesting, explaining all the different perspectives.'

'And what did Liz say to them?'

'She was invited to explain the mental health issues that people can experience. One of the key things she was pressing for, was for the manufacturers or the companies hosting the games to impose limits on playing time, to protect players from getting addicted.'

'And what did the manufacturers say about that?'

'They said it would spoil the games, though some people said they were focused more on their pockets. And she wanted the government to take a separate tax from them to fund research and treatment for addicts.'

'I bet they loved that.'

'It's happening already in the USA.'

'Has it? That's ridiculous though, isn't it, if you follow it through? You know a company is making and selling a harmful product, so you let it continue, as long as it helps tidy up the mess it created in the first place. Am I the only one to fail to see the logic or lack of morality in all of that?'

'Their argument is that most people game safely and we shouldn't deprive them of the pleasure they gain from that.'

'In the words of Mandy Rice-Davies, "they would say that wouldn't they?" Don't worry. Old person's reference. You can look her up later. Good work, though I imagine Liz made a lot of enemies with her stance. Finding someone who might have followed that up with violence – that would be like finding a needle in a haystack, although I do, perhaps, have a way in. Was it the Department of Health who set it up?'

'You know someone there?'

'I used to. I could probably pick up the relationship, if it would be useful.' Judith opened up a photograph of Liz Sullivan lying dead and ran her fingers across her screen. 'Can you send me the link to the sessions,' she said. 'I may as well have a look, together with everything else.'

'Does that mean we're not leading with the natural causes defence then? What did your pathologist friend say?'

'I think we need to explore every possibility for now, not keep our enquiries too narrow. I was being totally frank when I told Jaden that juries dislike random events, things which just happen. But I fear that, without the police doing more to look for another culprit, that may be our best bet.'

***

Constance returned home that evening with a long 'to do' list which she needed to trim. There was no way she could complete all these tasks and attend to her other clients. Judith had the luxury of one case at a time and could devote every waking hour to it, if she chose. Although, in some ways, Constance welcomed the distraction from Jaden and what might have happened in the bedroom of 38 Dunloe Close.

She thought back to her lightning tour of Liz's flat, with PC Thomas at her side. PC Thomas had been in a hurry – probably late for a date with an impatient partner – and had rushed Constance around at a tremendous pace, not allowing her to touch anything, despite the forensic team having finished long ago. At least she had been able to take some photographs. She called them up on her laptop now and flicked through them, one at a time.

It was funny. Despite lots of personal touches, Liz's flat hadn't felt homely. There were plenty of books on the shelves, a couple of landscape prints on the wall and evidence of a last meal still sitting in the kitchen. It was probably because there were so many examples of solitary living; one pair of shoes by the door, one umbrella propped up in the corner, one towel in the bathroom.

She tried to imagine them sitting together, Jaden and Liz, around the small table, laughing and joking. And then their progression to the bedroom. She was careful to take lots of photographs there, although she knew the pathologist would have plenty in her report.

Try as she might, though, Constance couldn't recall having seen any photographs of Will, Liz's husband, anywhere. Sandy had said she was unsentimental, or was pretending to be, and that was certainly borne out in the place where she lived.

There was one of Tom, a lovely snap, perched on top of the TV, of him running towards the camera, when he was much younger, his eyes shining with delight. And another image of a group of young men, attached to the fridge by a magnet. Constance was forbidden to pick it up, but she waited until PC Thomas took a call and then quickly pulled it off the fridge and checked the back where, scribbled in a looping scrawl she read *To Dr Liz from Nick and the rest of the A team xx.*

She had replaced it carefully and then taken her own photo of it, which she studied now. Four young men, arm-in-arm, all laughing and cheering. Family or friends; she couldn't say which. She would also mention it to Dawson, see if he had traced anyone in the picture.

Dropping off on the sofa, uneaten dinner by her side, she had another dream about Jaden. This time, Constance was, herself, tied by her wrists to a four-poster bed, with an orange, camouflage-pattern bandana wrapped around her head. She was watching a game unfold on an enormous screen, which spanned the whole of the ceiling. The game involved tiny ant-like creatures fleeing before an enormous pair of black and red trainers, which were marching across a desert landscape, trampling everything in their path, clouds of dust rising up in their wake.

***

Judith was feeling uncomfortable about her forthcoming meeting with Maisy Walton, former Minister for Health and an old friend of Martin's, even more uncomfortable because it was such an unfamiliar experience for her to be uncomfortable. She usually tried to avoid putting herself in that position, at all costs.

Judith had chosen lunch at the Bleeding Heart in Farringdon, tucked away from the hustle and bustle, hoping it would be quiet, but there were a fair number of people waiting for a table, as she spied Maisy crossing the courtyard to join her. Perhaps that was a good thing; if Maisy was unaccommodating, she could terminate things quickly, on the basis that they needed the table for the next lunch guests.

The two women greeted each other with the customary kiss on both cheeks, Judith thinking that Maisy looked well on her retirement, albeit forced by an unexpected reshuffle. She knew Maisy would understand that there was a reason for the invitation – at least two years had passed since they were last in touch – but both women also appreciated the need to go through certain preliminaries, before Judith would get to the point.

So, they ordered drinks and a light lunch and, after exchanging pleasantries, Maisy sat back, fixed her large, heavily-lined blue eyes on Judith and set the ball rolling.

'Is it one of your cases you wanted to talk about,' she asked, 'or something charitable?'

'Why would it be something charitable?' Judith asked, amused by Maisy's directness.

'Thank goodness for that. People seem to think that, since I retired, all I want to do is volunteer for charitable work. Not that it isn't worthwhile and I appreciate the very privileged position I am in, but I just can't do it 24/7 and they only want me as a figurehead – "former cabinet minister" and all that. They don't even care what I say. Actually, often I don't even have to say anything. Good. It's nice to be wanted for my brain again, but you'll understand that.'

Judith smiled and she wondered that she hadn't tried harder at a friendship with Maisy, over the years. It was only now that she could be more objective. Before, her friends had been neatly divided into her own and those Martin introduced into their relationship and she had dropped the latter, as readily as she had thrown out Martin's suits.

'It's about your consultation on online gaming and its impact on health.'

'I remember it well. I sat in on some of the sessions. What did you want to know?'

Judith wanted to know a million things, most importantly, why there were still no recommendations, but she was going to bide her time in getting there.

'It was a very extensive exercise,' she said.

'Yes.'

'I saw that you had contributions from a variety of sectors.'

'That's always the way.'

'How did you choose the contributors?'

'Usually, we have someone do research, find the most eminent people, from both sides of the fence.'

'Do you tell each contributor what the others have said, to give them an opportunity to put their side?'

'Not exactly. That would be too unwieldy and take forever. What we do is we give each person an advance brief of areas we want them to cover. But then, if someone else has highlighted something new, outside the brief, which is relevant to that participant, we do raise it on the day and people can come back, if needed.'

'And who reads it all and pulls together the recommendations?'

'A team in the relevant department, in this case, my former department.'

'How long does it usually take?'

The waiter arrived with their food and Maisy waited until he had deposited their plates and left before replying.

'Why are you interested in this?' she said.

'Elizabeth Sullivan was a doctor who gave evidence to the committee.'

'Yes, I saw her name. And she's dead now. I saw that too. Is that what this is about?'

'The transcript of the Q and As suggests things were all very polite. But tempers must have flared, given that you had families of addicts giving evidence too.'

'We tried hard to keep the different interest groups apart, asked them to come in on different days.'

'But they could see what each other said?'

'It was posted daily. You think someone we spoke to killed Dr Sullivan?'

'Her views were unpopular with everyone in the gaming industry.'

'You can see why. But that's life. We don't go around killing people we disagree with. If we did, we'd have to give up on freedom of speech and democracy. I don't see how any of this can help you?'

Judith began to eat her salad and Maisy followed suit. Then Judith paused.

'Is absolutely everyone who gave evidence named?' she asked.

Now Maisy put down her knife and fork.

'There were a few closed-door sessions – surprisingly, not from the addicts. You might have thought they wanted their privacy, but they were, generally speaking, happy to share. No, it was the gaming companies. They were worried about "confidential information", so they said, giving something away which might benefit their competitors.'

'And who were they?'

'You'll be able to identify them by process of elimination because the company name will appear in the list of contributors, but there won't be a record of any interview.'

'Is there any way I could get to see what they said, on a confidential basis?'

Maisy shrugged. 'What does that mean *on a confidential basis*? I'm not saying I don't trust you. I just mean it will be confidential until you decide you want to use it and then you'll find a no doubt perfectly legal way of doing so, but where will that leave me? I don't have access any more, even if I was willing.'

'That's a shame. As you say, someone who was prepared to assassinate a devoted doctor, just because she held a different view on an important national health issue, that kind of person must be a threat to the very fabric of our society…as well as a murderer, of course.'

Maisy frowned at Judith and carried on eating. But now was the time for Judith to ask the question that was really bothering her.

'All right, I understand there are limits to what you can say,' Judith said, careful to keep her voice even and matter of fact. 'Something less controversial, then, without making you give away any secrets. Why, eight months on, is there still no conclusion, no recommendation, no action?'

'It's tricky stuff, with lots of competing priorities.' Maisy answered quickly; clearly she had used this excuse before.

'Even so, there must be a date when a response is expected?'

Maisy finished one of her two fishcakes and wiped her mouth. 'There's no date of which I'm aware.'

'Oh come on. All that taxpayers' money?'

'It's been buried.'

'What?'

'But you didn't hear that from me, OK?'

'Why?'

'If you've read any of it, I should think it's patently obvious. Look, the government held a similar exercise in 2016, when they looked into regulation of our tech industry. They heard from all different areas, from big business, from pressure groups and the public. In the end, they decided not to impose any regulation – nothing at all, zilch – and to allow the industry to flourish unchecked. There was a push for the UK to become world leaders in technology and artificial intelligence – all of this was before Brexit of course – and, in order to encourage highly skilled people to come here, they wanted to make things as easy and lucrative as possible.'

'And gaming benefitted from that?'

'It is one industry, yes, that gained a lot and has garnered huge investment.'

'And the natural conclusion of this latest enquiry would have interfered with that?'

'Almost certainly, it would include some limitations. And the gaming companies would not only have been cross, but there were murmurings that they might sue.'

'Sue the government?'

'Only murmurings, like I say, but they would claim to have invested millions, perhaps hundreds of millions, in the industry, on the basis they could have free rein to create, develop, sell – to the UK public, at the very least – whatever they wanted. And that, for the government to come along four years later and curb all of that, potentially massively impacting their creativity – for "creativity" feel free to substitute "profit margins" – was wrong.'

'Quite apart from the government's own reduced tax revenue on profits?'

'That too, yes.'

'Will there never be a conclusion then?'

'That, I don't know.'

'Don't you feel bad about any of this?'

Maisy had just resumed eating, but she stopped again. Perhaps Judith had pushed things too far. Instead, she took a sip of fizzy water.

'I took my responsibilities very seriously,' Maisy said, 'and, if it had been my decision alone, then, notwithstanding all those other considerations, we would have recommended putting some framework in place. God knows it must be better to do it now, when the people making the decisions are, generally speaking, not people who play these games. Can you imagine what it will be like, if we leave things another fifteen years till Generation Z is in charge? It's bad enough having the odd millennial in the team.'

'Was it connected with your retirement, any of this?'

'I had had enough, for a variety of reasons, most of which would bore you to death. Look, I'm sure that when the pressure from concerned people gets too great, something appropriate will be done with all the information we gathered. But, when I left, there was certainly no impetus to bring that day forward. Of course, with the death of Dr Sullivan, there's one less voice to complain about it all.'

PART TWO

24

JUDITH WAS DELIGHTED that the trial was finally underway. Although it was the most stressful time for her, and she had to work day and night for its duration, it was the pinnacle of her practice, the culmination of years of training, cutting her teeth on parking fines and insurance fraud, to arrive at the point where clients' lives and futures depended on her performance.

She also knew how much she owed to Constance, who had tempted her back to work, after a hiatus of five years, brought on by Martin's sudden death and the issues it uncovered. She hadn't appreciated how much she missed the buzz of a new case, until then.

There was relief too, that this trial was not being filmed live, like her last. The justice system had dipped its toe in the vat of Court TV for a period of four months last year and was now evaluating the mixed results. So, while Judith would always dress formally for any trial, she didn't need to worry, this time, that every element of her outfit, down to her shoes, would be under scrutiny and subject to review on the evening show, often at great length, and – in preference to her actual performance as an advocate – that viewers would speculate about where she had her hair done or what face cream she might use in the mornings.

It was also liberating to return to the more mundane regime of anonymous entry to the court building. Last time, she and Constance had been surrounded by crowds baying for blood. This case was no less important, but you wouldn't know it. Where hundreds of demonstrators had congregated in September, blocking her way, cheering and cursing in equal measure, now the underground passageway was quiet and deserted. Judith never thought she would be so pleased to smell the sour air and inhale the faint whiff of stale alcohol, which signified the return to normality of the place.

'Who's here?' Judith met Constance one floor above their appointed court, having sent Constance in earlier, to take a look around.

'Tom's here with Mr Jenkins and Eve, Liz's sister.'

'Ah. The globetrotter. Did you talk to her?'

'I tried. I'm not sure I got very far.'

'Anyone else?'

'Her friend, Sandy, is here.'

'That's it?'

'I think so. There are other people, but I don't know who they are.'

'Anyone for Jaden?'

'I told Nathaniel not to come today, in case there was press interest. No one else who is obviously here for Jaden, no.'

'All right. Why don't you go back in and just *hang around* a bit.

I'm interested to know who else might be here.'

'Is there someone, in particular, you're looking for?'

'Not exactly. Can you do that? I'll be down in ten minutes, ahead of the start.'

Judith sat down quietly on a bench and collected her thoughts. She had no master plan for Constance. It was more that she knew Constance liked to feel useful and Judith had a sudden desire to be alone. She had written a rather unorthodox opening, this time, and it worried her that it was an "all the eggs in one basket" approach. Her discussions with her pathologist friend had persuaded her that the post-mortem evidence was equivocal, that Liz could have died suddenly and without warning, and that was likely to be more appealing to a prospective jury, than any kind of conspiracy theory, involving persons unknown, who didn't like what Liz had to say. All other leads, including the photo Constance had sourced from Liz's flat, having run cold, natural causes was the main defence they had settled upon for Jaden, on the murder charge.

Judith thought it had reasonable prospects. If she'd been the kind of person who liked to gamble – which she wasn't, well, just once in her life on the Grand National and she'd made Martin place the bet – then the odds would have been fairly good.

What remained, nagging away at her, however, was the feeling, fuelled by years of experience, that she was missing something very obvious. That, given Liz's uncompleted quest to impose limits on the gaming industry, her liaison with Jaden, a local gamer, was almost certainly no coincidence. Jaden had insisted he had no idea that Liz was a doctor, but she still worried that there was some information she hadn't yet found, which would show or might hint that Jaden had deliberately pursued Liz. And, if so, she wanted to find it – and defuse it – before the prosecution did.

As for the claim Jaden had raped Liz? Judith agreed, wholeheartedly, with Jaden that he should defend it, although she was slightly less confident of his prospects on this charge. It was more a question of appearances than evidence. If Jaden had been forty-five years old, white and a professor, she'd have fancied his chances more. Perhaps she would even weave that into her narrative, although it would be a foray into the realm of discrimination, which she usually avoided like the plague. But this damned, stubborn client of theirs would not be advised on the theft charge.

'I'm not a thief,' he had declared, his nostrils flaring, and Judith had, somehow, refrained from pointing out to him that his criminal record said something different. It must have been the pleading look Constance had flung in her direction which bound her lips, temporarily. Of course, Constance had been right. Point-scoring against your own client was not usually a productive use of a lawyer's time – as ineffectual as reflecting on the circumstances of her husband Martin's death, rather than his life.

Thinking about Martin, even for a second, made her melancholy. 'Love's Labour's Lost,' she muttered to herself, as she gathered up her books and headed down to court.

***

Judith nodded her greetings to her opponent, Sylvie Elliott, bilingual (French mother), counsel for the prosecution, as she organised her papers. Judith had never appeared against Sylvie before; she was part of the new breed of junior silks, state-educated and multi-faceted. Sylvie had three young children and was also champion of a breast cancer charity, in addition to running marathons in her spare time. Judith had reflected that she had never had any spare time, although if she had, she would not have spent it pounding the pavements in all weathers.

She wondered, then, what she might have done in her twenties and thirties, if work had not been all enveloping, if she had not always been trying to prove herself as equal or superior to her male counterparts. She liked to think she would have learned a musical instrument – something soulful like the oboe or cello. Anything too jolly would have irritated her. She had always preferred heavyweights like Bach and Beethoven over the more frivolous Vivaldi.

Or to paint: a universal, timeless pastime, which could endure into her silver years. She had enjoyed sketching as a girl; still life – a hockey stick, her gym shoes, a bag of oranges – but also outdoors – the wisteria outside her window at home, the apple tree in blossom, the dahlias her father favoured. Portraits had never been her thing, the entire process too personal, closeted with another person in close proximity, seeking to reproduce not just their physical features but the thoughts behind them, to capture what made them tick. She hadn't ever wanted that intimacy with anyone, not even Martin, which was ironic because, of course, now, in her professional life, she was seeking out people's motivation all the time, trying to probe them for clues which would expose their actions, when their words fell short.

In any event, there had been little time to indulge any crumbs of artistic talent in the busy academic schedule of her youth. Perhaps it wasn't too late now, if she could find a very patient teacher. Oils would be her palette of choice today; the use of chiaroscuro to bring depth and mood to an object. When she'd bought her flat, that was one of the ways the agent had sold it to her – the constant, cool northern light caressing the large arch window in the master bedroom. 'Perfect for painting…so I'm told,' he had declared, with an impish grin. And, just for a moment, she had been seduced by the romance of it all.

Her musings ended with the arrival of Judge Oliver: old school and a stickler for process, as well as being on the harsh side of the sentencing spectrum. Constance had been upset he was presiding over them, but Judith wasn't disappointed. In theory, he should be tough with the prosecution too, which might help if things were finely balanced. Given a choice, she would always prefer a hard-liner over a soft-touch judge.

Sylvie began just before 10am, her voice bearing the slightest trace of her European origin, but, if Judith had thought she might begin softly, brought up, as she must have been, on the language of love, she was mistaken.

'Members of the jury,' Sylvie began. 'This is going to be a difficult trial, not in the sense that there is any doubt that the right person is sitting here in the dock,' she paused for emphasis, 'but because the evidence you will hear about the waste of a woman's life will upset you, chill you and make even the most charitable of you wonder if there is any morsel of decency left in the human race.

'On the 2nd of November 2019, Dr Elizabeth Sullivan was taken from this world. Dr Sullivan was a mother and a committed consultant psychiatrist, devoted to her patients and to research which she hoped would have far-reaching impact for sufferers from addiction, everywhere. Jaden Dodds, who lived opposite, and was, in every way "from the opposite side of the street", snuffed out that life, callously, cruelly and without a thought for the consequences of his actions.

'I cannot even begin to imagine what Dr Sullivan's last minutes must have been like. This young man, Jaden, to whom she had chatted casually, her neighbour, turning all his considerable *brute strength* on her, using his six-foot height, thirteen-stone weight, to tremendous advantage, tying her up, raping her and terrorising her to such a degree that her heart, literally, exploded.

'But that wasn't enough. No. Jaden Dodds wasn't finished yet. He calmly and heartlessly searched around Dr Sullivan's flat until he found her handbag and stole her purse. Then, perhaps even in her bedroom, where her body was not yet cold, he used her credit card to buy himself a pair of training shoes he rather liked. And, finally, he returned to his own home and broadcast his regular show, without a trace of guilt for the terrible crimes he had committed.'

Jaden had begun the morning by surveying his audience and allowing them to get a good look at him. He had shaved, his hair was cut short, he wore a white shirt and tailored jacket and he sat with his hands resting lightly on his knees. But, despite the smartness of his appearance, nothing could hide his physical bulk. It was up to Judith to show the jury that whatever Jaden *might have done*, was totally irrelevant.

'Usually, when I defend a client, I am seeking to show that someone else was responsible,' Judith began. 'I am trying to demonstrate for you that another hand wielded the knife which delivered the fatal blow, another arm brought down the club, or another driver caused the lethal accident. In all of those cases, what is obvious to everyone is that the victim has been killed by someone; it's just a question of finding out who.

'In this case, things are rather different. I am going to show you that Elizabeth Sullivan was not killed at all. She died from natural causes. The condition which she carried around with her, every minute of every day, could have ended her life at any moment. Hypertrophic cardiomyopathy, conveniently shortened to "HCM", is a recognised genetic heart disorder, which causes a chamber of the heart to be enlarged and susceptible to failure. There are no symptoms and Elizabeth Sullivan did not know she had the condition. My learned friend, Ms Elliott's reference to an explosion is, therefore, particularly apt; Elizabeth Sullivan was, literally, carrying a time bomb inside her.

'Jaden Dodds was her neighbour, a young man, admittedly with few academic qualifications, but who, with true creative and entrepreneurial spirit, has been supporting himself financially for a number of years with a hobby, a website which attracts like-minded followers and which has become his profession. He jump-started Elizabeth Sullivan's car one cold autumn day and they struck up a friendship.

'On the 1st of November, a Friday night, she invited him over for dinner, they had some wine and they had sex, consensual sex, in her bedroom. Ms Elliott invites you to feel outraged that this happened, to believe that the gulf between Elizabeth Sullivan and Jaden Dodds was so huge – age, race, class – that he must have forced himself on her, that she could not possibly have consented, and that the very fact that he was larger and heavier than she was should be counted as damning evidence of his guilt. I am sure you don't need reminding of the simple, biological fact that, within any heterosexual couple, the man is often larger and physically stronger than the woman, but that is no reason, on its own, to assume coercion is at play in their relationship.

'When Jaden left Elizabeth Sullivan's flat, around 9pm on Friday

1st November, Elizabeth was alive and well. Some time afterwards, and before 10am the following morning, Elizabeth's heart gave out and she died, in her bed. Jaden Dodds returned home and broadcast his usual show and, if you watch that show, as I will be encouraging you to do, as part of the evidence in this trial, you will see that his demeanour is not that of someone who has just been involved in a violent episode, which has led to the death of another human being. Instead, it shows a young man continuing his life and his normal routine in order to earn his daily bread; a man who has done nothing wrong; an innocent man.'

'I'm surprised you didn't play the *cougar* card,' Sylvie leaned over and reprimanded Judith, when Judge Oliver directed a five-minute break at the end of their opening speeches.

'I'm sorry?'

'Or remind us of how some, educated white women find young, black men particularly attractive.'

'I was saving that argument for later,' Judith replied, 'but so pleased to find it resonates with you too. I knew the French were into free love, and all that. After all, you invented *laissez faire*.'

'Oh please,' Sylvie said. 'I can't believe you're even defending this case. And if you're so sure she died of natural causes, just accept a manslaughter charge and save us all a lot of time and money.'

'And spoil our fun! I was also thinking of evoking *white guilt*; perhaps tomorrow. I expect you'd like that argument too.'

For a second, Judith thought Sylvie might stick her tongue out. Instead, she just smiled and fixed the screen-save on her laptop, before turning to speak to her instructing solicitor.

***

'Inspector Dawson. Tell us what you found at Dr Sullivan's apartment on the morning of 2nd November 2019.' Sylvie was beginning her questioning of Charlie Dawson, after the lunchtime break.

Judith registered Sylvie's habit of leaning heavily over the lectern, her head tilted to one side, one arm passing closely in front of the other. It gave her interrogation a conspiratorial quality; she wasn't an accuser, merely a temptress, teasing the answers from her adversaries.

Constance had shared with Judith her concern that Dawson may be unwell and Judith scrutinised him closely for any signs of weakness. She had to concede that he had shrunk since their last court encounter and his suit hung loose around the chest, making him appear even more scruffy than usual. But his answers maintained their usual clarity and focus. Perhaps she would enquire after his health, if they had a chance to speak privately.

'I was called to Dr Sullivan's apartment around 11am on Saturday the 2nd of November,' Dawson began. 'Dr Sullivan was lying on her back in bed, one arm on top of the covers, eyes closed, and she was dead.'

'Who alerted the police?'

'Her cleaner found her. She has a key.'

'Was there any sign of forced entry?'

'No.'

'Any signs of violence?'

'No.'

'No upturned furniture? Items on the floor?'

'No.'

'What view did you form, then, of what had happened?'

'I couldn't be sure, of course, and Dr Sullivan was a young woman, but it looked as if she had died in her sleep.'

'Then, what happened to change your view?'

'One of my men, PC McConaughey, had noticed some faint marks around Dr Sullivan's arms, as if she had been restrained in some way.'

'Anything else?'

'There was a wine glass next to the bed and a second glass by the kitchen sink, each containing some red wine. This suggested she might have had a visitor the previous night. Then, we looked around for a handbag, mobile phone, car keys, that kind of thing and we couldn't find any of them. That made me concerned she might have been robbed. I called in the pathologist and the forensic team.'

'Thank you. And the pathologist will confirm this but, at a high level, can you tell us what evidence connects the defendant, Jaden Dodds, with this awful crime?'

'His fingerprints were in the apartment, including in Dr Sullivan's bedroom and on the second wine glass, the one in the kitchen. Also, Dr Sullivan had had sex shortly before death and tests confirmed this was with the defendant.'

Dawson stared at Jaden, who blinked heavily and lowered his head. Despite Judith having mentioned this in her opening, Dawson's choice of words, and their tone and direction, elicited a moan from the public gallery, evidencing Tom Sullivan's obvious distress.

'When you first spoke to the defendant, what did he tell you about his relationship with Dr Sullivan?' Sylvie pressed home her advantage.

'He said she was a neighbour and he had helped her with her shopping.'

'He led you to believe that they were friends?'

'More like acquaintances. He said that was the only time he had been in her apartment, to carry in the groceries.'

'Any other evidence linking Jaden Dodds to the crimes committed at 38 Dunloe Close?'

'Dr Sullivan's credit card was used three times between 5am on 2nd November – Saturday morning – and 11pm, so that's after her death. One of those purchases was for a pair of distinctive black trainers in a size 11, not Dr Sullivan's size. A pair of new trainers matching that description was found at the defendant's flat on 4th November.'

'What did the defendant say about those?'

'First, he said he didn't recognise them, that sometimes fans sent him shoes. Then he changed his mind and said they were a gift from Dr Sullivan.'

'A gift?'

'He said he had helped jump-start her car a few days earlier and she had wanted to repay him, that she'd ordered the shoes online for him the night she died.'

'So, first the shopping, then the car. Quite the good Samaritan then?'

'That's what he'd like us to believe, yes.'

'But you don't accept that?'

'No, I don't.'

***

'Chief Inspector Dawson, when you entered Dr Sullivan's flat, can you describe what you saw? It's a ground-floor flat, isn't it?' Judith was brisk in her cross-examination. She didn't need any ruses with Dawson. He was usually a straightforward witness, although she had upset him more than once previously with her directness. Luckily, he didn't bear grudges and he understood it came with the territory.

'Yes, all on one level,' he replied. 'First, I entered the living area. The curtains were drawn back, but the cleaning lady confirmed she had opened them, when she came in. It was fairly tidy but, well, lived in, if you know what I mean. There were some magazines on the sofa, a jacket hanging behind the door. Over in the kitchen area, the dishwasher was open and it was full of the dirty dishes from the night before. There was the wine glass I mentioned and a frying pan in the sink itself.'

'And, in the bedroom, can you describe the furniture?'

Dawson pursed his lips, squeezing his eyes shut momentarily to aid his recollection.

'The bed, a chair, a low kind of dressing table, where we found Dr Sullivan's laptop, a bedside table. That's it, I think. And the curtains were closed.'

'Thank you. I'm going to show you a picture of Dr Sullivan's bedroom. It's pretty much as you described. I want to ask you about the chair though, as I understand it was taken away for forensic testing. Why was that?'

'You'd have to ask the pathologist. Sometimes, they think it will help the enquiry.'

'You weren't the one, then, who asked for the chair to be tested?'

'No.'

'I have to say that I am not used to large items of furniture being removed from the crime scene but, as you say, we'll ask Dr Bailey when she gives her evidence. Did you smell anything unusual in the flat?'

Dawson's eyes flicked to Tom, who was staring daggers at Jaden.

'There was a smell of urine.'

'You don't mention that in your statement?'

'I didn't think it important. I thought Dr Sullivan may have… soiled herself. Given that I had concerns this was a murder scene, I called in the pathologist.'

'Yes, you've said. What led you to my client, Jaden Dodds?'

Jaden looked up and Dawson stared across at him again.

'Once we knew this was a murder investigation and a burglary, with her bag being missing, my officers went door to door and took fingerprints and DNA samples. Jaden's sample matched the prints and DNA in Dr Sullivan's apartment.'

'I think that's a very condensed summary of what actually happened, isn't it? Let's take it in stages, shall we? On the first day, your officers were sent out to speak to neighbours. What did they do?'

'They took statements.'

'Asking *did you see anything untoward last night?* – that kind of thing?'

'Yes.'

'And did they speak to my client or his flatmate, Nathaniel Brooks?'

'They spoke to the defendant, who said he knew Dr Sullivan, as a neighbour.'

'Jaden Dodds admitted knowing Dr Sullivan?'

'Yes.'

'When did your officers go back to question my client a second time?'

'The next day.'

'Why did they go back?'

'Another neighbour told us that Jaden had been chatting to Dr Sullivan the evening before she was killed. We became suspicious that he might have known her better than he was letting on and that he might be hiding something.'

'Any other reason?'

'No.'

'So, you began your inquiry with…what you might call "an open mind" then?'

'As I always do.'

'Then, at what stage did you become so very blinkered?'

'Ms Burton!' Judge Oliver had snapped his pencil in half and waved it to the court usher, until a pristine one was produced and handed up to him. Judith nodded her apology.

'Jaden Dodds and Elizabeth Sullivan were neighbours,' she continued. 'There was therefore no reason preventing them from engaging in neighbourly behaviour, was there?'

'No.'

'Yet you became suspicious of my client, purely because you were told he had been chatting to Elizabeth, even though he had told you, himself – volunteered, that is – that he had helped her with her shopping?'

'It's standard practice to follow leads, especially people seen with the deceased shortly before their death.'

'Did you take fingerprints or swabs of DNA from anyone else in the street?'

'Yes.'

'Who?'

'Nathaniel Brooks.'

'My client's flatmate?'

'Yes.'

'Anyone else?'

'No.'

'Why, was that?'

'Jaden's prints matched the ones in Dr Sullivan's flat.'

'So…a lucky guess, then. The prints and DNA you happened to take from the first person you tested, matched what you found in the apartment?'

'Not a guess. It was good policing. Like I said, my officers targeted the two boys because the defendant had been seen with Dr Sullivan shortly before her death. Then, once there was a match, no, there wasn't any need to look any further.'

'You were…what? Saving taxpayers' money?'

'We'd found the right person.'

'And the neighbour who reported to you that she had seen my client and Dr Sullivan having a friendly chat out in the street, she was female?'

'Yes.'

'White?'

'Yes.'

'Educated?'

'I don't know.'

'And how old?'

'I didn't interview her. I have no idea.'

'Let's just call this neighbour, whom you have just described, the one who told you that she had seen Jaden and Dr Sullivan chatting, the information which made you suspect my client of robbery, rape and murder, let's call her Mrs Smith. I know it's not her real name.'

'All right.'

'If my client had told you that Mrs Smith had been laughing, exchanging pleasantries with Dr Sullivan, would you have sent your officers to swab Mrs Smith's nose and throat, and that of her family members, hauled her into the police station for questioning and executed a search warrant on her home?'

'I was following a hunch and it proved to be right.'

'Unless you are going to argue that any of the evidence against your client is inadmissible, and I am assuming you would have done so by now if that were the case, move on Ms Burton.' Judge Oliver was scowling at Judith and the new pencil was in danger of going the way of the old.

'Can you describe the sequence of events on the night of Dr Sullivan's murder, given the evidence you uncovered?'

'I'll do my best. The neighbour – the one you just called Mrs Smith – she saw the defendant talking to Dr Sullivan at around 6pm. Another neighbour saw the defendant entering the house with Dr Sullivan, shortly afterwards. They ate together, drank some wine together. Then, at some stage that evening, before 9pm, the defendant wanted sex, Dr Sullivan said no, he restrained her with some ropes he had brought with him, raped her, killed her and, before he left, he stole her bag containing her purse and phone.'

'Can we, once again, take that in stages, please, and separate out the fact from the conjecture? You have factual evidence that Jaden was speaking to Elizabeth Sullivan around 6pm and that he entered her house just after?'

'Yes.'

'And my client accepts that. The rest, however – the alleged rape, murder and theft – they are all your theory of what happened. You have no direct knowledge of any of those matters?'

'That's right. But it's a theory based on the evidence we found.'

'And your theory is that Jaden killed Elizabeth Sullivan because she refused his advances?'

'Yes, coupled with the theft. Like I said, he went on to steal her credit card and used it to buy himself a pair of trainers.'

'That's pretty extreme, isn't it?'

'I've seen it happen before.'

'Have you? Can I ask how much the trainers cost, the ones purchased with Dr Sullivan's credit card.'

'Two hundred and forty-two pounds.'

'Do you think that's a lot of money for a pair of trainers?'

'I think so, but I know some kids, young people, like special ones and I know they can cost a lot.'

'I'm going to ask the jury to take a look at exhibit two, which is a pair of trainers. Thank you. Now these, as you can see, are a brilliant turquoise with the words "Human Race" on them. Can you see that? "Human" written down the right foot and "Race" down the left. I am told these come from a range made by Adidas and designed by a well-known music celebrity.'

'If you say so.'

'Next we have another pair, these burgundy high-tops are "Air Jordans" made by Nike, bearing the logo of the renowned American basketball player, Michael Jordan.'

'All right.'

'My Lord, I'm not sure why we are being treated to a fashion show by Ms Burton, but it does not appear to have any relevance to her client's defence.' Sylvie bobbed up out of her seat.

'These items are directly relevant to the theft charge, if you will allow me a moment to develop my argument.'

'Go ahead, Ms Burton,' Judge Oliver hardly looked up, as he bade Judith to continue.

'These two pairs come from Jaden's wardrobe and they are a representative sample of the trainers he likes to wear,' Judith explained. 'I think you will agree, whether you like them or not, that they are quite…flamboyant in style. Importantly, the first pair retails…well, retails isn't quite the right expression. These trainers are so sought-after that they sell out their original run and then a kind of secondary market operates, where the lucky buyers sell them on, via various websites, for a big profit. This pair was purchased for in excess of £900, but I have looked online only today and couldn't find a pair for less than £4,000. Does that surprise you, Chief inspector?'

'It does, yeah, I suppose it does.'

'The second pair, similarly, were purchased by Jaden for £799. Which leads me to ask the obvious question: why should a young man who can freely afford to buy designer footwear at £800 a pair – leaving aside for a moment, whether we feel that is a prudent use of his income; that's a matter for him – why should he choose to buy a much less expensive and more run-of-the-mill pair, when he has unlimited funds, aka Dr Sullivan's credit card?'

'I don't know why he chose that pair.'

'No, but the implication, surely, is that he never chose *that pair* because he never stole the card in the first place.'

'You're implying that. I'm just reporting what I found. Maybe he was worried that the card would be rejected if he went over £300. I don't know, do I?'

'But when we don't know the answer, we have to draw conclusions about the most likely chain of events and I submit that it is highly unlikely, given Jaden Dodds' very particular and expensive taste in footwear, that he purchased these shoes.'

'Then what were they doing in his flat?'

'We'll come on to that later,' Judith said, without turning a hair, although, privately, she was asking herself the same question.

Then Judith had a sudden moment of clarity and, as soon as she did, she reprimanded herself for not seeing it earlier. It wasn't the complete answer to the issue which had been gnawing away at her for days, but she felt sure it was part of the answer. In order to flush it out, though, she had to take a risk. She looked across at Jaden, then stole a quick glance at Constance. Finally, she turned her head, a few degrees, in Sylvie's direction, where Sylvie's supercilious expression provided all the confirmation she needed.

'Moving on, do you know what Elizabeth Sullivan's area of specialism was?' Judith asked.

'She was a psychiatrist.'

'That's right. Anything else?'

'I don't know the details, but she treated alcoholics.'

'Yes, she specialised in addiction; people who cannot help themselves but, through no fault of their own, they become addicted to alcohol, pills, online games, gambling – even pornography. She treated them with medicine and with therapy.'

'If you say so.'

'What does Jaden Dodds do for a living?'

'He has an online website.'

'What does he do on that online site?'

'He plays video games.'

'And is it secret, this site?'

'No, it's a public site.'

'Did you ever consider the link between what Jaden does for a living – that is, gaming; showing other people how to improve their scores in online games – and what Elizabeth Sullivan did – that is, treat people with illnesses relating to gaming?'

'No. I didn't. But it sounds like they might have had quite an interesting conversation that evening, over dinner.'

Dawson's eyes twinkled, as his joke spread out and settled in the minds of everyone in the court. Judith sat down and Sylvie bobbed up.

'Just one more question, Inspector Dawson.' Sylvie returned the sideways look at Judith. 'Were you aware that Dr Sullivan was a very vocal campaigner against online gaming?'

'I don't know much about that, no.'

'Then I will be taking this issue further with other witnesses. However, it's only right and fair to lay down a marker, at this stage, that the prosecution case will include a further possible motive for Dr Sullivan's murder. Jaden Dodds intentionally hunted down Dr Sullivan, to silence one of gaming's strongest critics.'

25

JUDITH AND CONSTANCE WERE packing up their papers when Tom Sullivan came bowling over, Mr Jenkins in hot pursuit.

'Why didn't you tell me?' His face was blazing and his fists were clenched. Judith wheeled around and soaked up the full force of his anger and humiliation.

'I'm sorry...' she began.

'Why didn't you tell me about what he did to Mum?' He began to sob and Mr Jenkins extended a protective arm around his shoulders, which he threw off.

'I wasn't able to tell you.'

'That's not true. You didn't tell me, because you knew, if you did, there was no way I was going to help you. You said he was innocent, when you knew what he did.'

'Tom, come away now. Leave these ladies alone. They're just doing their job.' Mr Jenkins intervened a second time, with a little more authority than before. Tom turned on him too.

'I don't see why you're being so nice to them,' he shouted. 'They tricked you too, unless you knew. You probably all thought it was funny, didn't you? Him shagging my mum. I bet he thought it was pretty funny too.'

'No one thinks any of this is funny,' Mr Jenkins reached out and pulled the boy towards him.

Tom flung his headmaster's arm away, growled at them all and then ran out of the court.

Outside court, Liz's sister, Eve, was waiting. Constance had pointed her out earlier, seated next to Tom. Judith wondered if they could possibly pretend they hadn't seen her. She really did not want another scene after Tom's outburst, but Eve was already walking forwards and speaking to Constance at the same time.

'Miss Lamb, hello. It is Miss Lamb, isn't it?'

'Yes.'

'I'm Liz's sister, Eve. We spoke. You remember?'

'Yes, hello.'

'Look, I understand that everyone is entitled to a defence and all that, but is this really necessary?'

'I didn't think anything in the opening statements or Inspector Dawson's evidence was…inappropriate. As you say, everyone is entitled to a fair trial.' Judith hung back. Constance could hold her own, she thought.

'It just seems really obvious to me that it was him, especially now we know… Well. I know my own sister. She wasn't in the habit of…casual encounters. Making us, me and Tom, sit through all of this; it's very cruel.'

'I understand it must be hard for you,' Constance said, 'but you wouldn't want the wrong person to go to prison, would you?'

Eve shook her head sadly. 'I knew there was no point saying anything,' she said.

'How is Tom doing? You know...what we talked about.'

'You think you can get around me that way, talking about Tom like you're his friend?'

'I... Maybe we should continue this conversation another time,' Constance said, glancing over at Judith for reassurance. Judith said nothing. 'I can see you're upset,' Constance said.

Eve's face softened. 'He's doing all right, considering,' she said.

'Have you thought of anything you might do to help him?' Constance asked.

'There are places you can go – you know, residential places – to wean you off it. I've been taking a look. It's just that, poor Tom, he's been pushed away so many times, I'm not sure that's what he needs right now.'

'I'm sure you'll decide what's best for him.'

'If only Liz was here to advise me, eh? She was very determined, you know, Liz was.'

'Was she?'

'I expect that, even if she'd known about the HCM, she wouldn't have changed anything. She always did as she pleased, thought she was invincible.'

'Sounds like you're pretty adventurous too, I mean, where were you in November?'

'Not really. You can't change how you are. Even though Liz had a serious profession, and a son, she was still the extrovert, the free spirit, the "no ties" one in the family, throwing herself into everything she did, heart and soul and damn the consequences. I had to go all the way to Nepal to prove it. She could do it, right here in London.'

***

Judith and Constance sat together in Constance's office, in the late afternoon and reviewed the first day's transcript, but Judith kept staring out of the window.

'What is it?' Constance eventually asked her.

'It's nothing.'

'It's never nothing with you.'

Judith laughed. 'I suppose you know me too well now for me to get away with that. I was having a moment, which we can ill afford. Thinking about poor Tom Sullivan and what he said.'

'Don't let it get to you.'

'He was right though. If he'd known that his mother and Jaden were lovers, he would never have spoken to us.'

'We couldn't tell him and we never forced him to help us.'

'I know all that and you're very sweet trying to make me feel better about it, but he was still right. Then I was distracted by all the things Eve said about Liz and then about Tom and what to do next. And then I was accepting, with considerable reluctance, that I would have failed despicably as a mother, if I'd had to deal with those kind of issues. That's what I was thinking about, OK?'

'Wow. Is there any space left in your head to think about the case?'

Judith laughed. 'I have a very big head,' she said.

'Dawson was on form today, I thought,' Constance volunteered, to get Judith back on course.

'Yes,' Judith smiled. 'Not taking any nonsense from me, was he? Did Jaden really spend that much money on his trainers?'

'That's what he said, and all the prices checked out, but I confirmed it with my brother too, just out of interest. He's not into his footwear, but some of his friends are. He's the one who first told me about all the queues you get when a new range is released. Some of his mates would do it, sneak out of the house before anyone was up, buy the shoes, keep them, all wrapped up and pristine, then re-sell them at a huge profit.'

'Very entrepreneurial, I suppose.'

'What was Sylvie Elliott saying to you?'

'You don't want to know.'

'I do.'

'She was going for the jugular, actually. Not at all as I expected. I mean, I heard she was a benevolent person. Certainly not in her approach to her legal work. And so pointed; barbed, even. I think I must have upset her in a previous life.'

'As opposed to the prosecution counsel when we defended James Salisbury, whom you really did upset in a previous life. What was she called?'

'You know her name.'

'Celia Mansome.'

'There you are. You remember everything. All right, now it's time to focus on tomorrow.'

'What do you want to talk about first?

'I've been reading Dr Sullivan's research. It all focuses on addiction of various types.'

'Yes.'

'But the most recent work was on gaming addiction, as I mentioned to Charlie. So – people who can't stop playing online games.'

'Dr Williams said that was her particular interest. Like the man in China who died of dehydration?'

'He's at the most extreme end, but I did my own research and there are other horror stories too. There's this couple in South

175

Korea who allowed their real-life baby to die, while they were tending for a virtual one.'

'Yuck.'

'They were so wrapped up in an online competition to be the best parents that they forgot to feed their own child. And that's what much of Elizabeth Sullivan's recent work focused on; people who withdrew from normal life, so that they could carry on playing a game.'

'I've seen that. So?'

'I also read that her team had been part of the group lobbying the World Health Organisation, to recognise gaming as a disorder in 2018 and, later, as a mental health condition.'

'Now that I didn't know. Is it important?'

'I don't know, but it feels like it is, and it was noticeably absent from the papers you sent me.'

'Those are the ones Dr Williams sent on. I can ask him for anything relating to that.'

'If you could, and quickly, please. I want to understand more about Liz's involvement and what the impact was of that WHO decision.'

'Who for?'

'For everyone. Start with addicts, but then branch out. It came to me in court this morning, when I was asking Dawson about the link between Elizabeth Sullivan and Jaden. It's been staring me in the face all along. It began with your very timely discovery about her involvement with the government enquiry. I don't believe the friendship between the two of them was unplanned – a random meeting.'

'You mean the stuff Sylvie spouted about Jaden killing Liz to stop her condemning gaming?'

'Yes and no.'

'What do you mean?'

'I'm hoping I've bowled Sylvie a googly on that one.'

'You've lost me this time.'

'It's a cricket expression. You could substitute "put one over" instead, I think.'

'You don't think Jaden deliberately targeted Liz Sullivan, because of her views?'

'No, I don't. You heard what her sister said – that Liz didn't appreciate conventional boundaries. I think it was the other way around.'

26

LUKE STOOD, OPEN-MOUTHED, gazing down into the atrium from the first floor balcony. Hundreds of people were pouring into the space-age conference centre. Arriving at the airport had already set his expectations high; the plane swooping down low over the bluest sea – they didn't call it the Côte d'Azur for nothing – and dropping fast onto the small, sandy spit of land, with the snow-tipped mountains in the distance. And the balmy temperature of 15°C, as he stepped onto the asphalt, only served to lift his spirits even further. Which was just as well, because there was a considerable amount of angst jostling for position inside his body, and it ran the risk of overflowing, if he didn't keep it at bay.

Naturally, he was chuffed to bits that Eric had asked him to attend, even with the challenge of the new game and the speechwriting elements. But now that both were complete – the former having filled almost every waking moment since that November morning he had taken Eric a coffee, the latter having required five nights of research and some help from his sister with the English – it was always good to have a sounding board for your ideas – he should, in theory, be able to relax.

They had arrived early this morning, checked into their hotel (overlooking the beach) – separate rooms, what a relief – and then taken a short taxi ride to the convention. For the first hour, Eric had introduced Luke to people he knew. In fact, Eric appeared to know everyone they encountered, or have at least one common acquaintance. And, even if he didn't know the people he met, he had heard stories about them, some of which he recounted to tremendous hilarity. This was Eric at his most affable and charming, all traces of threatening behaviour or martial arts tendencies banished. And with every handshake or back slap or kiss on the cheek, Luke began to believe, for the first time, that Valiant might be in with a shot at the top prize.

Now, one hour into the afternoon session, and after a quick reminder of the key points, delivered in part via a timely trip to the men's toilet, Eric was on the podium and everyone was listening to him. Not only the 700-strong delegates, but thousands via the online stream. And there was his name in lights: 'Eric Daniels, CEO, Valiant Enterprises'.

'Thank you so much for having me,' Eric began, enveloping the audience in his broadest smile.

Luke felt his pulse begin to rise and sweat broke out across his forehead. Although he was no showman and preferred to stay behind the lens, being the coach rather than the contestant did nothing to reduce his apprehension as Eric opened his mouth again, to speak the words Luke had prepared.

'I've been asked to appear today to represent the small, independent game manufacturer. My company, Valiant, is tiny in comparison to some of the big names. But we're one of one hundred UK-based manufacturers – many more worldwide – who are absolutely committed to the future of online gaming and to creating the best user experience; that principle guides us always. And, like our name, we are brave, heroic and intrepid in everything we do.

'I'm here, today, specifically, to talk about what it would mean for me, and for Valiant, for Esports to be recognised as an Olympic sport, but I have to include in that, the impact on our fans too – on all the people who play our games – because, without them, without our audience, I think everyone here must acknowledge, we are nothing.

'What will that recognition, that inclusion, do for Valiant and every other game manufacturer? I'm going to be honest. It will give us credibility and legitimacy. It will send a long-overdue message to the world that what we do is worthwhile and valuable. It will mean that this slight whiff of the dishonourable, which has been associated with gaming since its beginnings, will be vanquished for ever. And that's important.

'Next, it will bring us to a new audience. People may not even be aware of where you can watch Esports – especially people over the age of twenty-five – and they're missing out on the tremendous enjoyment it can bring. And with a new audience, we may also encourage more people to play. Not only do we human beings watch what we play, we play what we watch. Our researchers believe we could easily double our followers, as a result of the international exposure, in the first year alone.

'But it will also be good for gamers, yielding national gaming heroes, elevating the status of the world's best players, and they deserve it, don't they? There are lots of well-known players with their own following, but to be the best in your country and then the best in the world – that's something different; that's worth the hours and days and weeks and years of hard work to reach the pinnacle of success, which is represented by the Olympic Games.

'And the beauty of it is, it will bring together gamers from all over the globe. There's been this feeling that maybe, in some parts of Asia, they're ahead of the rest of the world, there's more of a tradition of playing these games at a high level. Now they get to test their skills, going head-to-head with the best in Europe, the best from the Americas, the best in Africa.

'And that's another point in favour of giving us entry. Unlike some more elite sports, gamers come from all different socio-economic backgrounds.' Eric paused and Luke felt he was seeking him out, sending him a message, in that moment, that he appreciated the words Luke had arranged on the page for him. 'The Olympics is all about channelling spirit and universal acceptance, but it has to be said that not all of its sports are accessible to everyone. Take show-jumping, or fencing, or even tennis. They tend to be the preserve of the more wealthy members in society. But gaming? Anyone can do it. Anyone has a chance to be the best.

'And with the increased revenue, the games manufacturers and the Esports teams can invest in the gamers, in their training, including in making them more media-savvy, more resilient and free from exploitation. It's a situation where everyone wins.

'So that's what gaming can do for games companies and gamers: provide support, credibility, legitimacy, build our audience and fanbase, make our players heroes. But it's a symbiotic relationship, I promise you. It will bring tremendous benefits to the Games too.

'Let's begin with demand. Twenty million people watched

the recent *Call of Duty* tournament in the USA alone; around sixty million worldwide. We're not quite up to the numbers who watched Usain Bolt win his 100 metres gold, but we're on a steep trajectory towards it. Staggering, isn't it? In fact, for some years, I've been hearing from my friends in traditional sports – and I do have a few – that we're not managing to attract young people to watch the Olympics, that track and field events don't carry the hearts of our youth.

'Of course, we can stick our heads in the sand and chastise those young people, tell them they *ought* to be interested in traditional sports, try to drag them kicking and screaming to watch it. Or we can listen to them, listen to our viewers, our supporters, our fans, the future sportspeople of the world. We can ask them what sport they want to view and how they want to view it; that's important too. And there will be only one resounding response. We want Esports. And we want to view it on all our devices. And we want it in the Olympic Games. Thank you.'

Eric was pleased with himself, Luke could see that, even from this distance. And he could also see a number of the Olympic officials, conspicuous because of their distinct name badges, whispering and nodding, before, themselves, breaking into moderately enthusiastic applause.

'Thank you so much, Mr Eric Daniels, CEO of Valiant UK, top indie manufacturer, here from London. We do have time for a couple of quick questions, before I invite our next speaker to the stage. Any questions? Yes.'

Luke bit the inside of his mouth. This could be tricky, but he had primed Eric on the kinds of things that were likely to come up and how he might be minded to answer.

'Hi Mr Daniels. I am so delighted we have representatives here today from small companies like yours. I think it's important for creativity, to make our games more imaginative, that we can benefit from the nimble way smaller companies can bring their offering to market.' A woman a few rows back was given the microphone and her face was projected on to the big screen. Luke recognised her as someone he had met that morning. She had kissed Eric on both cheeks and given him her number before moving off.

'Thank you.' Eric was beaming again.

'But, and I am saying this as a gamer myself, and as a supporter, I just don't see how your offering can fit the Olympic message. The last game you put out, *Hellraiser Dawn*, contained a series of automatic weapons, together with traditional items like clubs and swords and, in order to win, the player had to stab sixteen opponents and decapitate the seventeenth. How can that be in keeping with the *non-violent* ethos of the Olympic Games?'

Luke stared at Eric. They had rehearsed this one. He didn't know why the questioner was looking so smug. This was the most basic question, the one the anti-inclusion campaigners wheeled out at every opportunity, albeit rather 'the elephant in the room' with the Olympic selectors in earshot. Eric stood back from the lectern and then walked around it, owning the stage and Luke saw, in his eyes, that he was confident he had this covered.

'I'd like to answer that question in two parts, if I may. First of all, Ruth, I accept that, certainly at the outset, when we begin to acclimatise new enthusiasts to Esports, allow them to experience our creations in all their glory, to begin to understand what they're about and what pleasure they bring, we should be selective about the games we play, on this vast international stage. NBC has been doing it for a while, with its Universal Open. They selected *Rocket*

League, which some of you may know.

'So, no, I'm not advocating *Grand Theft Auto* or *Man Hunt*, yet, for the Olympics, not for one moment deprecating either of those offerings. I accept that would be like asking a toddler to ride a motorbike. However, there are myriad games which would be suitable to ease people in. Valiant is currently developing a fantastic new game called *Midas*, a game of spectacular strategy and skill, a game with green credentials and a game which operates from beginning to end without any blood being shed. That's what I would recommend.

'Second part of my answer is crucial too. In our games, the violence is online. It's not real and it does not translate into the real world. All that stuff of ten, fifteen years ago – people trying to say that gaming encouraged copy cat violence – it's been shown to be scaremongering and totally false. Gamers understand what they are doing is not real. And that is in stark contrast to some of the sports the Olympics reveres, the most obvious being boxing, an Olympic sport since 1904.

'There are, what, around 18,000 professional boxers…and far more amateur boxers. If you asked me what profession I would prefer my own child to undertake – boxer or gamer – from a safety perspective, I know which I would choose. And then there are the extreme sports that have crept in more recently: the luge; snowboarding. Many people die each year participating in those sports. And look at fencing, which I mentioned earlier, with its origins in real-life duels to the death! We have to be objective, not swayed by hysteria, and then, when we reflect, I doubt there will be many level-headed people who still believe that *violence* in gaming is an authentic reason for rejecting this vast industry, closing your doors to us, refusing to allow us in.'

'Time for just one more I think?' Luke could hardly believe it when the compere turned to one of the Olympic committee representatives, seated on the front row. Even holding this man's interest for long enough for him to ask a question would thrill Eric, regardless of its content.

'Mr Daniels. That was a rousing and heartfelt speech you just gave. Turning things around again, you spoke about what the Olympics would gain from Esports joining its fraternity. I'm interested: do you think that live sport can have an impact on how you design your games?'

'Absolutely! Where's Luke? Luke. Are you there? I'm just looking for my colleague, Luke; he's in the audience. He's a bit shy. Luke, just wave your hand and I'll see you.'

Luke gulped, then decided that he had to give up his anonymity or fear Eric's wrath later on. He raised his hand and felt all eyes upon him.

'There you are. So, Luke is a brilliant designer. I brought him with me so that he could speak to you about the games he's designed, especially that one I mentioned – *Midas*. It's the one everyone's going to be talking about. But he's also a proficient sportsman. And he channels that passion he feels from playing competitive sport, that rush of adrenalin you get when you walk on a pitch and a crowd roars, when you shoot that basket from ten metres, when you cycle through the pain to beat your previous best. All of that goes into our virtual games, so we're back to that interdependence, that synergy between physical sports and Esports. And strategy too. People forget that some games are not just about speed, strength and reaction time, they're about strategy, like the best games of chess, like *Midas*.'

Luke puffed out his chest, threw his shoulders back and tried to resemble the gifted athlete Eric had identified, as hundreds of eyes looked him over. The truth was that he did occasionally jog around his local park, but had never been good enough to be chosen for any team sport. But Eric was continuing, regardless of the lies he was disseminating.

'In fact, I am going to make a prediction, ladies and gentlemen, slightly off-piste, continuing the snowy theme, but follow me for a moment, if you dare. I am going to predict that, within five years, young people will be headlining their gaming skills on their CVs, not hiding them. Employers will recognise that superior gaming techniques have real value in the workplace; the ability to assimilate information, react swiftly, coordinate actions, play or lead a team, remain calm under pressure – all valuable attributes which any employer will treasure. You have a Top 100 ranking in *Overwatch*, you're going to start shouting about it. And why not? We've sat in the shadows for too long. Now is the time for Esports to come racing forwards into the light.'

27

DR SUSAN BAILEY, FORENSIC pathologist, was sworn in as the prosecution's second witness on the second morning of the trial. She was neatly dressed and heavily pregnant and she took a few extra moments to settle herself down.

'Another wonder-woman,' Judith had quipped to Constance, as they walked past her on their way into court, her arms resting lightly on her distended belly.

'What do you mean?'

'She has a fabulous CV and she finds time for a family. I bet she also makes her own pasta.'

'She's forty-two though, and it's her first child, so I wouldn't be too jealous.'

'How do you know that?'

Constance tapped the side of her nose with her finger. 'You know everything's available online, on everyone, these days.'

'Only if you allow it to be,' Judith said. 'That's why I've never operated in the virtual world.'

'Are you sure that's why?'

Judith smiled. 'All right, and because I don't know how to; there is that, too. But I've never understood this desire to share such personal information with complete strangers. I mean, it's so self-centred, so opinionated. I didn't see Dr Bailey in that category.'

'You didn't see her as a mother either. You must be slipping.'

'Let's hope, for Jaden's sake, that I can hold things together for a little longer.'

***

'Dr Bailey. Can you tell us how Dr Sullivan died?' Sylvie Elliott had smiled and wished Constance and Judith good morning, as if they were the best of friends. Judith had responded with a nod. Now Sylvie was leading the expert pathologist, briskly, through her evidence.

'She had a heart attack.' Dr Bailey was softly spoken and she gestured with her hands as she spoke.

'Can you say when this occurred?'

'Not with any great precision. Sometime in the twenty-four hours before she was found. As she was last seen alive at 6pm, sometime between 6pm and 9am the following morning.'

'And what caused the heart attack?'

'Dr Sullivan had a condition called "hypertrophic cardiomyopathy" or "HCM". It's inherited, and around one in five hundred people in the UK suffer from it, with varying degrees of seriousness. Essentially, the wall of the heart – the myocardium – becomes thicker, making it more difficult for the heart to pump blood around the body. Most often, it's the left ventricle which is affected and this was the case with Dr Sullivan.'

'Did Dr Sullivan know she had this condition?'

'I believe not. For many people there are no symptoms and it was not in her medical records.'

'What about treatment?'

'Well, again, you have to know you have the condition before you can treat it, and, like I said, I don't believe she did. But it's a mixture of medication to relax the heart muscle or thin the blood, instructions to keep fit and eat a healthy diet, subject to not undertaking particularly vigorous activities and, sometimes, surgery, depending on seriousness.'

'You've described her condition, but why, in your expert opinion, did Dr Sullivan have her heart attack *at that moment in time*?'

'I mentioned not undertaking very vigorous activities. That's because, if the heart rate goes up too much, in this defective heart, which is having difficulty pumping blood around the body, that can bring on a heart attack.'

'Other than vigorous exercise, what kind of things can make the heart rate go up?'

'Fairly obvious things; excitement, shock, fear.'

'Fear?'

'Fear prepares the body to respond to danger. It results in a cocktail of hormones being released into the blood, and these, in turn, speed up the heart rate. It is my belief that Dr Sullivan experienced *something* which made her very frightened, and this pushed her heart rate up. It couldn't cope with the increased blood flow and it shut down.'

'What makes you believe that she was frightened?'

'I found increased levels of adrenaline in her urine. Also, when I first examined the body, it was clear that she had been sweating. It's quite basic, but you can smell if a dead person has been sweating a lot before they die, as well as detecting sweat on the skin, which helped corroborate my view that she had been raped. And that the rape, even over a fairly short period, would have terrified and traumatised Dr Sullivan sufficiently to bring on the heart attack.'

'Could she have been saved?'

'It's impossible to say for sure. If someone had been with her and had immediately dialled 999, perhaps, depending on the severity of the attack. Of course, if she went into cardiac arrest, that person could also have tried CPR, which would have doubled or perhaps even tripled her chances of survival.'

'Death would not have been immediate?'

'It would have taken some minutes for her to die, in my view.'

Sylvie paused again. Oh she was good, Judith admitted to herself. Sylvie wasn't going to say that Jaden left Liz to die, because the prosecution case was that he murdered her. But, just in case any juror had a doubt in his or her mind, independently, when it was mulled over in bed at night or on the train on the way into court that, perhaps, the boy hadn't hurt her – Liz really had spontaneously gone into cardiac arrest – the boy was still at fault because he could have saved her; he had ample time to save her and he never even tried. Research a few years back had demonstrated that people hated passers-by who failed to intervene –with venom. And now Sylvie would move on, but the seed had been sown.

'And what makes you believe that Dr Sullivan was raped?' Sylvie asked.

'There was some redness in the genital area and the marks around her arms, of course.'

'What were those marks?'

'Dr Sullivan had some faint marks around each forearm. It appeared she had been tied down, and I reached the conclusion that this was during sex, to prevent her from resisting.'

Sylvie Elliott allowed her eyebrows to arch high into her hairline, she nodded knowingly and then moved her head slowly to look at Jaden. Every eye in the room followed suit and Sylvie allowed the silence to be filled with everyone's private thoughts and opinions jostling for position. Then she administered her coup de grâce.

'Can you determine when Dr Sullivan was untied?' she said.

'No.'

'Might it have been *after* she died?'

'It's possible, yes.'

A juror coughed out her displeasure. Sylvie gave a slight bow and sat down.

'Thank you. No further questions,' she said.

Judith had felt weary, briefly, as she listened to Sylvie's questions. Of course, hers was a privileged position and a career she loved, but the forensic evidence was depressing to hear, representing, as it always did, the demise of a person; cataloguing the last hours or minutes of life of a human being. Their views, loves, achievements now immaterial; all that mattered was what factors had made that life come to an end.

She was a little surprised that Sylvie had stopped so soon, had not pressed Dr Bailey to conjure up a vision of what Liz's death might have looked like – pulse racing, gasping for air, heart overloading – to match her opening statement. But, most likely, she was saving all of that up for Jaden himself. Sometimes, having a doctor calmly and precisely reflect on cause of death could make it all feel rather sterile. Far better in terms of impact on the jury, to challenge the accused directly and robustly, and trigger an equally forceful response. In any event, Judith was going to spend longer with the pathologist. It was key to Jaden's defence to obtain some concessions from her.

'Dr Bailey, good morning. You have kindly explained HCM, the condition from which Elizabeth Sullivan suffered and which, you say, led to her heart attack and subsequent death. You've also expressed the view that it was unlikely she knew she had the condition, as it was not in her GP's notes and she did not appear to be taking any medication for it. That much was very clear, thank you. I wanted to ask you what the symptoms are of HCM.'

'Some people experience shortness of breath, headaches, light fainting, that kind of thing.'

'I see. But I heard you say, I think, and I couldn't believe this was correct, that others have no symptoms at all?'

'That's right.'

'Really. You can have a major, life-threatening heart condition and no symptoms?' Judith screwed her face up tight to illustrate her level of scepticism directed at the doctor's evidence.

'I can assure you, that's right. Sometimes, patients are totally unaware they have the condition until they have a heart attack. I had a patient only a month ago, a man of forty-two, who worked as a fireman for twenty years, who had no symptoms at all, until he suddenly died.'

'As abrupt and unforeseen as that. That example really puts things into context for us.' Judith's face relaxed, now her trap had been sprung. 'Isn't it possible, therefore, that this also happened to Dr Sullivan? She and Jaden spent an enjoyable evening together and then, sadly, as might have happened at any time – as you've just said happened with your otherwise healthy fireman – she suffered a sudden and unexpected heart attack in the night and died?'

Dr Bailey paused before replying, clearly regretting her moment of exposition and the point she had conceded so early in Judith's cross-examination. She stole a quick look towards Sylvie.

'It is possible,' she said, 'but, in my opinion, like I said, it was the events of the evening which caused Dr Sullivan's heart to be forced to work harder, and that is why she had the heart attack, at that moment.'

'And that's because you believe she was raped and your view is that a rape would have caused Dr Sullivan considerable fear and trauma?'

'Yes.'

'You mentioned finding adrenaline in Dr Sullivan's urine. I noted that. Could adrenaline have been secreted during the heart attack itself or in the lead up, if Dr Sullivan had experienced shortness of breath or fainting symptoms? Being a doctor, in particular, she might have worried that something quite serious was wrong, causing the release of that same *fear* hormone you mentioned.'

'It is possible, yes.'

'There were also traces of two drugs, medicinal drugs, in Dr Sullivan's system, weren't there?'

'Yes, one is bupropion; sold as Wellbutrin. It's an effective anti-depressant, although it's also used in the UK to help things like smoking cessation. The other is a tricyclic clomipramine, usually sold as Anafranil, also an anti-anxiety and anti-depression drug.'

'Why would Dr Sullivan have been taking both of these drugs?'

'It's unusual to take both simultaneously. I am assuming she was crossing over, finishing taking one drug and beginning the new one, but traces of both remained. It's recommended that you leave a gap between the two, and, in fact, you should not simply stop taking the Anafranil, you can have withdrawal symptoms, but, as she was a doctor, she may have decided she knew better.'

'Were these drugs prescribed by her doctor?'

'The Anafranil was, the Wellbutrin, no.'

'So…what? She bought it herself? Self-prescribed?'

'Either is possible. Doctors are not supposed to self-prescribe, but sometimes they do.'

'Dr Bailey, you mentioned not taking the two drugs together. Why is that?'

'The literature records that they can react together with certain side-effects, but it would be uncommon.'

'Is one of those side effects to increase blood pressure?'

'It is, although Wellbutrin on its own can increase blood pressure.'

'And what would the impact be of elevated blood pressure, for someone with HCM?'

'Unhelpful.'

'Unhelpful?'

Dr Bailey hesitated again, and this time she looked at Jaden. He was watching her with considerable interest, his hands interlocked, thumbs pressed against his lips.

'It would cause the heart to have to work harder, so, increasing the chance of cardiac arrest,' she said.

'You also said, in your report, that Dr Sullivan was raped. Why did you say that?'

'Because that's my professional opinion.'

'Was that your opinion before you knew Jaden Dodds was her

sexual partner?'

'What's that supposed to mean?' Dr Bailey's expressive hands were suddenly stilled and drawn back against her body.

'I'm asking you, at what point you formed the conclusion that Dr Sullivan had been raped, rather than the sex having been consensual?'

'When I saw the marks on her arms...'

'We'll come to that in a moment. Anything else?'

'When I saw her heart had burst.'

'Now let's take this slowly because, members of the jury, this is incredibly important. If we ignore the heart attack for a moment and the marks on Elizabeth Sullivan's arms – and I do appreciate their significance; I will come back to them – but what *other signs* were there that led you to the conclusion that she had been raped?'

One women juror let out a sudden sob and Tom Sullivan threw off Aunt Eve's arm and ran out of the court, the door banging behind him.

'There were signs of redness in the vagina, like I mentioned, indicating that the sex had been quite vigorous.'

'Anything else?'

'No.'

'That's all?'

Now Jaden sat back and lifted his chin defiantly. Dr Bailey was careful to avoid his stare.

'Yes,' she said.

'Could normal, consensual, vigorous sex have caused the redness?'

She thought hard before replying.

'Yes...it could,' she said.

'There were no internal injuries, which might otherwise have been consistent with forced penetration?'

'No.'

'No bruises or other marks anywhere on her body, other than those on her forearms?'

'That's right.'

'Is that usual? I mean, Ms Elliott was at pains to tell us what a *lusty* young man Jaden Dodds is. If he had forced himself on Dr Sullivan, tied her up and raped her, would you not have expected some other bruising, somewhere?'

'It would have helped to corroborate my view if there had been bruising, but it's not always the case. Sometimes the victim is too scared to resist and just complies.'

'All right, so the factors which...let's not say change your opinion; perhaps it's more *tipped the balance* in this particular case...leaving aside those marks on her arms again, they were not related to any injuries suffered by Dr Sullivan anywhere on her body?'

'That's right.'

'I said we would come on to the marks. Can you show me, on your own arms, whereabouts the marks were on Dr Sullivan?'

Dr Bailey pointed to the area halfway up her forearm.

'Thank you. We can see the marks on Dr Sullivan's arms on this photograph too, and they are exactly where you say. What do you think made those marks?'

'The marks were left by some kind of flat strap, not a rope.'

'And you suggested to Ms Elliott that Dr Sullivan sustained those marks because she was tied to the bed by Jaden Dodds?'

'I did, yes.'

'Let's take a look at a photo of Dr Sullivan's bed again, shall we? It has a solid wooden headboard with these little wooden finials at each side. I suppose you could, maybe, wind a strap around one of those, but she could lift it off – can you see that there's no means of fastening it in place?'

Dr Bailey opened her mouth and looked at the judge.

'What I mean is that, if Dr Sullivan had straps around her arms, there was nowhere secure on the bed to attach them, was there?'

'Maybe they were attached lower down, around one of the legs?'

'That is possible, but if you look at the configuration of the room, the bed is up against a wall, and there is barely one metre on the other side. Not much room for one person, let alone two, and it would be incredibly difficult to secure both hands around the same bed leg, in that constricted area.'

'I accept there isn't much space, yes.'

'And you called these "faint" marks, when you were talking to Ms Elliott – your own words?'

'Yes.'

'If Dr Sullivan had been struggling, fearing for her life, wouldn't you expect those marks to be more pronounced, as the straps pulled and tightened?'

'They were certainly quite…indistinct.'

'On a scale of one to ten, with ten being the most obvious marks sustained by a person struggling desperately against a restraint, and one being the least, where would these marks sit?'

'Around a three, I'd say. But, like I said, some people just give in, faced with a stronger opponent.'

'Dr Bailey, there was a chair in Dr Sullivan's room, wasn't there?'

'Yes.'

'A wooden-backed chair with a soft seat. Again, there's a picture up on the screen. Is that the chair?'

'Yes.'

'And you directed that it should be removed from the flat and tested. Why was that?'

'The seat was stained with urine.'

'You thought that was unusual?'

'Yes, I did.'

'Me too. Did you test the urine?'

'Yes.'

'And?'

'It probably came from Dr Sullivan herself.'

'Probably?'

'This will sound surprising, but it's very hard to know who urine has come from. It can contain cells from the urinary tract, but if someone has been sitting on the chair, that makes it much more difficult to tell.'

'And had Elizabeth Sullivan been sitting on the chair?'

'There were some marks in her groin area, suggesting she had, but they were inconclusive.'

'Curiouser and curiouser, I say. If Dr Sullivan was tied to her bed and raped by Jaden Dodds, and then she had a heart attack and died, why is her urine on the seat of a chair, 6 feet away?'

Dr Bailey was silent. She moved one hand over her stomach.

'I agree that it's strange,' she eventually said. 'I didn't see how I could possibly guess how or why it happened. I just confirmed it was probably Dr Sullivan's urine.'

'And you stopped there, because, like inspector Dawson, you felt you had your man, when Jaden Dodds' fingerprints and now his DNA were a match.'

'Yes.' Dr Bailey took a deep breath. 'Look, perhaps she was tied to the chair and not the bed?'

Sylvie coughed into her hand, a clear signal to the pathologist to stop hypothesising. But Judith had planned for this very eventuality.

'All right. Let's examine that theory. If you can wait one moment, I have a very similar chair, which I am going to bring into the courtroom, from a well-known furniture manufacturer. Here you go, and my instructing solicitor, Miss Lamb, is going to assist me. Miss Lamb, can you sit in that chair please? Thank you. Dr Bailey, the usher will hand you two leather straps and I'm going to ask you to tie them around Miss Lamb's arms, as close as you can to where you think they were on Dr Sullivan. Can you do that please?'

Dr Bailey rose to her feet, waddled down the steps to the floor of the court and tied the straps around Constance's forearms.

'Just one moment. You've tied those straps very tight, I can see, but your report mentions faint marks.'

Dr Bailey nodded. 'You're right,' she said. 'The straps would have been looser.'

Judith herself went to join Dr Bailey on the floor of the court as she loosened the straps. Now Constance's hands were free to move around and she waved them at the jury.

'If Dr Sullivan's arms had been strapped to the chair, in the place where the marks appear, then, as you can see, she can move around and, if you look carefully, you can see that the straps are constantly shifting up and down and would have almost immediately caused a chafing or rubbing of the skin. Do you see that?'

'I do.'

'Was there any of that chafing on Dr Sullivan's arms?'

'No. There wasn't.'

'So we've discounted being tied to the bed, because of the logistical difficulties, and now we've discounted being tied to the arms of the chair because the marks on Dr Sullivan's skin would have been different, leaving to one side in its entirety, the… logistical difficulties of having sex on the chair, particularly non-consensual sex.'

Constance stood up a little abruptly and Dr Bailey returned to her seat.

'While you are here, Miss Lamb, can you remain standing please, as I complete this point. Dr Bailey, do you know when those marks were sustained by Dr Sullivan, how many hours, or days, even, before she died?'

Dr Bailey looked across at the jury. 'In my opinion, somewhere in the twenty-four hours before she died.'

'Twenty-four hours. So we're not just looking at the twelve hours or so after Jaden left at 9pm that evening but also, at the absolute minimum, the nine hours *before* he visited – the whole of that day.'

'Yes.'

'Now these straps – you say straps rather than ropes; I'm using straps too, by way of illustration – have they ever been located?'

'Not as far as I am aware.'

'Do you know how Dr Sullivan travelled to work in the mornings?'

'No. Do you?'

'Yes. She used to walk or, on cold or rainy mornings, she would catch the number 30 bus. This is a photo of the bus, one of those smaller, single-deckers which can navigate London's narrower streets. And this is a photo of what it looks like inside the bus on a busy morning. This photograph was taken a week ago on a Friday at 8.30am in the morning. What do you notice?'

'It's very full.'

'It is, yes. No seats, standing-room only. If you focus, for a moment, on this woman standing in the foreground, what is she doing?'

Dr Bailey turned her heavy-lidded eyes onto Sylvie. She knew what was coming next.

'She's holding on to something – looks like a bar by the door,' she said. Constance stared at her, as she began to follow Judith's gist, too.

'She is, so that if the bus were to lurch suddenly to one side or brake abruptly, she wouldn't fall over. Usher, can you bring in exhibit 3, which is Dr Sullivan's handbag.' Judith allowed the bag to be shown to the jury. Then she dug underneath her desk and pulled out the identical bag. 'I took the liberty of purchasing this last week and, as you probably saw from Dr Sullivan's bag, it has quite a wide leather strap. Now Dr Sullivan didn't just use this bag as a handbag, she used it to transport notes and books. And that made it fairly weighty.'

Judith stepped forward and placed the bag, replete with one of her court files inside, over Constance's arm. 'If you, Miss Lamb, could reach out, as if you were holding on to that vertical bar, on the crowded bus, please.'

Constance did as she was told and, within seconds, the bag slid part of the way down from her shoulder to rest half way between her wrist and elbow. She shoved it back up onto her shoulder and, almost immediately, it slipped down again, to hang from her forearm. Judith allowed it to remain there for a few seconds only. When she removed it, there was a wide red band on Constance's arm.

'Dr Bailey. The journey from Dr Sullivan's flat to the hospital can take anything between ten and twenty minutes, depending on the traffic. Isn't it possible that there never were any restraining straps used to hold Dr Sullivan down, in her bedroom? That's why no straps were ever found? The way she sustained those "indistinct" marks on her arms was from carrying her own bag, full of papers, to and from work that day, or over a few days?'

'I don't think so.'

'It's possible though, isn't it?'

Dr Bailey was silent. Judge Oliver stopped writing and looked up.

'Please answer the question, Dr Bailey,' he said.

Dr Bailey nodded to him. 'Yes. If the bag was heavy enough, it is possible,' she said.

'Thank you. One final area I wanted to explore – and this involves some close scrutiny of the photos taken immediately after Dr Sullivan's death.' Judith looked across at Tom and Mr Jenkins as she spoke. Tom had only just returned to his seat after his hasty exit, when Sylvie had taken Dr Bailey through the rape evidence. 'My Lord, I am aware of members of Dr Sullivan's family in the public gallery; may I suggest a moment, in case they would like to leave or turn away.'

Mr Jenkins whispered to Tom, but Tom shook his head violently and scowled at Judith. He wasn't going anywhere this time.

'Do go on, Ms Burton.'

'If you look at Dr Sullivan's forehead in this photograph, I've blown it up for you, can you see some very faint circular marks – four of them, on the skin?'

Dr Bailey took a moment to examine the photograph.

'Yes, I can.'

'Do you know what those are?'

'No.'

'Can you hazard a guess at what they might be?'

'If I had to guess, I would say that she had been wearing some kind of headband which had left those marks.'

'I'm going to show you a photograph of Dr Sullivan taken the following day, from your post-mortem.'

'All right.'

'Are those circles apparent now?'

Dr Bailey looked carefully again. 'I can't see them, no. Now that you mention it, though, there was a tiny amount of something sticky on Dr Sullivan's forehead, like an adhesive, which I detected.'

'It's not in your report?'

'Given the cause of death, I concluded it had absolutely no relevance, as I do now.'

'I see. Thank you. No further questions.'

28

'YOU WERE BRILLIANT WITH Dr Bailey,' Judith was back at Constance's office, a box of cold pizza in front of them on the table.

'Thank you kindly. She was a fair witness, I thought. I mean, her assumptions were not necessarily wrong, and I imagine pathologists hate to conclude the victim died of natural causes; it's so mundane. But they were all premised on Jaden tying Liz to the bed and terrorising her, when it almost certainly never happened.'

'I'm not sure we're out of the woods, though.'

'I agree. There's a long way to go yet.'

'That's a funny point about Liz and the anti-depressants, isn't it?'

'I'm sure doctors get depressed as much as anyone else. And she'd been widowed and had all those issues with Tom and his problem gaming.'

'But why have one medicine prescribed and the other one secret?' Constance tapped her fingers against the side of her head.

'She was probably impatient. She'd been prescribed the Anafranil by her GP; it didn't work; she couldn't get another appointment for two weeks, so she got hold of the other stuff – the Wellbutrin – somewhere else. I understand it's incredibly easy to do these days.'

'Maybe.'

'I think it's not worth you spending more time musing over it, as we'll never know why. Let's talk about the chair, shall we? Sorry I had to drag you into the demonstration.'

'It's all right. I'm used to it by now.'

'At some stage in the hours or days before she died, Liz was tied to that chair. Assuming it wasn't Jaden and we can't be certain of that – if he's guilty, he might have done anything to frighten her – but, assuming it wasn't him, who might have tied her to the chair? Who else had access to the flat?'

Constance's hands fell to the table with a thud. 'I thought you said she got the marks on the bus?' she said.

'I got Dr Bailey to admit that Liz *might* have sustained the marks that way, but, hand on heart, I don't think that's what happened. We can't ignore the urine on the chair, which suggests she was sitting there for a long time, and not voluntarily. And before you say anything else, she couldn't have been tied to the arms, it must have been to the upright back of the chair. I saw that as soon as we did the demo in court, which means that she couldn't have tied the straps herself.'

Constance's mouth opened and then closed again. She had thought Judith's impromptu performance with the bag full of books, a moment of genius. Now Judith was saying it was just a distraction.

'All right,' she said. 'A friend or a boyfriend we don't know about might have had a key. Or Dr Williams? Or Tom?'

'Yes, Tom. Let's double-check when he was last home, shall we? And who was that friend you spoke to? Sandy something. Press her hard. Maybe Liz had a boyfriend, someone who was abusing her, and Sandy didn't want to say. Ask her about Dr Williams too.'

'All right.'

'And now I recall, when we spoke to Jaden, the two of us, do you remember he said that Liz wanted him to leave, that she was checking her phone a lot? It could have been for messages from another boyfriend. Jaden might have misinterpreted her casual brush-off. Perhaps she wasn't embarrassed at all. Instead, she needed to check in with someone else and she didn't want Jaden to hear.'

'You mean like "coercive control"?'

'It's possible. Maybe not that extreme, but someone who liked to check up on her, or a regular Friday-night call. I just think the chair is important and we shouldn't just push it to one side and move on.'

'Does that mean you think this was a murder, after all?'

'Oh Lord. I hadn't even considered that. Yes, I suppose it does. What a mess. I need to give this some further thought, don't I? Why don't you go home and call me in a couple of hours? When I've had some time to reflect.'

***

Judith's doorbell rang an hour after Constance had headed home. She pressed her intercom.

'Yes?'

'Take away for Ms Burton,' a man's voice announced.

Judith frowned. 'I haven't ordered a takeaway,' she said.

'Ms Judith Burton, ordered half hour ago.'

'Which takeaway are you from?'

'Lady, I have some other deliveries, please, so can you let me in, so I can get on.'

Judith buzzed the door downstairs, opened her front door to the communal corridor and straddled her doorway. Greg took the stairs two at a time. When he reached the top step, he held the takeaway bag out towards her.

'Hello Judith,' he said. 'I thought you might be hungry.'

29

CONSTANCE THOUGHT ABOUT calling David, Tom's room-mate, but then she noticed the time, and that he was most likely still in lessons and unable to answer his phone. It wouldn't take her too long to get to Mill Hill, although if Mr Jenkins had not yet returned, she wondered if she would be allowed to speak to David. In the end, she messaged Mr Jenkins to tell him she was travelling to school to speak urgently to David, and then messaged David separately with her estimated arrival time.

David was waiting for her in the entrance hall of the school, his anxious face peering out through the window.

'Am I interrupting your lessons?'

'It's PE last lesson. And I can join late.'

'Do you need someone with you? I did message Mr Jenkins, but I didn't hear back.'

'We didn't have someone with us last time,' he said.

'No, we didn't. You weren't at the trial?'

'I asked Tom if he wanted me. He wasn't sure, but Mr Jenkins said no.'

'I see.'

'I think he was worried I would talk about it to the other boys.' He stared at his hands. 'What was it you wanted? You said it was urgent.'

'It's about home visits. Did Tom go home a lot? You see I got the impression from Dr Williams – he's a colleague of Tom's mum – that he did, but Mr Jenkins seemed to think it was just holidays.'

'Mr Jenkins is wrong. But there's a surprise.'

'Tom did go home more than usual?'

'He knew she needed to see him, his mum. She really missed him. And sometimes she had to be away during holiday-time; all these conferences she went to. Mr Jenkins wouldn't give Tom permission, except once when it was his birthday. Said it was too disruptive.'

Constance waited. She had a feeling that David was about to divulge something to her. She wasn't disappointed.

'It wasn't far to his house,' David continued. 'Not like some kids who are from Reading or places like that – even Somerset. He could get there in forty minutes, door to door, if the trains were running OK. Sometimes, he just went…and I covered for him. Just to see her for a couple of hours.'

'Tom went home, without telling anyone?'

'Yes.'

'And no one found out?'

'I think Mr Pritchard, the caretaker, might have seen him coming back one time, but he never said.'

'Aren't the gates locked at night?'

'There's loads of ways around – at least four or five. But mostly, Tom would cycle to the station, leave his bike, bomb it down the

Northern line and be back before lights out.'

'The night his mum died. Did he go and see her that night?'

David shrugged and looked away. When he looked back, he appeared to be on the verge of tears.

'I don't know,' he said. 'He didn't say he was going, but I can't be sure. He didn't always say first. Sometimes, I would just find him gone. That day, I was playing rugby near Oxford. We didn't get back till around eleven. There was an accident on the road and we were stuck for ages. Then we had stuff to unpack and we got something to eat. I probably didn't get to bed till around midnight.'

'And Tom was in your room, when you returned?'

'Sitting up in bed. And we talked about the match.'

'He didn't say he'd been to see his mum?'

'No, but I saw his coat behind the door and it was wet.'

'His coat was wet?'

'When I asked him, he said he'd sneaked out for a cigarette with one of the other boys.'

'You think that wasn't true?'

'I think it probably was true. Tom did go out to smoke in the woods sometimes, not that often at night, but, maybe as I was away, he was bored. I'm just saying I can't say for sure where he was that night. Then, the next day is when the police came.'

'How did Tom react when they told him about his mum?'

'I wasn't there. He was in Mr Jenkins' office. But we all heard him. He kind of screamed. Then nothing. Just nothing.'

***

Judith and Greg tucked into their takeaway, Greg having

insisted they eat from the foil containers. He said it was to save washing up at a time when Judith was busy, and that it made the experience more authentic. Judith watched him as he spoke; the lights gleaming in his eyes. Even with this simple gesture, Greg was challenging her again; she knew that. He was aware of how difficult she would find it not to decant the chicken curry on to a plate, but he wanted to see if she could restrain herself, like forcing a cleaning fanatic to sit in front of a pile of dust on the floor, or an arachnophobe to hold a spider. The one concession he made was metal cutlery. Even he balked at eating with a short-handled wooden fork.

'I messaged you,' Greg said, in between mouthfuls.

'I know. It was rude of me not to reply. I've just been so busy,' Judith said.

'You stood me up at Delamina?'

'You can't stand someone up if you haven't agreed to meet them in the first place.'

'I should learn not to argue with a lawyer, shouldn't I? What's keeping you so busy this time?'

Judith paused and laid down her fork.

'I know you're in regular contact with Constance and our trial has been in the news – not front page, but still up there.'

'All right. I know about the Elizabeth Sullivan case. That's why I thought you might need some sustenance. I remembered how you forget to eat when you're working so hard. How is it going?'

'It's going well, in the sense that we may get Jaden acquitted, of the murder at the very least, but I can't work out what really happened that night.'

'You always say that doesn't matter, to focus on getting your client off. Connie's always the one seeking the whole truth.'

'Yes, but I also don't want to put forward an argument in court which I don't believe in. It isn't right. I've been trying to persuade the jury...and myself, that Liz Sullivan just died, just like that and it was a pure coincidence that it happened after Jaden's visit. But the more I delve into things, the less I believe that was the case. There are some...conflicting pieces of evidence.'

Now Greg stopped eating.

'Tell me what's bothering you. Use me as your sounding board. It may help to have a fresh perspective.'

Judith sat back and thought for a moment. Then she pushed her food to the centre of the table.

'All right, the key points, without breaking any confidences,' she said. 'Liz Sullivan was an accomplished and dedicated psychiatrist, who specialised in gaming addiction. She asked Jaden Dodds, a well-known local gamer and her neighbour, to help her with her car and then invited him in for dinner and sex. She ended up dead – cardiac arrest – turns out she had an undiagnosed heart condition. But here are the loose ends. First, she had traces of two kinds of anti-depressant in her body, only one prescribed by her doctor. Second, and this one's really odd, I think that, at some stage in the one or two days before her death, she was strapped to a chair in her bedroom for so long that she urinated on it because she couldn't get to the bathroom.'

'OK.'

'Connie and I want to know who tied her to the chair and why, but it may be totally unconnected to her death. At the same time, I know her meeting with Jaden wasn't random. She was researching the impact of gaming on the behaviour of young men. I believe she targeted Jaden and Nathaniel, his flatmate, for her research. Maybe, if she hadn't died, she would have told them who she was and asked them to participate in one of her studies? But I can't prove it. Then, it seems she had also contributed to a government enquiry into the impact of gaming, which has been mothballed at the request of someone on high. Maybe, someone heard Liz's testimony, or read it online, and decided to get rid of her. And her phone was stolen, so we don't have her contacts or messages.'

'He has a website, your Jaden?'

'He's on this service called Twitch, and YouTube also.'

'Did Liz Sullivan follow him?'

'I haven't checked. I wasn't sure how to?'

'You have her laptop?'

'I leave those things to Connie.'

'All right. I can't help you with the drugs, the chair, the government enquiry. You'll need to work those out or put some more manpower on the job. But I can easily help with the other stuff – what your dead doctor was doing online. I'll need to take a look at her laptop, at her browsing history. It will almost certainly shed some light on what she was up to with Jaden. I'll go over to Connie's as soon as we've finished.'

'But we don't know what name she used?'

'She won't have been too cryptic, I can guarantee. I've cracked countless passwords in my time, as you know. And people like Liz – doctors, lawyers, teachers – they're not good at hiding their identities, because they can't see the point. You wait. I can guarantee it'll be more obvious than you think.'

Judith watched Greg as he rejected his empty foil container and peered into hers to see what she had left behind. Quite apart from his usefulness on this particular aspect of the case, and the fact that the food had been welcome, she was genuinely pleased to see him. She had forgotten how much she enjoyed speaking to him and how, on occasion, it was refreshing for someone else to take control.

***

Constance caught Sandy on the phone, on her way to a gym class. She was apologetic, but it was her one luxury of the week, she said. But she could spare five minutes, if she could find a quiet place to speak.

Despite Constance's probing, she was adamant that Liz hadn't told her she was seeing anyone. Only that slight feeling she had had that Liz was out somewhere and keeping it a secret. Constance had sent her the photo of the four men she had found in Liz's flat, before the call, but Sandy had replied with a question mark, followed a few minutes later with one word: 'patients?' Constance had sighed. She had considered that possibility herself, but there was no way she could find information on any of Liz's patients. All their identities were hidden in the studies she published.

Constance decided to grasp the nettle, and asked Sandy if she thought Liz and Tony Williams might have been romantically involved. Sandy had guffawed with laughter.

'Oh no! Definitely not. I mean, they were perfectly good friends and worked together, as you know, but he was far too cautious for Liz. She liked men with big personalities, like Will. Those were the people she was drawn towards. And she was critical of colleagues having work relationships – thought it compromised their professionalism. Sorry I can't help more.'

30

LUKE WAS WAITING FOR ERIC at the bar of their hotel. He had already been hanging around for more than half an hour, but he didn't mind. He had downed a delicious cocktail and was savouring a second, while people of all shapes and sizes wafted past. Not only did he feel comfortable from his vantage point, but the layout of the bar had sparked off an idea for a backdrop to use in *Midas*, which had lifted his spirits even further.

'Midas'. He rolled the name around in his head, as he had been doing for days now. It had taken a little time for it to bed down. It was like when his best mate, Simon, had a baby. He and his wife called it 'the baby' for at least the first month and, even now, Simon sometimes forgot his son's name. But now Luke was finally used to 'Midas', accepting of it, embracing it and everything associated with it, and at just the right time. 'Mi-das', 'Mi-das', 'Mi-das'. Eric had been right. It was a superlative name and he couldn't wait to hear everyone shouting it from the rooftops. He took a deep breath and allowed the sweetly-scented air to fill his chest.

The two days had been a triumph – hence the cocktails and relaxed frame of mind. Numerous people had congratulated Eric on yesterday's speech, and more still had been enquiring about Valiant, its games and what *Midas* looked like. Most importantly, despite some predictions from the pessimists, the Olympic committee had stayed the distance, had engaged with a number of the speakers and conversed freely with the other delegates. They had listened and clapped and nodded in the right places, indicating, at the very least, some careful thought being given to the various proposals. It was a huge step forward for Esports.

Luke checked his watch. He would have to wait at least another half hour, he decided, before he could reasonably give up on Eric. He had seen Ruth, the woman who had asked the first question, hovering in the lobby when they had both returned and it had crossed his mind that she might have been looking out for Eric. Luke had to hand it to Eric. He could turn on the charm whenever he wanted, and he seemed to have all the right people eating out of his hand.

And, of course, there was Luke's own future. He had picked up a few contacts too, as modestly and self-effacingly as he could, while continuing to pretend to be the great sportsman Eric had publicly lauded. Eric clearly considered it a great joke, compounding matters by intervening when Luke was asked which sports he particularly enjoyed. 'Basketball is his best sport,' Eric had winked at Luke from behind his glass, before adding 'and rowing. Our office is right by the River Thames.'

Twenty minutes passed, his enthusiasm began to wane and he was considering heading out to grab some dinner, alone, when Eric appeared, swaying slightly as he crossed the room, his face a mass of smiles. He seized Luke by the shoulders, as he had that day in the office, and Luke braced himself for another kiss, which never came. Instead, Eric encircled him in a tight bear hug, followed by a hearty slap on the back.

'Here you are,' he said, his speech leaning towards slurred. 'This is where you've been hiding.'

Luke decided this wasn't the time to remind Eric of their arrangement to meet almost an hour earlier.

'Yes, I'm here,' he replied weakly. 'Would you like a drink?'

'Would I like a drink? I certainly would. Whisky would be good. Jack Daniel's straight up. My shout.'

He collected their drinks from the barman and beckoned Luke to follow him into one of the booths. Luke suddenly began to feel nauseous. Maybe it was drinking on an empty stomach. More likely it was the recollection of his terrifying encounter with Eric, the one involving the bottle, the Sellotape and Major Valiant. However much he tried to shrug it off, however much he reminded himself of what he owed Eric, it still encroached on his thoughts in moments of tension – and that included Eric being obviously on a journey to inebriation and carrying a glass in his hand: *'minnow', 'domino', 'dodo'.*

'You never know who's listening in these places,' Eric confided, oblivious to Luke's inner torment. 'So!' he announced, grinning again and throwing his arms out wide. 'What a trip!'

'What a trip,' Luke repeated, with what he hoped would pass for genuine gusto. He sipped at his drink and pushed away the dark thoughts clouding his mind.

'Such wonderful feedback for my speech…well, your speech. Credit where it's due. Who'd have thought you were such a master with words? Ideas, yes – a creative genius – but so good with words too. You could write speeches for a living. People would pay you a lot of money, you know that?'

'I'd rather design games.'

'Is the right answer!' Eric downed his drink and waved for another. 'Anyway, let's catch up now. So many names, contacts, meetings I've set up – some of them for you too. We're going somewhere. I'll tell you that for nothing. This time next year, your name will be in lights.'

Luke nodded and lifted his glass to his lips again, but this time he didn't drink.

'Listen, I'm just remembering. I was supposed to meet you here at 8 o'clock, wasn't I?' Eric was suddenly serious.

'Well…'

'And, what time is it now?'

'It's nearly nine.'

'I got a bit delayed, that's all. I am sorry. You know that woman, Ruth, who asked me the question yesterday?'

'Yes.' Luke's hunch had been spot on.

'She wanted a bit more info on *Midas*. I gave her a few hints. I only just managed to get rid of her.'

Luke suddenly felt panic rising inside him.

'You didn't tell her much about it, did you?'

'Nothing important; don't worry.'

But Luke was still worried.

'What's the matter?'

'Nothing,' Luke said, rather too quickly. '*Ex post facto*', '*out the window*', '*ELMO*', he thought.

'You think I told her all about *Midas*. You think she wheedled it out of me, the way some women do.'

Amazing, wasn't it? If Eric were a dog, he would be a bloodhound. He could be half-cut and still sniff out Luke's innermost thoughts and fears. Maybe that came with the martial arts training. All those Southeast Asian techniques; people thought they were just about fighting, but Luke knew they were all about the senses too.

'No… I…'

'She was a plant, OK?'

'A plant?'

'I got her to ask that question. I wasn't sure she'd do it, but I thought it worked pretty well.'

'I would never have guessed.'

'So, I had to take a few minutes with her, earlier this evening, to…show my gratitude. You must appreciate that.'

'Uh…yes. And the other guy?'

'Oh no. That was the real deal. I haven't got to anyone on the Olympic committee; well, not yet, anyway. I was on my own for that one.'

Luke laughed then, relieved that all the secrets of his game had not been relayed to the pushy woman in the red trousers.

'Listen, there is something I want to…canvass with you. No obligation; of course not; very much your own decision.'

Luke's bullshit radar twitched sharply and then careered off the scale. He knew exactly what those words meant, especially when delivered by Eric; something was coming that was totally non-negotiable.

'It's something Ruth alerted me to,' Eric said. 'It's that maybe we need to rethink the name…of the game. Another company has used "Midas" in the past. Nothing like our game – something pretty tame – but we may not want to risk it. I remember you weren't so keen on the name anyway.'

Luke swallowed hard and tried to control his pulse, which was also leaping around erratically. Didn't Eric realise how much time and energy Luke had expended on the new game? That he had embraced the new specification and the new name, despite some early reservations, and that everything he had done since that fateful November day was to build *Midas*?

'There are lots of other names of kings we could use, if we had to and if you wanted to, I mean. There's Julius Caesar or Arthur or Richard the Lionheart or even older ones like...Tutankhamen. That would help with the gold, too. You wouldn't have to change all the gold stuff.'

Luke tried to steady his breathing. This just wasn't fair. He knew, if he was rational, that Eric was trying to do the right thing, but he wasn't feeling rational. He was feeling perverse and stroppy and downright angry. '*Ego*', '*fiasco*', '*overthrow*'.

Why hadn't Eric done his research, before he insisted that Luke make all those changes? The game was all built around Midas now, and the gold mine. And even though he acknowledged that the Tutankhamen guy was kind of linked to gold, with that great big golden scary-eyed mask, it wasn't the same, and no one could spell his name anyway. *Midas* it was and *Midas* it had to be.

'I can see you want to think about it,' Eric was saying. 'And that's no problem. We should revisit it, though, once we're back in London, before we do any more marketing. I didn't realise what an asset Ruth was, I have to admit that. She's come up trumps on so many levels this time.'

Luke was no longer hungry. He just wanted to sleep. And despite his enormous disappointment, he was holding it together – just.

'Not that they're all as reliable as Ruth, you be warned,' Eric's mouth kept on going. 'Lucky, I didn't tell that other bitch too much, before I knew about her,' he said. 'Gerry's still having kittens about it, but I was careful, I told him. I never showed her the storyboards or the prototypes; a bit of banter and a few numbers here and there won't have given her anything to go on. Bitch!' Eric downed his refill and snarled his words at Luke.

Luke immediately reconsidered his assessment that there was anything appealing about Eric. Maybe his sleuthing skills came from advanced military training for mercenaries or his experiences with his various ex-wives (Gillian had mentioned two to him now; Samantha, known as Sam, and Bev), which had made him so suspicious. Even so, Luke checked over each shoulder that no one was close enough to witness Eric's meltdown. After the tremendous success of the conference, he wouldn't want to spoil things now.

'I'm feeling a little tired,' Luke tried to find a way out, away – anywhere but seated in this bar with his volatile, double-dealing boss.

'Now you want to change the subject,' Eric joked. 'I told Sam – my first wife – that I'd learned my lesson, that I wouldn't trust women who chased after me, and I have. Funny thing is, I thought Liz was after my money, like all the others, but I was willing to risk it. The car always gets them, gets their juices flowing. What can I do? I'm not going to give up my Porsche, just because it attracts the women. God, I love that motor. But I was wrong. It wasn't the money with her...Liz...Elizabeth! She was after secrets.' He tapped his fingers on the side of his head. 'She wanted what was up here. Do you know what she told me?'

'No,' Luke was wondering who Elizabeth was. She wasn't one of the wives Gillian had mentioned. But Eric was continuing his tirade.

'She was in HR. HR! That was a joke. Unless HR stands for

"fucking spy". Can you get me another drink? The waitress seems to have gone AWOL.'

'Sure. But listen, Eric, I'm not doubting you.' Luke took the view that empathy might be the best way to cut things short and he hovered on the edge of the bench.

'I'm telling you, this Elizabeth, she took me for a ride. I don't take kindly to being taken for a ride. You remember that. People who try to take me for a ride end up on their own one-way ride. You get me? Maybe I should have realised when she would never stop talking, asking me questions all the time – so interested in our work. Well, I put paid to that, stupid bitch. Ha! She can't do any more talking now, anyway. I told Gerry I would sort it out, and I did.'

Luke thought back to the punch bag and the phone call he had overheard in Eric's office some weeks before, as he finally eased himself out of his seat and their compartment. Had those words been addressed to this Elizabeth? He walked over to the bar and waited to be served. When he looked back at Eric, he was gone. A moment's search, with his eyes, located him introducing himself to two women and then squeezing himself in between them, at a table in the far corner. He appeared to have completely forgotten about Luke or his diatribe involving Ruth, Sam and Elizabeth.

Maybe Eric wasn't quite as successful with women as he thought he was. Although Luke accepted he was in great shape physically – he had seen that the night with the punchbag – Eric was pushing forty, and his hair was beginning to recede at the temple. Maybe it suited Eric to boast of his conquests, that he kept his women on their toes, when the reality was that, at least some of them lost interest or didn't answer his calls: '*micro*', '*solo*', '*dumbo*'. He laughed to himself. That was why he had to continually chase them; it was his insecurities ruling him.

'Can I help you, sir?' There was the barman, attentive as ever.

Luke looked over again at Eric, who was throwing his head back and guffawing at a joke he had been told by one of his new female friends. But Luke couldn't forget what Eric had just said: 'people who take me for a ride, end up on their own one-way ride. You get me?' Eric's face had twisted nastily as he spoke.

'No, actually, I changed my mind. I'm pretty tired. No thanks,' Luke said to the barman. Then, keeping his eyes keenly fixed on Eric, all the time, he backed away from the bar and, once out of sight, he picked up his pace as he headed back to his room.

31

CONSTANCE STOPPED BY AT Nathaniel's before court the next morning. She had forewarned him of her visit and his crumpled clothes and red eyes hinted strongly that he had not yet gone to bed from the night before, rather than having roused himself early, especially for her. He invited her in and she settled herself in the kitchen, among more empty pizza boxes.

'Hi Nathaniel, or should I call you Nath, now we know each other a little?'

'Hi.'

'You said you wanted to talk about tomorrow. You're not feeling nervous, are you?'

'I'm not great talking in front of loads of people.' He hovered by the sink, waving his hands over the dirty dishes, as if that might magic them clean.

'I don't believe that. You have thousands of people watching your show.'

'But they ain't there – not in the same room. I can't see 'em, when I'm talking. I told you.'

'Then, you just need to tell yourself it's the same. Pretend you're on your show and they're listening in.'

'What if they don't believe what I say?'

'That's always a worry. But if you tell the truth, that's all anyone can ask of you. That's all JD can ask. And it's not as if you're the one on trial. You're just a witness. If you want to come by today and sit in for a while, see the court room layout, where everyone stands, you can do that.'

'JD said he don't want me to come.'

'Do you know why that was?'

Nathaniel nodded, clasped his hands together, then un-clasped them, then he rose and walked over to the window.

'Is there something that's bothering you?'

'Yeah. I told you. I'm not good with an audience.'

'Something else? JD tells me what a brilliant friend you've been to him, all these years. Mr Mason told me too – your old teacher – when I went to see him. He said how close you two were. I know it must be hard for you, with Jaden away.'

'You talked to Mr Mason?'

'He said to send you his best wishes. You and Jaden were clearly his favourites. He's the headteacher now.'

'I always liked Mr Mason,' Nathaniel stared out of the window. 'He's the kind of person you could tell stuff to, do you know what I mean?'

'I got that feeling as soon as I met him.'

'If I…found something that would help JD and I gave it to you, do you have to say where you got it from?' Nathaniel stopped fidgeting and he focused on Constance for the first time. Constance felt heat flood her cheeks. She had worried that

Nathaniel was the weak link, that he may not come through for JD. And, despite having sought to reassure him about how easy he would find the process, she knew, from experience, that it was risky having him testify. Despite the potential benefit of any clear evidence he could give of Jaden returning, calm and well-fed, at 9pm from Elizabeth Sullivan's, she had worried what he might say. But this last question, this probing, this hint, albeit hypothetical, that he knew more than he was letting on, was truly worrying.

'You mean, if we imagined that, not something really happening?' she said, playing along as best she could.

'Yeah, that's what I mean.'

'So, if, say, I was to go to the bathroom, and leave my bag here on the chair and, later on today, I found something…unexpected in my bag, then I wouldn't know where it came from, would I?'

Nathaniel nodded. 'I suppose not.'

'Was there anything else you wanted to know about?'

'No, that's it. I was just wondering about that. Well, how's it going? The trial.'

'It's going well, but the bit that's really tricky for JD is the theft charge, explaining how he got those shoes. He just keeps insisting they were a present from Liz.'

'She was a nice lady. She baked us a chocolate cake. Some people might think that was a bit strange, too, but it happened.'

'I'm sure you're right. Some people are just generous. So, I'll see you tomorrow at 9am. You remember where?'

'I'll be there. Anything for JD.'

'And if you think you want to come by today and take a look, just send me a message first, OK? I'll come out and meet you.'

'Sure.'

'But, before I go, I'll just use the bathroom, if that's all right.'

***

Constance checked her bag three times, including on the x-ray security at court, but found nothing new deposited there. It disappointed her to realise that either she had been wrong about Nathaniel after all, or she had not done enough to garner his trust, or heighten his sense of obligation to his friend, despite her best efforts.

Then her phone hummed in her pocket. Reading the message, she shook her head from side to side. She sent a short response, before zipping up her bag and running out of the court building, waving her arms around to hail a cab as she went.

32

Sᴛʟᴠɪᴇ Eʟʟɪᴏᴛᴛ ᴀᴘᴘʀᴏᴀᴄʜᴇᴅ Judith outside court, as they waited for the door to be unlocked. Constance hadn't appeared yet and Judith was prepared to work solo today, if necessary. She knew that Constance would be following some lead and that it was almost always important. It was just that, invariably, things were better viewed through two pairs of eyes and it was hard to reproduce the atmosphere of the courtroom, the tone of the words used, the body language of the witnesses, simply by reading through the transcript afterwards. That was the one useful element of the Court TV pilot they had endured last time around.

'Are you ready to throw in the towel yet?' Sylvie asked, smiling as she spoke. The woman really was a walking antiphrasis.

'Are you like this with all your cases, or just the ones you're worried about losing?' Judith said.

Sylvie shook her head. 'I never lose,' she said, 'and I'm not about to begin now.'

They both heard a key turn in the lock and, as Judith pressed on forwards, Sylvie caught her arm. 'We may be prepared to offer him manslaughter, if he pleads now,' she said.

'What?' Judith could hardly believe Sylvie's audacity. Judith had no problem with confidence – she understood how important it could be to the presentation of a case – but when it overstepped the mark into impudence and pushiness, then she was unimpressed. The one advantage was that Sylvie's unpalatable behaviour would make it easier to gloat, if Judith's carefully placed hints sent her off in the wrong direction. But Sylvie was speaking again.

'Maybe, just maybe, he thought she wanted sex,' Sylvie said, 'he really did; when she said "no" he couldn't stop himself. And when he saw she was ill, he tried to save her, but he panicked and ran. He's only young, after all. I may be able to persuade my team to accept manslaughter, but I'd need an answer today.'

'The answer's no. Why on earth would an innocent man plead guilty to manslaughter?'

'You know as well as I. This isn't about being innocent, it's about persuading them that you're not guilty. You think you're so clever with the chair and the straps and the handbag. Juries don't like lawyers who are too clever. You know that – you've been doing this far longer than me – but you still can't resist showing them how clever you are, can you?'

Judith said nothing and Sylvie pressed home her advantage.

'And I don't know if you've been watching them as closely as I have – your precious jury – but they haven't warmed to your boy. I'll share that with you for free.'

'They haven't heard from him yet,' Judith said, knowing, as soon as the words came from her mouth that they were ill-thought-out.

Sylvie withdrew her hand from Judith's arm and gave a short, sharp, high-pitched laugh. 'If that's what you're relying upon, then I have underestimated you massively. We both know your client giving evidence will be nothing short of a car crash.'

As Judith clattered her way through the swing doors into court, Sylvie followed close behind, and while Judith was dropping her books down on the bench, Sylvie leaned across into her space with the words: 'Let me know, today, if you're interested. A bird in the hand...and all that.'

***

Judith had seen Dr Williams out of the corner of her eye, seated outside court, during her exchange with Sylvie. He had been moving his hand repeatedly to his pocket, bringing it out empty, his fingers strolling aimlessly up and down his thigh. Then he had settled upon his wedding ring and begun to roll it around his finger, first one way and then the other.

She wondered if he and Liz had been more than colleagues; Constance had agreed to make further enquiries. She could easily imagine that all those hours of 'collaboration' which would have been part and parcel of their joint book – the late nights arguing over titles and correcting typos and agreeing on the acknowledgements or cover – would have led into bed.

Then she checked herself; Greg would call her a cynic for those thoughts, say she was an enemy of romance, true love and fidelity, although, of course, it was what had happened between herself and Greg back in the day... Well...almost. Selective memory: the perfect companion for self-preservation, she thought.

'Dr Williams. You worked closely with Dr Sullivan on various research projects?' Sylvie was on her feet again, arms wrapped around her notes, her voice like liquid honey.

Tony Williams wore a jacket over his jumper, something Martin would have considered a massive fashion faux pas, but which, at the very least, would keep him insulated from the cold February day outside.

'I did, yes,' he replied.

'And you last saw her on the day she died?'

'We were discussing some work over tea. Liz left around 5pm. That was the last time I saw her or heard from her.'

'What were you discussing?'

'Over the years, we worked together, like I said. Liz's hospital trust and mine – she was based in Hackney, I was in Kennington – we'd collaborated on projects to tackle addiction of various kinds. Then, three years ago, I joined her in Hackney and we continued our work.'

'How would you describe Dr Sullivan?'

'Immensely dedicated. She cared deeply about her patients and went out of her way to help them recover and lead normal lives.'

'Was she worried about anything, when you met?'

'She didn't mention anything.'

'Are you aware of her ever having received threats from anyone?'

'No. Well, as psychiatrists we do tend to run more of those kind of risks than other doctors, but she never raised this with me.'

'What about anyone in her personal life?'

'Again, not as far as I know.'

'Were you aware that she suffered from this heart condition, HCM?'

'No. She never said and I certainly never noticed any symptoms. She always appeared healthy. She was slim, perhaps a little underweight, even, but she never had time off work for illness. I wouldn't have guessed.'

'Did she ever mention the defendant, Jaden Dodds, to you?'

'She did, yes.'

The hairs on the back of Judith's neck stood up and she scribbled some notes down in her pad, seeking out Constance, but cursing to find her still missing. Where had she gone, at this crucial moment? Dr Williams' head turned towards Jaden, before slowly turning back.

'Can you explain the circumstances?'

'It was just a throwaway comment and she didn't say his name. Just that there was a boy on her street who was a gamer, who operated a gaming website. That she'd met him. That was all.'

'Did she indicate who made the first move, whether Jaden had approached her?'

'I don't think so. I had the feeling they met in the street.'

'So, he, Jaden, he could easily have approached her?'

'Yes.'

'And Dr Sullivan was well-known, locally, as a doctor treating gaming addiction?'

'You could say that. Local people with those kind of problems would be referred to her and some of her papers were available online. And her book...our book.'

'That day, Friday the 1st of November, did she say if she was planning to meet Jaden Dodds, in the evening?'

'She didn't say anything but...'

'Go on.'

'She had this look in her eye, like there was something she wasn't telling me. Maybe he had asked to see her again and she was thinking about it.'

'Thank you, Dr Williams.'

Judith sat reflecting for a few seconds longer than usual on Dr Williams' words, before rising to her feet.

'Is it right that gaming addiction is now considered a recognised disease by the World Health Organisation?' she began.

Dr Williams' eyes widened and he sat up straight. Perhaps he hadn't expected his appearance in court to provide an opportunity to talk about his work, but it seemed to enthuse him, nevertheless. 'Yes, since May 2019,' he said. 'It's classified as a mental and behavioural disorder.'

'And what are the signs of this addiction?'

'Severe. We're not talking about someone who plays video games for recreation, then switches off and goes and joins their mates for football. This disorder is so intense that it will be distressing for the sufferer and will significantly impair how they function in every area of their life. They may stop speaking to anyone, stop eating, stop washing, they may drop out of school or lose their job, be unable to sleep, either because they are gaming all night or, when they do stop, they simply can't switch off sufficiently to allow their body to rest; total withdrawal from normal daily life.'

'And do sufferers come to you voluntarily?'

'It's almost always family members who ask us to intervene; sufferers most often can't appreciate the state they're in.'

'What is the impact of the WHO recognising gaming addiction as a disorder?'

'Enormous. It provides a standard definition of the disorder, based on symptoms. That means, where treatment is available, patients can expect it to be provided, as they now have a recognised disorder. It also allows doctors to reliably communicate with patients or other doctors to enable trials to take place, so treatments can be developed. And, as we can standardise eligibility criteria for participants, we can be assured that the treatment is correctly targeting people with the disorder and compare treatment outcomes across different studies, to identify which treatments are working best.'

'And does everyone agree with you that it's a good thing?'

'Most people and certainly most doctors. Not surprisingly, the companies who produce these addictive…potentially addictive games are up in arms, protesting, decrying it as nonsense, lobbying for a reversal of that decision.'

'Now you and Dr Sullivan co-wrote a paper entitled "Behavioural Addiction, Holding Back the Tide," in 2017, at the end of a joint study.'

'We did.'

'And what impact did that paper have on the WHO?'

'It was cited as one of the factors they considered, when they made their decision.'

'You mentioned your book a moment ago. You co-authored a book with Dr Sullivan, *The Good, the Bad and the Problematic*, a year earlier.'

'Yes. That was also referenced by the WHO, as having major impact.'

'Gosh. You and Dr Sullivan were materially involved in the changes it adopted. So, you could stop there, couldn't you?'

'I suppose so.'

'But Dr Sullivan didn't stop there, did she?'

'No, she didn't.'

'She wrote eleven papers over the last two years, all on the subject of internet gaming, covering genetic and environmental influences, reward dependence, possible links with autism, proven links with self-harm and suicidal behaviour, and including a swingeing critique of the gaming industry.'

'That's right, yes.'

'Were you involved in that research?'

'I moved towards gambling as my main area of interest. Like you said, Liz stuck with gaming.'

'She must have made some enemies then, among the gaming community?'

'She wasn't flavour of the month, no.'

'Can we take a look at one of Dr Sullivan's papers? It's this one, entitled "Impulsiveness, Decision-making and Reward Dependence". You're familiar with it?'

'I am, yes.'

Sylvie was on her feet, even before Judith had opened the paper on her laptop. 'My Lord, the details of Dr Sullivan's work, however fascinating, are a total irrelevance.'

'My Lord, Ms Elliot insisted, if you recall, on "laying down a marker" that she wished to show that my client deliberately targeted Dr Sullivan *because of her work* and wanted to punish her for it. She has pursued this argument, just now, with Dr Williams, albeit without a shred of evidence. Knowledge of what Dr Sullivan did, including the studies she conducted in this particular area of gaming addiction is vital, therefore, to rebut the prosecution's case in this area.'

Judith held her breath. She was pretty sure she was right on the law, but some judges would be thinking about their lunch or their day off and would want to curtail testimony, which may only be of peripheral relevance. But Judge Oliver was not one of those judges. He prided himself on his strict adherence to the rules. He waved his pencil at Judith to continue. She located the paper on her laptop and read its title out again.

'Yes,' Dr Williams said. 'It was based on a study involving sixty individuals aged between fourteen and thirty, most of them male.'

'What were they being tested for?'

'These kind of studies address a number of aspects of the behaviour of gamers, but the key elements are whether problem gamers perform less well than the control set in our tests, suggesting their brain functions are impaired by their gaming habit. Then we can draw conclusions about whether their cognitive functions have been impacted by the gaming – things like working memory, behaviour control, including impulsive tendencies, or attention deficit.'

'How do you test them? Do you watch them gaming?'

'Not usually. We ask them questions about their gaming habits, to see if their use is problematic, then we assess those cognitive functions I mentioned, using a variety of tests. The form we use most often is called the Stroop test.'

'Can you explain that please, in general terms.'

'Yes, so the Stroop test is named after a psychologist and dates back to the 1930s. It involves using different stimuli and asking participants to read out what they see. The test then records how quickly they respond and if they get the answer right.'

'Thank you, so I have an example here on the screen. You can see the words "green", "blue" and "pink" written up in different, non-matching colours.'

'Yes. The word "green" is in pink text, the word "blue" in yellow text. The participant might be asked what colour is the word "green"? In order to respond correctly, the meaning of the word "green" has to be mentally suppressed. We then record how long it takes them to reply and that gives us the information I was talking about, on whether their brain is processing information normally or not.'

'And Liz's research showed that volunteers who admitted they gamed a lot – their functions were impaired, when compared with other people who didn't?'

'That's it, in a nutshell.'

'But if you had succeeded, you had the WHO classification, and a big multi-national taskforce was to be formed to take the research forwards, why did Dr Sullivan still feel it necessary to write all these papers, involving all this testing? All this, no doubt, on top of her usual clinics.'

'She said it would take years to coordinate and she recognised that, for people with addiction, every day was a day wasted or, worse still, a day closer to ruin.'

'She was impatient?'

'She was dedicated.'

'Was Dr Sullivan working on any specific trial, of which you were aware, immediately prior to her death?'

Dr Williams looked at Tom before answering. Tom was watching him closely, his expression hostile.

'She handed in some work a couple of weeks before she died. After that, I don't know. She could be a bit secretive. She did discuss things with me, but she liked results first, so that we really had something to talk about.'

'Were you aware that Dr Sullivan was taking anti-depressants?'

'No.' Judith thought Dr Williams hesitated a second too long before replying.

'Two, in fact. One called Wellbutrin, the other, Anafranil; only one prescribed by her GP. You are familiar with both of those?'

'Yes, of course… I didn't know.' Now he had spoken abruptly and colour had flooded his cheeks.

'You didn't prescribe the Wellbutrin for her?'

'Absolutely not.'

'You seem agitated.'

'I'm just upset to hear that Liz was on that medication and I didn't know about it.' He drew his hand across the lower part of his face. 'We knew each other so long and she never let on,' he said. 'If I'd only known, perhaps I could have helped her.'

***

'How was Dr Williams?' Constance caught up with Judith at court, after it adjourned early, Judge Oliver having another hearing to preside over for the remainder of the day.

'I'm not sure. I wish you'd been there.'

'I'm sorry. I was occupied with something really important.'

'Go on. Lay it on me.'

'I have Liz's mobile phone.'

'What?'

'Liz's phone.'

'How?'

'Mr Mason, Jaden and Nathaniel's old headmaster. He gave it to me.'

'And how did he get hold of it?'

'He wouldn't say; said he was sworn to secrecy.'

'I see.'

'But I happened to mention him to Nathaniel first thing this morning and I don't believe in coincidences. I think it gave Nathaniel a neat solution to the tricky situation he found himself in.'

'Ah. I understand, I think. Have you taken this up with Nathaniel yet?'

'I thought it more important to get the phone to Dawson and to update you. I… I asked Greg to help out. He was at my place anyway, looking at Liz's laptop, like you asked, and so it wasn't far for him to meet me at the police station. You know what he's like with things like that. He got the phone open straightaway and the police are reviewing the messages. Dawson's going to call me back this afternoon.'

'Wow. Well done you…and Greg. On balance, I agree that was a good enough reason to miss Dr Williams.'

'So, what did I miss?'

'You've met him. Did you find him…evasive?'

'Not really. OK, if I think back, he was in a rush to be somewhere else. Then, again, I did get him at the hospital in the middle of the day.'

'Did he tell you that Liz had mentioned Jaden?'

'No, he never said.'

'I thought you wouldn't have forgotten to tell me that. Thing is, I didn't believe him when he said it. I can't remember why, whether it was too off-hand, or it sounded rehearsed. But it didn't ring true.'

'Why would he lie about it?'

'I don't know. I mean, if you analyse it carefully, it's not evidence against Jaden – Liz telling Williams that she had met Jaden. Jaden accepts they met.'

'Maybe you were right about the affair thing and he's trying to show he's relaxed about Liz knowing Jaden, to keep us off the scent. Although I spoke to Sandy last night and she was very clear they were just friends. Said he wasn't Liz's type.'

'Not everyone sticks with type – that would be very dull. Well, if she's wrong and they were involved, there's bound to be stuff on Liz's phone that will give him away.'

'Let's hope so.'

The two women laughed companionably.

'Another strange thing he said, though,' Judith continued. 'He claims he didn't know what Liz was working on when she died, which seems odd if they were so close.'

'I agree and I'm sure he told me something different. I'll check my notes. And I had to message a few times before I got all Liz's research papers. Did you ask him about the government committee?'

'I couldn't see the point. It's all public. And I was already on thin ice with the judge, trawling through Liz's research. I wasn't sure it added anything. Dr Williams didn't give evidence to them – I checked – but that's not surprising, as his focus has moved more to gambling recently, although...'

'What?'

'Oh, I don't know. I wonder whether Liz stole the limelight and that's why he shifted his focus. That there could only be one expert in Hackney on gaming addiction.'

'There's nothing wrong in that, is there?'

'No, you're right. There isn't. And he didn't strike me as a man with a big ego, whatever his failings, so forget I said anything.'

'OK. Listen. Two more things on my list. Greg is still working on the copy of Liz's laptop, to follow up your theory that she was watching Jaden online, as part of her research,' Constance said.

'I want to get a handle on what she was up to, yes,' Judith replied. 'And this seemed the best way.'

Constance had to hand it to Judith. Greg could just reappear in the picture and Judith felt she didn't need to provide any explanation. She was certainly not owning up to their impromptu dinner date.

'Any news on Tom's home visits?' Judith neatly changed the subject.

'That was the other thing I wanted to tell you. David said Tom might have gone home that night.'

'Might have?'

'Tom would sneak off to see his mum, without getting permission. David was away, himself, that evening, so he doesn't know for sure, but Tom was definitely back by midnight.'

'Hm. Not good to have yet another possible suspect. But it doesn't feel like Tom did this.'

'He wanted to keep on gaming. We both heard what David said. Liz wanted to stop him.'

Judith shook her head slowly.

'Listen, if we are adjourned till tomorrow and you can spare me, I'm off to see Nathaniel now,' Constance said. 'It means I won't get on to those last research papers of Liz's till later.'

'That's fine. I'll take a look at them too.'

'I'll call you as soon as I hear from Dawson, and if Greg finds anything.'

'Great. And I'll be preparing for Nathaniel tomorrow.'

Constance opened her mouth, then closed it again. She knew Judith shared her concerns about Nathaniel, but she was not going to formally accuse him of anything until she had confronted him herself and given him the opportunity to explain.

33

TOM SAT ON HIS AUNT'S SOFA, while she busied herself in the tiny kitchen.

'I thought I'd make you pancakes. They were always your favourite, when you were little. I've got bananas and Nutella, whichever you prefer. Or both together! And, if you like, you could stay here tonight. You don't have to go back to school.'

Should he tell his aunt he no longer liked pancakes? That wasn't true; they remained a firm favourite, but he wanted to do something to assert himself, to have some impact, even at this pathetically low level. He wanted to be heard. He also wanted her to stop pretending everything was OK, when it wasn't.

Eve had already mixed the batter and was spreading the fat around the frying pan. She was singing a tuneless song to herself. Maybe he should be particularly cruel and allow her to make a huge stack and then refuse to eat any of them. That would show her not to make assumptions that he was hungry, or about what he liked to eat.

Tom reached for the TV remote and pressed some buttons. Then he looked around at the sparsely furnished room. Apart from the sofa he was sitting on, there was a single bed in the corner, with a lamp on the floor, some bookshelves and a half-built wardrobe, with brightly coloured fabrics peeping out.

Evidently, Eve liked vibrant colours; the scatter cushions were orange and pink, the lampshade was yellow and the bed throw was red with purple flowers. Tom thought the room the complete antithesis of his mum's flat. How could two sisters be so very different?

'Yes, I know, there's only one bed, but it's very cosy. You could have it. I'll sleep on the sofa. I'm used to it. I've slept in a lot of uncomfortable places, I can tell you.'

Tom thought back to the rare occasions Eve had visited them over the years. Maybe only a handful of times, usually on her way back from some trip or in the process of planning another. She had always brought them gifts from her travels; he remembered a poncho from Bolivia which had given him a rash, a hat from Australia with real crocodile teeth in the brim, which had fallen down over his face, and a laughing carved buddha from China, which had sat on the mantelpiece for years. Eve had told them that rubbing its stomach brought good luck. Tom had rubbed it every day for around a month before concluding it didn't work. Had she really believed any of that? Clearly, it hadn't worked for either of his parents. He had no idea where it was now.

He flicked through the channels. He wanted to check his phone, but he thought his aunt might think him rude. He'd had it on all the way back here, in the taxi.

'I'm hoping it's all going to be finished this week,' Eve carried on, 'the trial. If that daft judge hadn't had something else slap-bang in the middle, we might have been finished already. Then we can try to get things back to normal,' she said.

Tom's fingers hovered over the remote and then his bottom lip trembled. Before he knew it, his shoulders were shaking and choking noises were coming from the back of his throat.

Eve turned off the gas hob, rested her spoon down in the bowl of batter and went to him.

'I'm sorry, love,' she said. 'I wasn't thinking about what I was saying.'

She glided around the sofa and sat down next to him. As she reached out towards him, Tom sprang up and ran away to the bathroom, slamming the door behind him. He searched for a lock, but there wasn't one. God, Eve was pathetic! Who didn't even have a lock on their bathroom door? Then he sank down to the floor, hugged his arms tight around his body and he cried as hard as he could.

34

'How did you get it – the phone?' Constance barely managed to control her anger, as she barrelled her way past Nathaniel and into his flat. This time, his creased pyjamas bore testament to the fact she had awakened him. He could have only had five hours sleep at most, given that she'd left him at eight-thirty. He closed the door and, this time, he followed her into the kitchen.

'I don't know what you're talking about,' he said.

'Someone hand-delivered Elizabeth Sullivan's lost mobile phone to Mr Mason at your old school.'

'So?'

'Just after I left here and we had talked about him.'

'It wasn't me.'

'I'm sure it wasn't. That would have been too risky. You asked someone else to do it for you. Perhaps one of his pupils. Oh come on, Nathaniel. How did you get that phone?'

'I don't know what you're talking about.'

'All that, "if you happened to find something". Do you think I was born yesterday?'

Nathaniel picked up a glass from the draining board, filled it with water and drank it down.

'OK. You want to play the silent type? Wait here.' Constance marched out of the room and into his bedroom. She went straight to his wardrobe, opened both doors and then stood back, surveying its contents.

'You can't do that!' he stormed in behind her.

Constance knelt down and her eyes wandered over his shoe collection. She pulled out the first pair of Yeezys trainers and threw one over her shoulder. Nathaniel ducked and it narrowly missed him and ricocheted off the wall. Then she pulled out a second and waved it at him. 'Here!' she shouted. 'Here!'

'What! Stop throwing my shoes around, will you?'

'My brother told me. He said they weren't the kind of shoes he thought JD would wear, especially when I told him about JD's other trainers. But you, you're a different matter. Evidently, they're your shoe of choice.'

'That don't mean nothing.'

'No. It means lots of things. And when were they delivered? Those shoes the police found, shoved behind the kitchen waste pipe. Was it after JD was arrested? I could check. I could easily find out what deliveries were made to this flat that week.'

'That would take forever.'

'No, it wouldn't. Because my brother, I just mentioned – he used to work as a delivery driver. And he knows everyone who delivers round here. I could find out in ten minutes, maybe even five. Now, you are going to get dressed and we are going, together, to see JD right now. And if you want to keep denying to me that you stole Elizabeth Sullivan's bag and bought those trainers with her credit card, that's fine. But let's see you deny it to JD.'

***

Nathaniel was silent the entire journey to Eastleigh prison. That suited Constance fine, as she was boiling with anger. She hadn't made up the whole story about her brother; he had done some delivery work, but he was not always easy to reach, so she couldn't be confident he could provide the input she wanted in double-quick time. But Nathaniel didn't know that. Although now she had seen his shoe collection, it was blindingly obvious the trainers belonged to him; she kicked herself for not working it out earlier.

As they waited for Jaden to be brought in, Nathaniel spoke for the first time.

'Let me see him on his own, please, just for a minute,' he said.

'What, so you can dream up some story to tell him?'

'Just a minute. Then you can say whatever you like. Please?

Constance allowed Nathaniel to enter the interview room first, following after a few minutes had elapsed. When she did, Jaden, still in his court clothes, was sitting with his head in his hands and Nathaniel was facing the opposite wall. They both turned around at her entrance.

'Have you told him?' Constance asked.

'He didn't need to tell me,' Jaden replied.

'What?'

'As soon as I heard they was Yeezys, all those weeks ago, I knew it was Nath or someone sending them for Nath. And when he didn't say he knew nothing about them, I knew it was him. I'm not stupid.'

Constance looked from one boy to the other, finally focusing

247

on Jaden.

'Why didn't you tell me?' she said.

'What? And drop Nath in it? Then we'd both be in here.'

'I don't think so,' she said. 'Without the theft of the trainers, the police don't have much else connecting you and Liz.'

'Apart from they had sex together in her bed and then she ended up dead,' Nathaniel said.

'All right, yes, apart from that. I'll have to tell Dawson, see if we can get the theft charge dropped.'

'Aha. You're not telling no one.' Jaden stood up and he towered over Constance.

'I have to.'

'If I'd wanted you to tell the police, I'd have said.'

'But you may go to jail, when you're innocent.'

'I don't want you to tell the police, and you're my lawyer. You have to do what I say, don't you?'

'I'll tell them, then, when I go into court tomorrow. I'll tell them it was all a mistake.' Nathaniel also rose and he rested his hand firmly on Jaden's shoulder. Jaden placed his own hand on top and shook his head.

'I don't want you to do that,' he said.

'It might save you, man.'

'I'm telling you, the time's passed. It's too late. Now, we'll both go down together and then who'll visit me when I'm inside? And who'll keep the show going for when I get out?'

Nathaniel's whole body drooped. 'Constance. Tell him. I'll tell everyone tomorrow, when it's my turn to speak,' he entreated her. 'I should've let on at the beginning. I just got scared.'

'Nath. You made a mistake. You never stole the card or bought the trainers. He gets confused sometimes. He's just doing it to try to save me.' Jaden was standing taller than ever.

'What?' Nathaniel said. 'But you just said…'

'I was…mistaken. All the pressure of the trial. It's nice of you to do this, to protect me, but I can't let you.'

Nathaniel turned to Constance, his face a mass of confusion and disbelief.

'If JD doesn't want to put your evidence forward, I can't call you,' Constance said.

'What?' Nathaniel repeated.

'I can't call you as a witness. That's it.'

'This is all your fault,' Nathaniel shouted at Constance. 'You dragged me here, you forced me to talk to JD and now you're saying I can't even tell everyone the good stuff. If you hadn't made me come, I would've just done it in court tomorrow. I was all ready.'

'It's not her fault, Nath,' JD said. 'It's just how it is. And I know you weren't looking forward to being in court, and I really appreciate you were going to do it, even so. I won't forget that.' He turned to Constance. 'What now?' he said.

'I'll tell Judith,' Constance said, 'and we'll think of who to put in tomorrow morning to replace Nathaniel.'

Then she turned to Nathaniel, who was staring at the floor. 'But before I do,' she said, 'if you really want to help, you can tell me how you got Liz's credit card in the first place. Then maybe we can salvage something from this mess.'

35

CONSTANCE ARRIVED AT JUDITH'S two hours later, armed with the copy of Liz's hard drive and her own laptop. Judith was sitting on the floor, with Liz's research papers strewn all around her and a worn-out expression.

'Any joy?' Judith asked, groaning as she eased herself up onto the sofa.

'Nothing from Dawson yet, but he's promised to call me by ten pm latest, with an update.'

'And Liz? What was she doing when she wasn't seeing patients, in that spare time Tom said she never had? Has Greg waved his magic wand?'

Constance thought Judith not only eager for news, but keen to hear that Greg had been useful too. Perhaps she wanted to justify to herself allowing him into her life again.

'I have lots to show you. The best way is to have Liz's laptop open next to mine, so we can see what was happening at Jaden's end too.'

'OK.'

Judith sat back, plumping some cushions behind her.

'Here I am looking at Jaden's past shows, starting with 14th October, a Monday night, a few days before he jump-started Liz's car. Jaden is online, there we go. He's live at nine-thirty pm and here's the YouTube follow-up. Now let's cross-check it against Liz's browsing history. Greg showed me how to do this.'

Constance sat the two laptops side by side. It wasn't always possible to track exactly what Liz had been watching, but she was visiting YouTube over and over again, often at exactly the time Jaden's show was replayed. But the most interesting aspect was the chat on Jaden's Twitch stream.

'Here,' Constance paused the chat and pointed to an entry in pink.

'Hay JD & Nath. Great show tonite @ES77.'

'Oh my God!' Judith hands enveloped her face. 'You think that's her? @ES77. What's 77?'

'Her date of birth.'

'It is her! Greg was spot-on. So simple. That's her. It's easy once you know.'

'Greg's not had time to go back that far, but she'd been a subscriber to JD & Nath for a month before this; she'd made a few small donations too. She was beginning to earn their confidence, little bits of support, here and there, working up to this, a few days later. Look.'

'Do you ever meet up with fans? @ES77'

'And listen, JD picks it up in his commentary. "Hey there ES77. I'm a bit shy of strangers. But you can ask me all you like online".'

'I was right, then,' Judith said. 'She's researching gaming and its impact on young men and, here, right on her doorstep, she finds a young man at the centre of the industry. She tries to approach him this way, gets the brush off. So, she had a convenient flat battery and suddenly they were friends. Brilliant. This is brilliant.'

'I don't see it as so significant.'

'Look, you're right. It isn't *directly* linked to what happened on the night of 1st November. And maybe it's a massive side show. That's what Sylvie will say, and Judge Oliver will agree, because he does everything by the book. But I'm sure it's connected. I've never been more sure. Here is evidence – clear evidence – that Liz was interested in Jaden, making contact with him anonymously, way before they met. We can use it to show she was stalking him and not the other way around. I'll have to handle it really carefully though. I mean, if I try to say Liz initiated everything, including the sex, and all for her research, that may be a step too far, even for our enlightened 2020 jury.'

Constance leaned her head back against the arm of the sofa. She was pleased to have something positive to bring to Judith, after all her efforts, although the prospect of even more work to prove this in court, opened up before her.

'Where did you get to with Nathaniel?' Judith asked.

Constance's mood plummeted further.

'Ah,' she said. 'That's not such good news, after all.'

36

IT WAS RAINING HEAVILY when Constance exited the underground station and began her walk home, her conscience pricked by barbs of self-reproach. How could she not have guessed earlier that Liz had pursued Jaden? She had been too fixed on Jaden himself – those ridiculous fantasies about him invading her dreams – rather than the wider picture, and it had been left to Judith to work it out.

Usually, it was the other way around; Judith pleading with Constance to stay focused on the case, not to stray too far from their brief, in case they turned up something unhelpful, and Constance insisting on finding the truth regardless. Why had she been so reticent this time?

Instead, she'd missed the obvious signs of Nathaniel's guilt and then her forcing him to confess in front of Jaden had been downright stupid. Judith had tried to make her feel better, said she wasn't to know that Jaden would be so protective of his friend. But she should have joined the dots; Mr Mason had told her how it was between those two.

Constance had progressed only a few metres along Old Street when she felt it again, the same tingling sensation she had experienced that night outside Jaden's flat, an overwhelming impression that someone else was invading her space. She turned around and saw only a homeless man, settling himself down for the night in a doorway, drawing his feet in tight to keep them out of the wet.

She walked on and it was busier now; a couple running, shoulder to shoulder, a plastic bag raised aloft to deflect the rain, an old man shuffling along, a broken umbrella fitted snug to his head, one spoke poking forward like a wayward bayonet. The window of the bakery on the corner of Vine Street was still lit; its rows of doughnuts and cup cakes shining out, garish and florid.

As she turned into Hackney Road, she heard footsteps, muffled by the rain and punctuated by the occasional splash, but definitely footsteps. She whizzed around and a shadow disappeared behind a van. She advanced two paces to stand beneath a streetlight and waited, the rain heavier now, plastering her hair down onto her head.

Nothing happened for a few seconds. A car sped past, its headlights illuminating the gutter. Constance shivered. She wanted to move on, but she also wanted to know who was following her. She waited some more. Rain began to trickle down the back of her neck. Then a man stepped out onto the pavement. He began to walk towards her. He stopped about two or three metres away, blinking, as the rain lashed across his face.

'Who are you?' Constance asked.

'I'm Nick. I'm sorry if I scared you. I just want to help,' the man said, his voice light and cheerful, despite the storm.

'Help who? Why are you following me?'

'You're the lawyer defending JD. I was in court today.'

'Have you been…'

'I saw you once before, outside Dr Sullivan's flat. I have information which could help you, help JD.' The man walked forwards, bouncing on the balls of his feet.

'Why do you want to help JD?' Constance asked, taking a step back. Nick stopped beneath a streetlight.

'Because Dr Sullivan was my doctor,' he said. 'And I think I know how she died.'

Constance peered at the man through the rain, and then she reached for her phone. She scrolled through her photos till she found the one Liz had stuck to her fridge. It was impossible to be certain in the poor light and the rain, but the man in front of her could be one of the four pictured in the photograph. She scrolled on to the next photo and read aloud, 'To Dr Liz, from Nick and the A Team.'

The man laughed. 'Yes!' he said. 'How do you know about that?'

'The A team,' Constance repeated it to herself. And 'come on, then,' she said to the man. 'Follow me.'

***

Luke's trip back to the UK had been uneventful. Eric, clearly exhausted from thirty-six hours without any meaningful rest, had slept in the taxi, in the airport lounge and throughout the flight, providing welcome relief to Luke, and time for him to read the paper, for the first time in weeks. But an article on page 7, tucked between a story about the havoc caused by Storm Dennis and the government plan to abolish criminal sanctions for failure to pay the TV licence fee, drew his attention and he read on, his breathing becoming increasingly laboured as he did.

Now, back in his new-build flat in Canary Wharf, Luke was mulling over what to do next, including whether there was any prospect of taking a few days' holiday, before things ramped up even more with *Midas*. He suspected pushback from Eric. But, even as he closed his eyes and tried to focus on the game, to allow the images he had created to cavort around inside his head, he kept coming back to Eric, last night in the bar and the things he had said.

And then his mobile rang and interrupted all those thoughts.

'Hi Luke. It's Gerry Collier here. How's it going?' Gerry was Valiant's accountant and trusted adviser.

Luke sipped at his can of Heineken and nodded twice, before remembering that would not communicate well over the phone.

'Good, yes, thanks. How are you?'

'Fine, listen. Can you give me five minutes update on your conference? I tried Eric last night and got nothing and the same first thing this morning. Then, I've been trying him again for the last hour, but his phone's off and I need to report to one of our investors by six-thirty latest, on your Nice trip.'

'He's probably gone straight to bed. It was full on while we were out there.'

'It wouldn't have hurt him to call me first. Well? Spill the beans.'

'Um. Yeah. It was brilliant. The Olympic committee was there. We met them, they liked Eric's pitch. We met loads of other people from the bigger companies, potential investors, TV and media.'

'And Eric's speech?'

'They loved it. One of the Olympic guys even asked him a question. He pitched *Midas* to a few people and the feedback was really positive. I know he's set up a whole string of meetings for the next two weeks or so.'

'Great. Fantastic. Was there anything bad? I just need to know because if I pass this on and then there's something I don't know about…'

'Not from me. I wasn't with Eric every second, but everything I saw was positive.'

'Thanks, you've saved my life. These guys at Anthem Capital, they like me to be prompt.'

'That's fine. They want to protect their investment. I get that.' Luke hesitated for a moment. This was his chance to find out if Gerry knew anything about what Eric had been shouting in the bar, and to address the creeping sense of dread he had felt since he had immersed himself in the news on the plane home. 'Can I ask you something? It's a bit random,' he said.

'Go ahead. Today, you've got my undivided attention.'

'Who's Elizabeth?'

'Elizabeth?'

'I think Eric went out with her recently and he's pretty cross about something she did.'

'Elizabeth.'

'Or Liz, maybe?'

'Oh, you mean *Liz*. He told you about that?'

'Just bits and pieces.'

'Listen, I don't think you need to worry about it. I told him to get rid of her and he did. Sometimes, Eric lets his…let's just say he likes a pretty woman.'

'He said she was a spy.'

'He picked up some woman – Liz, Elizabeth, whatever. I don't think I knew her second name – took her out. She said she was interested in investing in the company. Said she had inherited some money and wanted somewhere to put it, that she had been advised Esports was up-and-coming. He insisted I prepare some papers for her, give her information from our business plan. I didn't think it felt right. I did some digging and some of the info she had given was false. I told Eric I was fairly sure she wasn't an investor, that she was working for a competitor. He didn't take it kindly, as you can imagine.'

'When was this?'

'A few months back, October time.'

'Did you ever meet her?'

'Really briefly. One time I was having coffee with Eric and he hooked up with her right outside. I could see why they sent her; she was just Eric's type.'

Luke took a deep breath. 'Can I send you a photo? You let me know if it's the same Elizabeth?'

'What's this all about?'

'It's probably nothing, but I'll send you across the photo. Just message me back. I know you're busy and you need to get on. Will you do that?'

'Is this going to get me into trouble?'

'No, nothing like that. It's just for me.' As Luke spoke the words, he hoped against hope that they would turn out to be true. That Gerry would send back the right answer, that he could forget all about what Eric had told him when under the influence, and that he could go on to achieve worldwide adoration with *Midas*, or whatever new name Eric wanted, with Eric behind him all the way.

'Then, sure. No problem,' Gerry said.

Luke ended the call and then searched, online, for the photo which had accompanied the article on page 7 of today's *Times* newspaper, about Elizabeth Sullivan's murder. Surprisingly, given his secular upbringing, he found himself whispering a prayer to himself as he located the image and forwarded it on to Gerry, for confirmation of his worst fears.

37

TOM WAS SEATED AT his desk, laptop open, when David entered, fresh from rugby practice, his cheeks flushed, his hair tangled, his legs coated in mud. He grabbed his towel from behind the door and then stopped and closed the door behind him.

'Hey mate. What's up?'

No reply.

'Mr Jenkins said you might stay out with your aunt, but I'm pleased you're back.'

Still no reply.

'And he said I could come with you tomorrow, if you like. You know I won't say anything to anyone.'

David sat down on the edge of Tom's bed in his dirty shorts. This usually provoked a ferocious response, but today, nothing. Then Tom began to speak.

'They say the dead can't hurt you. Did you know that?' he began.

'Yeah, I suppose so,' David replied. 'Is it the trial? I was thinking. You don't have to go. Mr Jenkins could go and let you know what's said, or your aunt Eve. If it's too much.'

'I'm not talking about the trial,' Tom said.

'Oh.'

Tom touched his keyboard and his screen flashed into life.

'Read this,' he said, his voice trembling around the edges.

David stood up, leaned over Tom's shoulder and read the message to himself, his lips moving as they travelled over and deciphered the words:

'Hey Sully. When we made you the offer to join our team, we didn't know about your family background. We've now been informed that your late mother, Dr Elizabeth Sullivan, was the author of various publications critical of the Esports industry and, in particular, of manufacturers of online games. In the circumstances, we hope you'll understand if we withdraw the offer to join us. We have to think about the team as a whole and how people will fit in. You are clearly talented, so we're sure you will find a place somewhere else. Wishing you the best of luck.

Yours, Stephen Turner

Team Co-ordinator, The Wanderers'

'I'm sorry,' David said.

'It's all I've wanted to do, for so long,' Tom mumbled.

'It's just stupid.'

'Loads of people have parents who do crazy things. It's not our fault. We can't control them. Why can't they see that? I'm not my mother.'

'It's probably just 'cos of the trial. It'll settle down in a couple of weeks.'

'You think?'

'I do.'

'I bet some idiot rival told them. There's this kid I've been battling all week and I keep beating him. He started messaging, asking me personal stuff. I didn't reply, but I bet it was him. He wants my place on the team.'

'Could be. Or they might have worked it out themselves. Maybe your aunt said something? You said they had to contact her, for her to agree stuff.'

'She wouldn't. Aunt Eve is cool with it all. She knows how it's all I've got. She wouldn't.'

'It was probably this kid after your place then, like you said. I'm going to grab a shower. What do you say? After that, you come down and get dinner with me, in the hall? It's fried chicken tonight. Your favourite. Then, in a few days, you try again, once the trial's over.'

Tom closed his laptop and then looked at David.

'I'd like that,' he said.

'Good.'

'Don't be too long in the shower. I'm starving.'

David grinned at Tom, pulled off his socks and then raced off down the corridor, punching the air as he ran.

***

Constance took a taxi back to Judith's flat later that evening. It was a rare luxury for her, but she had already been soaked that day and covered a fair amount of ground travelling. She had called ahead and asked Greg to meet her there too. When she arrived, Greg opened the door.

'She let you in?' Constance whispered.

'You know I was here yesterday,' he whispered in return.

'That was when you took her by surprise...and you brought dinner,' Constance laughed. 'Where is she?'

'Just finishing a shower. Coffee?' Greg led the way to the kitchen.

'Have you talked to her about anything yet?'

'She said she was desperate to get clean. That it could wait five minutes till you arrived.'

'That's not like her.'

'I think she's pretty tired, actually. Won't admit it, but she needs to clear her head.'

'That makes two of us.'

Greg poured water from the kettle into the larger of Judith's cafetières.

'Have you...have you talked, at all, about why you split up?' Constance tried hard to keep her face neutral, matter-of-fact, but it collapsed into a mass of wrinkles and creases.

Greg shook his head.

'I'm not sure that's a good idea. You know what she's like. The personification of "never look back".'

'Then how will you know what you did wrong?... I mean, what you did which she thinks was wrong. I know you wouldn't have done anything intentionally.'

'Just leave it for now,' Greg said. 'None of us needs those kind of distractions. I'll talk to her, later on, after the trial...if we're still speaking.'

'Don't let her bully you,' Constance said, but regretted her words immediately, as Greg's cheeks flushed red. It must have been hard for him to swallow his pride and return, after Judith dismissed him so abruptly last time around. He didn't need reminding of how much more he might have to abase himself before Judith might be willing to open up to him.

'What's that you two are saying about me?' Judith wafted in, her damp hair clipped up tightly on the top of her head, trailing the scent of coconut.

'Just surprised you're pampering yourself at a time like this,' Constance said, forcing her tired limbs to project her into the living room, towards the work they needed to cover before any of them could retire for the night.

'I will treat that comment with the scant respect it deserves. OK, Council of War time. Who's going first?' Judith announced, placing the coffee in the centre of the table, with three mugs around it.

'Would you like to know who Dr Sullivan was messaging the evening she died? Dawson has sent everything through,' Constance began.

'Yes please.'

She nodded to Greg and he opened up a file on his laptop.

'None other than the eminent Dr Williams or "Tony" as she called him,' Greg began.

'All right. Not too suspicious. They were colleagues,' Judith said.

'Except that would be another thing he neglected to tell us,' Constance added.

'That's true. Can you read them out, the messages?'

'Nothing would give me more pleasure,' Greg said. 'Here we go. "*5.55 Are we still on for tonight?*" That's Liz. "*Yes. I'll be round about 8.*" That's Tony. "*Can you make it after 9 please?*" She sends that later; not sent till 7pm.'

'That's because Jaden's there. She doesn't want them to meet.

Hm. Go on.'

'That's it for the 1st November.'

'All right. So, Dr Williams lied about when he last saw Liz. Dirty rotten scoundrel. Why?' Judith was up and pacing the room.

'Is he married? Were they having an affair?' Greg asked.

'We've debated that at length,' Judith said.

'He is married, but Sandy, Liz's friend, was adamant there was no affair. She implied he was too boring for her,' Constance added.

'From what I've seen on her phone, I would agree. I've looked back a fair few days and the messages between them are not romantic – more like between colleagues or friends. I'm going to keep going through what Inspector Dawson sent over to Connie, but I thought you should get the headline.'

'Thank you Greg. That's wonderful,' Judith said, and Constance knew she meant it. 'So Dr Williams might have been the last one to see Liz alive. What about Tom?'

'No messages from Tom that night. If he did come over, it was unannounced.'

'There is someone else she's messaging though,' Greg added, 'and that does sound a bit more serious.'

'Someone else?'

'She's saved him as "Eric Valiant" in her contacts. Looks like they met up a few times, nothing too over the top, but these messages do end with an X.'

'Eric Valiant? Has anyone else mentioned him?'

'Never heard of him. So Liz might have been romantically involved with Dr Williams, Eric Valiant and Jaden?'

'I'm not sure how much romance there was with Jaden, even by his own admission. Leaving that aside, maybe one of the other two found out and killed her?'

'My money's still on Dr Williams,' Constance said.

'Really?'

'Because he's a doctor, so he would know best how to cover it up.'

'And he didn't tell us Liz knew Jaden until we got into court. Wait a minute. Connie. Look up "Valiant", quickly.'

'She doesn't need to; they're a gaming company,' Greg said. 'If you'd have let me get a word in, I would have said earlier. Making quite a lot of noise recently with a couple of their offerings.'

Constance opened Valiant's homepage and shared it with Judith.

'Valiant also gave evidence to the government committee. That's where I've heard the name before,' Judith added. 'Although they're one of the organisations who insisted on keeping their interview private. What a woman. She must have been pursuing Valiant too. If the government wouldn't take action, then she was going to tell Valiant exactly what she thought.'

'If that was what she was up to, she kept it well-hidden,' Greg said. 'Like I said, the messages are very friendly.'

'Look, I hate to break up the party, but there are some things I need to share with you, urgently, maybe more important than this Valiant stuff.' Constance had been patient with her news, but now she was almost bursting.

'Yes, of course,' Judith said. 'I was getting carried away with conjecture and Liz's bravado. Go ahead,' she said.

'I have someone else for tomorrow, a replacement for Nathaniel.'

'OK?'

'What's happened to Nathaniel?' Greg asked. Both women ignored him.

'Who is it?' Judith asked.

'His name's Nick Marsh. He was one of Liz's patients.'

'Are either of you going to tell me what's happened to Nathaniel?' Greg persisted.

'Nathaniel stole Liz's handbag.' Judith said.

'He says he found it, but we don't believe him,' Constance continued.

'Found it?' Greg asked.

'He went over to Liz's flat when JD was there. He says JD wasn't answering his phone and he wanted to remind him to get back in time for the show.'

'JD doesn't strike me as the kind of person who needs Nathaniel as a babysitter.'

'Either he was jealous that Liz had invited JD in and not him, or just plain nosy. Mr Mason – that's their old teacher – he knew the boys quite well. He says Nathaniel was always in JD's shadow. Either way, Nathaniel accepts that he went over there, the front door wasn't locked. He went in and took Liz's bag, containing her mobile and purse, says he couldn't help himself when he saw it lying there. JD and Liz were otherwise engaged in the bedroom.'

'And then what?'

'He used the credit card to buy the shoes – the ones the police found – then he had a pang of conscience, so he went to put the bag back, but he saw Jaden coming out of the flat, so he hid it instead; thought he would return it the next morning. Then the police were all over and Liz was dead. He disposed of the wallet and keys, kept the phone and the bag took a trip to NW3, where it was thrown in some bushes.'

'You believe him, that he's not just saying it to get JD off?' Greg asked.

'Nathaniel has form,' Constance said. 'Jaden kept him on the straight and narrow, even took the rap for something similar Nathaniel did at school.'

'So, why isn't Nathaniel giving evidence tomorrow then, saying he stole the credit card. He can say he found it if he likes, can't he?'

Judith shrugged. 'You may as well tell him the rest,' she said.

'Jaden won't let him testify,' Constance said.

'What?'

'Jaden says Nathaniel is lying to protect him, just like you said, and has forbidden us to allow him to give evidence.'

'Oh.'

Greg looked at both women. 'So that's it?'

'We can't put forward a defence, on JD's behalf, that Nathaniel stole the credit card, if JD doesn't agree. And we can't call Nathaniel to the stand, knowing he is going to say something contrary to JD's case.'

'But you could tell Dawson?'

'Not without JD's instructions we can't.'

'Right.' Greg poured himself some more coffee, a puzzled look on his face.

'Ok, tell me all about this Nick Marsh,' Judith asked Constance.

Constance took out her phone and showed Judith and Greg the photo of the four men she had found at Liz's flat.

'He's one of Liz's former patients. He's the one on the far left in this photo, from Liz's fridge. I'd been showing it around, but no one knew who they were. Then he, Nick, turned up a couple of hours ago – followed me home.'

Judith scanned the image and looked hard at Constance.

'He's willing to give evidence about a secret study Liz asked him to take part in.'

'Oh?'

'A study where she watched him, and the others, gaming and recorded the results.'

'Why was it secret?'

'No one's done it before, got gamers to actually play games. They're always asking them these random questions. Nick got the impression she wanted to make a name for herself, being the first to conduct this kind of research.'

'Look, I hate to burst the bubble.' Greg said, 'but how is any of this connected to Liz's death?'

'Connie. Do you remember that study Liz referenced in one of her earlier papers, all about brain imaging? Can you find that one for me?' Judith was beginning to smile to herself and Constance was hurriedly flicking through the screens on her laptop.

'You're not going to tell me?' Greg asked.

'Here it is,' Constance replied. 'I'll send it to you again. And I'll also send over the paper from the public study Nick participated in. It's one of her big ones. He's player A. You'll see his results at the end of the paper.'

Judith began to read the academic papers on her screen, at some speed, Greg drinking his coffee and watching her.

'I see. I'm only good for cracking passwords and fixing the boiler,' he said, with feigned annoyance.

Constance looked over at the radiator, then at Judith. She had forgotten Judith's comments about how cold her flat was, as, whatever the problem previously, it was certainly warm this evening, perhaps even too warm. Taking the hint from her guest, Judith shoved the window open three inches and took some deep breaths of the fresh air. 'I am appreciative; you know that,' she said to Greg. Then she strode across the room to the thermostat in the hall, frowned at it and fiddled with it for a few moments before returning to the table and reading some more.

Then, 'Nicholas Marsh. Was that his name?' she said to Constance.

'Yes.'

'Nicholas Marsh, Player A, wherever you are tonight, I love you,' Judith announced.

'Not far from here, actually,' Constance answered.

'Don't take it personally, Greg,' Judith spared him a quick glance. 'I'm not quite there yet, but we are on the cusp of answering your very important question. Tell me everything Nick Marsh told you; don't leave out any detail,' Judith directed her comments to Constance. 'And we'll want Tony Williams back. Can you arrange for that?'

'Straight after Nick?'

'Yes. That would be best. That way the delightful Sylvie doesn't have a chance to get her claws into Jaden.'

***

Constance's phone rang out and she pulled it from her bag. 'Dawson,' she announced, as she marched to the kitchen and listened to his call, returning a minute later.

'What did he want?' Judith asked.

'You're never going to believe it.'

'Try us.'

'They have a man at the police station; claims his boss killed Elizabeth Sullivan. They're interviewing him now.'

'What? Who is he?'

'They don't know. But Dawson told me the boss's first name. He's called Eric.'

38

Judith and Constance arrived at Hackney police station at 8am the following morning.

'This is such a dreary place,' Judith said, louder than she had intended, as they deposited themselves in the public waiting area. The desk sergeant looked up at her and frowned, before continuing to write notes in a ledger.

'It's a police station. What would you like? Velvet cushions?' Constance replied.

'It's still a workplace and a place the public come when they need help. They could jazz things up a bit; some prints and, yes, softer chairs would be nice.'

'You mean a bit like at the dentist?'

'Yes, I do.'

Constance giggled. 'You suggest that to Dawson. I'm sure he'd agree.'

'Talking about Dawson, I just wish he'd hurry up. Did you tell him we'd be here early?'

'He said he'd do his best. He knows we're in court this morning.'

Then, just as the hands of the utilitarian clock on the wall shifted to two minutes past the hour, Charlie Dawson arrived, stamping his feet on the mat. This time there was no mistaking the all-pervading grey hue of his skin, the bloodshot eyes and the shuffle, as he passed them and led the way to his office.

'You want to know about the visitor we had last night?' he said.

'Anything you can tell us. Have you reopened your enquiry? Are you going to stop Jaden's trial?'

Dawson sat down and switched on his PC. He unlocked his drawer and pulled out some papers, which he quickly perused.

'OK. Here's what we have. Male Caucasian, late twenties, walked in here around 9pm. I had gone home but they called me back in. Very agitated; said he wanted to talk to someone *confidentially* about a murder. His name is Luke Smith and he's a games designer for a company called Valiant. They make computer games.'

Judith and Constance exchanged glances.

'He told me this long story about how his boss, one *Eric Daniels*, is a bit of a psycho, into kung fu and he knew Elizabeth Sullivan.'

'Did he now?'

'Apparently, she posed as a wealthy widow, interested in investing in Valiant; took Eric in; he wined and dined her and showed her their business plan. I would have just told him to get lost, called him a crank, but we'd just found those messages on her phone I sent over. You know – the ones from "Eric Valiant".'

'Yes. We made the link too. Do you think he killed Liz?'

'This is where it gets a bit woolly. She was rumbled by Valiant's finance guy as a spy, and they stopped seeing each other. Eric started telling Luke, when he was drunk, that he had "sorted her out"; that kind of thing. That's why Luke thinks his boss might have killed her. Again, we might still have thought it was nothing. We all know that people say lots of things to their mates in pubs. But he also told us this Eric Daniels drives a very distinctive car, a black Porsche with personalised plates, and PC Thomas remembered the CCTV searches we did at the time picking up on a black Porsche in the area that evening. The boys are looking back at the footage, right now, to see if the plates match.'

Judith stood up and paced the room a couple of times, one finger pressed against her lips. Dawson waited till she returned to her seat.

'Have you told the prosecution any of this?'

'We sent the phone messages over to them late last night, same time as we sent them to you. This information about Mr Daniels, not yet, but, of course, I'll pass it on now. What do you think?'

'I think Elizabeth Sullivan was truly intrepid and very determined. Her sister doesn't know the half of it. Valiant gave evidence at the government review Liz participated in last summer. She must have latched on to this Eric after that – and maybe others too. We've been pushing for natural causes; you know that. Now I'm worried that she may have been murdered after all, Charlie, but not by Jaden. Will you pull him in, this Eric?'

'We'll have to, at least to see what he says about the messages on Liz's phone and what he was doing on the night of the 1st of November. And we'll swab him; look for matches.'

'And Dr Williams? Don't forget him. He was messaging her too.'

'I spoke to him last night. He was very cooperative, claims he never came to see her after all. He has offered an alibi, which I have not yet checked out, given this latest development.'

'So, you'll stop the trial?'

Dawson's eyes blinked in slow motion. 'I might have burst in like Rambo last time your friend Mr Winter asked me to, but I don't have enough evidence this time around.'

'Surely, you have *more* evidence than last time,' Judith pressed.

'If you remember, *last time,* as we keep calling it, I was under investigation. I didn't really have anything to lose. This time I have…what? An edgy guy who says his boss knew Elizabeth Sullivan, that the boss was shouting stuff about her when he was drunk, and a colleague exchanging messages with her, with an alibi. And your client was still in her bedroom – and in her knickers – just before she died. I need to follow the correct procedure.'

'All right,' Judith said. 'Keep us posted. We need to get going. Connie, can you wait for me outside please, just for a minute?'

Constance frowned, then obeyed Judith's order. When she had left, Judith pulled out her notebook, scribbled something down, then put it away and fixed her eyes on Dawson.

'Are you ill, Charlie?' she said. 'I thought you might not want to say, in front of Connie. Pity of the young and all that.'

Dawson sat back in his chair and tapped his fingers on the desk. 'Is it so obvious?' he said.

'Perhaps more to me, as I hadn't seen you in a while.'

Dawson shrugged. 'I had this pain in my back for weeks, took paracetamol, ignored it, thought it was just middle age. Turns out it's pancreatic cancer.'

'Ah. I'm sorry.'

'They say they caught it early. I've been having treatment for a few months now. It's not been too bad and I had a few pounds to lose. The wife is bitter, though; thinks the investigation last summer didn't help; that bloody glove. She might be right.'

'Will you keep working?'

'For now. They may operate. Then I'll be out for two months at least. I'm just taking one day at a time for now. But I know I don't look great.'

Judith got up and then, on the spur of the moment, she squeezed his arm companionably.

'You can always call me, if you want to talk about it.'

'Thanks. I generally prefer to ignore it, though; pretend it's not happening. You know how it is.'

'I do, yes.'

Judith turned to go.

'You know, I'm not afraid to admit it if we got the wrong person,' Dawson said, 'even though my reputation seems to take a hammering every time you and Constance get involved. Thankfully, I have enough convictions to my name to keep my stats healthy – healthier than my body, anyway.'

'I know that.'

'So, like I say, we'll bring this Eric in, today, this morning and I'll let you know if I got it wrong about Jaden, especially as I'm not really focusing on the long term, at the moment.'

'I know you will. You're a good man. Take care of yourself.'

39

NICK MARSH WAS SPRINGING lightly from one foot to the other, as if he was walking on hot coals, as he waited for Constance and Judith outside court. Judith stumbled on the steps on her way in and Constance caught her arm, before she fell.

'Are you OK?' she asked.

'I'd be better if I'd had more than one hour's sleep, but, hey ho, it'll all be over soon.'

In court, Constance looked over at Jaden. He was staring at his feet, both thumbs in his mouth and, in that moment, she felt the weight of her responsibility. Jaden Dodds was just a boy playing at being a man, with no one in the world to show him the way. She wanted to hug him and tell him that everything was going to be just fine; that the trust he had placed in her and in Judith would be rewarded. But they had a way to go yet. All the steps of their complex dance routine had to fit together and they had had so little time to choreograph it.

'My Lord, the defence is no longer intending to call Nathaniel

Brooks. Instead, we will be calling Nicholas Marsh,' Judith announced, when everyone was present.

'I see. Is there a reason why Mr Marsh is not on my list?'

'Yes, My Lord, the defence only became aware of his identity yesterday evening and, since that time, we have been speaking to him to understand the value of his evidence. We haven't had time to put very much in writing, but my instructing solicitor, Miss Lamb, sent you an email, early this morning, with a summary of the areas he intends to cover.'

'Oh yes, I did see that, thank you. You are saying, what? That Mr Marsh's evidence shows that Dr Sullivan manufactured her meeting with the defendant, rather than the other way around. Is that the gist?'

'That's part of it, yes.'

'Because she wanted his help in her studies?'

'Mr Marsh's evidence relates to one of those studies. In fact, the secret study Dr Williams mentioned that Liz Sullivan was working on, immediately before her death.'

Nick appeared considerably more normal in a shirt and tie and with his hair combed back off his forehead, than his rain-soaked condition of the night before. But the jauntiness remained, a reminder of his anxious, on-the-edge state of mind. Constance had briefed Judith fully on what he could say, but there was always a chance he might clam up on the day.

'Mr Marsh. How old are you?' Judith began slowly.

'I'm twenty-six.'

'And when did you begin to understand that you might have a problem with online gaming?'

'I don't think I did understand, at first. But my parents started to complain about it, when I was around thirteen, I think.'

'And what were they complaining about?'

'It was things like I wasn't doing my homework, because after school all I did was play games. And the games were different then. You really needed an X box or Wii console; you couldn't just play off your phone or your laptop. But I'd saved my birthday money up, so they couldn't say no to me and, at the beginning, it was fine. I would have friends over and we would play together. Then, like I say, I started to play all the time I could and my schoolwork suffered.'

'How many hours, approximately, per day, were you playing?'

'At least four hours on a weekday, more than six at the weekend. But it started to become more than that. I would get up to play, after my parents had gone to bed.'

'What happened next?'

'I stopped going out. It didn't happen all at once, but I just preferred to be gaming. And, once the multi-player games came along, I was in heaven.'

'What are multi-player games, Mr Marsh?' Judge Oliver brandished his pencil in the air.

'Games where you can link up with lots of other people online and play against them. They're incredibly popular now. My parents thought I wasn't interacting with anyone. They saw gaming as this lonely pastime. But there was a whole community for me out there, of like-minded people. OK, I hadn't met any of them in the flesh, but they were still my friends.

'Then, next stage, I flunked my GCSEs and had to leave school. I signed up to a college course, but I never went. I played on my laptop and I hardly came out of my room. I went down to eight stone, because I would forget to eat. I was hospitalised for dehydration, because I once played non-stop for nineteen hours.

When I was eighteen, my parents persuaded me to see a therapist and I did pretty well for a while, stopped playing, found a job and I met a girl, Madeleine. We moved in together.'

'And how long did this continue?'

'I was OK for a few years. Maddy knew about my problem. I never hid it, but I got a bit complacent, I suppose. I'd been told by the therapist not to play at all, a bit like alcoholics – you know, they mustn't have even a tiny sip, in case they relapse. But I thought I was stronger than that. And it had been ages since I had played; I thought I was over it. So, one evening, I was at some friends and one of them had a new game. They were all pushing me, saying they had heard how I used to be really good. Anyway, before I knew it, I was playing again, keeping it secret from Maddy. And it started to take over, I lost my job, I got ill and Maddy left.'

'When did you meet Dr Sullivan?'

'About a year ago. I'd taken part in an online survey. Then, I progressed to some face-to-face sessions, where I was tested. I told Miss Lamb, I was patient A in the paper Dr Sullivan sent in to the WHO. She said I was "textbook" because of my symptoms.'

'What did she tell you about the results of those tests?'

'Well, it wasn't anything secret. She said my tendency to be impulsive was higher than normal, my self-control was much lower and that I was super-competitive. She also said I had low self-esteem, which I hadn't realised, but I think it was right. My reflexes were incredibly quick, but I had poor decision-making skills. That last one bothered me.'

'I'm going to show you a photograph now. It's up on the screen.' Judith projected an image of the picture Constance had found on Liz's fridge.

'Yes,' Nick said, smiling as he recognised it.

'Can you tell me who everyone is?'

'That's me on the left and the others were on the trial, – the one I just mentioned.'

'Did Dr Sullivan take the photograph?'

'My sister took it on my phone and I sent a copy to Dr Sullivan, I remember. Is that where you got it?'

'My Lord, this photograph was located at Dr Sullivan's flat. She kept it prominently displayed. There was something written on the back.'

Judith showed an image of the message on the back and Nick laughed aloud.

'I'd forgotten. I was patient A, like I said, and A was the worst. When I sent her the photo, I called us *the A team*; just a joke. It's nice she kept it.'

'And where are the rest of the A team now?'

'Left to right, Ed is doing good, like me, back at work. Josh, I haven't heard from in a while and Marc...' Nick looked over at Judge Oliver and his shoulders gave an involuntary twist. 'Marc died,' he said.

'I'm sorry,' Judith spoke softly and was about to move on, when Constance dug her in the ribs.

'Ask him how?' she mouthed.

Judith frowned at Constance and Constance nodded at her to do as she was told.

'How did Marc die?' she asked.

'Suicide, they said,' Nick replied. 'Not one of the lucky ones, sadly.'

'No, how very sad.' Judith glanced over her shoulder at Constance. She wasn't sure what that intervention had added, but she had a further thought. 'Did Dr Sullivan know that Marc had died?'

'Yes.'

'And, after the study you were involved in, how did Dr Sullivan help you?' Judith moved on.

'Ah… I volunteered to be part of another special trial, an *unofficial* trial. Dr Sullivan gathered information about how my brain was working, while I was gaming, which she could use in her research. Not just me; she persuaded lots of others too, but it was always a bit close to the edge.'

'What do you mean?'

'To do the research she had to ask us to play a game, when there was always a risk it would cause a relapse.'

'Couldn't she just ask other people to play?'

'The whole point was that she wanted to see if addicts – like me, and the others in the photo – if our brain patterns were any different from non-addicts, and, in particular, what happened inside our brains, *when we were playing*, especially for long periods of time.'

'I have a photo here of you being tested in Dr Sullivan's secret trial. This is one of your own personal photographs, I understand. Who took this?'

'One of the other volunteers. We weren't supposed to. But he thought I looked funny with the sensors on my head.'

'And these sensors. What were they made of?'

'I don't know. They were soft, rubbery pads, a bit like those mats you can stick on the bottom of your bath. Dr Sullivan would carry them around with her, in her bag, and just stick them on us. They didn't hurt, but they did leave a small mark on the skin, for a few hours afterwards.'

'And then what?'

'At the end of the trial, Dr Sullivan recommended I take a drug called Wellbutrin. She explained that it was usually used for anxiety. She also taught me some strategies to help avoid getting into situations where I would begin gaming, like I had used before, but more focused on me.'

'And what happened?'

'It's only six months, but I've completely stopped gaming and I have a new job.'

'Ms Burton.' Judge Oliver gave an exasperated sigh. 'I am very delighted, as I am sure many of the jurors are, to hear both of Mr Marsh's return to rude health and Dr Sullivan's dedication. However, at present, I cannot see how any of this is associated with Dr Sullivan's death?'

Judith held up her index finger and nodded amiably. Now Judge Oliver's lack of imagination was doing him a dis-service. Thankfully, the facial expressions of at least half the jury and the public suggested they were one step ahead of him.

'I understand and all will be revealed very soon. Mr Marsh, why did you come forward yesterday and offer to give evidence?'

'I was in court and I heard what the doctor said about the marks on Dr Sullivan's head and the sticky stuff. And then what you said, about them fading later. She must have been wearing them herself, the brain sensors. They leave marks for a few hours and, sometimes, a trace of the glue is left behind.

'I don't know precisely what it's got to do with her death, but I'm certain Dr Sullivan was testing herself, with the sensors on her head, in the hours before she died, the way she tested me and the others, in our secret trial.'

***

Luke wondered where Eric was now. He pictured him seated in a police interview room, perhaps even the same one he had occupied last night, the taste of blood in his throat, his hands cuffed tightly behind his back. Would he be ruing the punch he threw at the police officer or persuading himself 'the guy had it coming'?

Luke had known it would end in tears, from the moment he saw the policeman arrive and ask to be shown through to Eric's office, a young, brawny guy; not the sensitive type. But how was the police officer to know that they had a key meeting with an Olympic representative in an hour, or to even begin to appreciate just how difficult it would be to re-schedule? Standing back and looking at things objectively, there were probably very few people who could have persuaded Eric to leave quietly, at that moment in time.

Luke hadn't seen precisely what happened in Eric's office, but everyone had heard it. A loud curse, followed by a crashing noise and then Eric had emerged in handcuffs, blood pouring down his chin. Luke imagined the officer asking Eric to accompany him, recommending Eric calm down, maybe even tapping at his arm to emphasise his point, before Eric, high on adrenalin ahead of their big pitch, and with false confidence after months of shadow-boxing, had swung his right at the officer's face. Luke visualised the officer, broad-shouldered and streetwise, ducking and then countering with a punch to Eric's ribs, swiftly followed by a fist to the nose. Had the officer even mentioned Elizabeth's name? Did Eric know he had been rumbled? Was Elizabeth his only victim? Luke's imagination went into overdrive: *'bimbo', 'imbroglio', 'inferno'.*

Then, as the policeman had dragged Eric out through the open-plan office, leaving cranberry sprinkles on the carpet, with all the staff trying to pretend this was just another normal day, Eric had caught Luke's eye and Luke had tried, as hard as he could, to appear surprised and shocked, as well as concerned, to hide his real feelings.

And what was he feeling? He wanted to feel triumphant, perhaps even proud of himself, for his superior snooping skills and public-spirited behaviour. Instead he felt only guilt, shame and dishonour.

***

Constance sat with Jaden for a few minutes through the short recess, while Judith went to check that Dr Williams had arrived. Jaden was animated, more than she had ever seen him, walking up and down the room, his eyes thoughtful and bright.

'He was good, wasn't he? That Nick,' he said.

'Yes. He was good.'

'Where did you find him?'

'He found me. He followed me around until I noticed.'

'You think those marks mean that Liz was testing herself, then, like he said?'

'It seems likely.'

'And what about the medicine he took. It was the same that Liz was taking.'

'It was.'

'So what's next?'

'We're re-calling Dr Williams. He had an arrangement to go over to Liz's, after you left.'

'I told you she was checking her phone!'

'You did. And maybe I should have listened harder.'

'You think he killed her?'

'He told the police he never went and, so far, we can't prove he did.'

Jaden tutted and shook his head from side to side.

'I don't get it,' he said. 'I don't see that guy killing her, you know. I didn't like him much. That I'll say. But I can't see it happening. Liz was tough, you know. She had an edge to her. She would have put up a big fight.'

'I know. Judith's working on how to get the truth from him. You need to trust her.'

'What she said – Judith – that Liz wanted to get to know me, only because of the gaming. Do you think that's true?' Jaden's face was a mass of confusion. He looked just like his fifteen-year old self, in the photograph on Mr Mason's wall.

Constance hadn't foreseen that this might have been an issue for Jaden, that he might feel slighted. But she decided this certainly wasn't the time to tell Jaden anything about Liz's undercover operation at Valiant, or about the suspicions the police had about its boss.

'I'm sure she was going to tell you,' she said. 'And invite you to take part in one of her trials. She probably thought if she just asked you and Nath, out of the blue, you wouldn't agree.'

'She went to a lot of trouble, if she just wanted a bit of help. Maybe it was all false then, that she liked me and Nath?'

'I'm sure she enjoyed your company too,' Constance said, feeling the heat rise in her face as she spoke. 'And that she was happy to bake the cake and cook for you. Like you say, she could have just asked you. But maybe, in the past, she had found other people needed to get to know her a bit first, to trust her.'

Jaden nodded and sat himself down.

'Is it going to end here, today?' he asked. 'Or am I going to have to listen to that silky woman ask me loads of questions?'

'Silky; you mean Sylvie?'

'She's silky smooth, but I can see it's just on the surface. She's like one of those spiders I saw on TV. They attract their partner, mate with them and kill them straight after.'

Constance laughed. 'She'd probably love to hear you say that. I can't say for sure whether you'll still be giving evidence. But we are going to do our best to end things today.'

For a second, tears sprang to Jaden's eyes, but he blinked them away. Then Constance went to him and hugged him tight. At first, he seemed shocked by her actions and didn't respond. Then, he allowed himself to wrap his arms around her too. Constance pulled away after a few seconds and smiled at him again.

'You keep strong now,' she said. 'Don't let your guard down, not for a second,' she added, 'but I promise we'll try to end things today, if we possibly can.'

40

'DR WILLIAMS, THANK YOU for taking the time to return again today. I know you have patients to see, so I will keep this as brief as I can. My Lord, before I turn to Dr Sullivan's murder, I do want Dr Williams to explain a little more about the work Dr Sullivan undertook. It will take some minutes to take him through the evidence, but, I respectfully submit, it is crucial to understanding what will follow.'

This was Judith's strategy, not only to pave the way for the critical part of his testimony, but also to lull Dr Williams into a false sense of security. He wasn't in court as an expert witness, but she wanted him to feel as if he was, that she was consulting him for the benefit of his expertise. It had worked with him last time around, had made him more cooperative than he might otherwise have been.

'Very well, but we've had quite a lot of "education" in this trial already. Not that I'm against it in principle, and I heard what you said with the last witness, but that isn't why we're here now, is it

Ms Burton? Don't go on too long. I shall be watching the clock.'

'Noted, of course. Dr Williams. What makes games addictive?'

'That's a huge question, with so many different answers, but I'll do my best to condense my knowledge, such as it is.' Dr Williams was clearly taking the bait. 'The people who design these games are not, on the whole, trying to make the game fun. That's the first thing you need to understand. It's not about fun. Instead, it's all about making money – not surprisingly – and that, in turn, is about keeping the player interested and playing. You often hear them say, it's all about *player experience.*

'Let me go back, for a moment, to ten years ago, to illustrate my point. Then, you paid forty pounds for a game, you uploaded it to your Playstation or Xbox and you played it, either alone or with your friends. You probably got to the end fairly quickly and the aim was to make it sufficiently enjoyable that you would play it a few times, then buy the next iteration when it was released the following year.'

'What changed?'

'Everything changed, with the advent of these free multi-player games, like *Fortnite.* Heard of that one?'

'Perhaps you could explain?'

'It's a survival game where you are competing, online, with hundreds of other players – people you have never met, except in the virtual world. You're dropped on an island, all sorts of hazards come your way and you have to survive and be the last person standing. It was launched in 2017. It was immensely popular and, importantly, it's free.'

'And why is that significant for your work?'

'Because if it's free, the developers have to find ways to keep you playing on and on, so that they can recover their investment in different ways. Usually, this is by way of online shops and rewards, which you pay for with real money. And the game designer has to find ways of making the player perform what are often boring or repetitive tasks, to keep them playing.'

'Can you expand on how the games hold players' interest?'

'It all goes back to Harvard University in the 1950s and Professor Skinner, who was a psychologist. He was experimenting with how to reinforce learning and he kept small animals: mice, rats, some birds, in a box and gave them various stimuli to see how they would respond. For example, he would train the animal to press a lever in response to a coloured light and that would deliver a reward. What he quickly discovered was, that if you wanted the animal to keep on pressing the lever repeatedly, you shouldn't deliver the reward every time, you should deliver it at random intervals. This principle is used all the time in slot machines; the player doesn't get a reward every time, but doesn't stop playing, because they keep on thinking that *next time* will be the time they hit the jackpot.'

'Anything else?'

'Oh yes, I've only just begun. Skinner also studied "shaping" – little incremental stages that lead, cumulatively, to a final reward. Once you're part of the way into a lengthy task, you keep going, so as not to lose the benefit of all the work you've already done. Examples in the gaming world might be a suit of armour, where you have to undertake highly repetitive chores to obtain each piece, in a precise order. Or there's a wonderful example in a Chinese game, where you have to open a treasure chest with a key. You have to buy the key first, with real money, and you may not buy the right key. On top of that, there's a prize each day for the person who opens the most treasure chests. So, even though the activity is incredibly dull – simply clicking your mouse over and over – many, highly intelligent people spend hours and hours trying to select the correct key or open the most treasure chests and be the winner. And, of course, they never are.'

'What about punishment?'

'Yes. Another Skinner discovery was the tactic of punishing animals if they didn't press the lever. This is replicated in so many ways in gaming. If you don't continue to harvest your virtual crops, which you have worked hard to cultivate, they all wither and die. If you don't clean your castle obsessively, it will decay and crumble. And what is also crucial to understand is that all these activities I am describing – they are sidelines to the aim of the game. They are pure money-spinners for the manufacturer. There is little or no skill involved in them, absolutely no fun whatsoever and they are designed to make you play on and on and on.'

'If they are no fun, why do we engage with them?'

'Well, some people don't; you're right. But others get hooked. One theory is it's all about filling a void. Some psychologists say that we all need three things in our adult lives in order to feel fulfilled. We need autonomy – that is to be in charge – we need complexity – so, not a dull, repetitive job – and we need to see a connection between what we do and our reward. Everyone knows that a flat salary, without any performance element, is not appealing.

'Gaming provides all of those things, when, sometimes, particularly for young men in unskilled work, their jobs don't. That's generalising a lot, but it gives you an idea of what might encourage a young person to get involved in gaming and shun everything else. And that's even before you start with the whole Esports industry and the tantalising chance to win huge prizes, which is only just beginning and which will definitely lead to more addicts.

'Look, it can be an escape for some people, into a virtual world which is better than their real world. We know from our studies that chemicals are released in the brain while you play, which help provide a feeling of satisfaction or gratification, like you might get from a physical sport.'

'But without the associated health benefits,' Judith interrupted. 'I just want to digress for a moment, but my reasoning will become clear shortly. Can you explain to the court what "brain imaging" is?'

'Certainly. It's a relatively recent technique, and quite varied, but, in essence, it's all about discovering which areas of the brain are being used, when we carry out different tasks. It involves a scan of the brain. The way I am most familiar with is by an MRI – that's a "magnetic resonance imaging" scan.'

'And Dr Sullivan referenced brain imaging in one or her older papers, didn't she?'

'Yes, she was interested in determining which parts of the brain were used during gaming and if they became more well developed in gaming addicts as a result. But, like you said, it was covered in one of her older papers; 2016, I believe.'

'So, that's incredibly useful background, thank you Dr Williams. You did explain it clearly and succinctly and it all fits with the evidence Nicholas Marsh gave this morning.'

'Nick was here? How is he?' Dr Williams' face came to life, for a second.

'He's well. He's back at work.'

'That's good. I know Liz showed particular interest in him. She so wanted him to be able to lead a normal life.'

'And he is. Now I know you've just said that Dr Sullivan's paper, with the brain imaging, was already three, nearly four years old, but Mr Marsh told us about another study Dr Sullivan was conducting just before she died; a secret study. Can you tell us about that?'

'I don't know anything about her secret study.' Beads of sweat broke out on Dr Williams' top lip.

'Really? Mr Marsh told us he was one of a number of young men who were monitored playing games, for her study. When you were in court yesterday, you said, I accept, that Dr Sullivan could be quite secretive. But you were her closest colleague and confidant and this was a big deal for her. You must have known what she was doing with Nick and the others. Would you like to reconsider your last answer?'

Dr Williams ran the palm of his hand over his face from top to bottom. He looked at Constance, then at the judge.

'She swore me to secrecy. I don't want to say.'

'Dr Williams, Dr Sullivan is dead, and this involves the study she was working on when she died. I think you had better tell us what you know. I suspect it will merely corroborate what Nick Marsh said, in any event.'

'All right. Liz had been doing some covert testing, with addicts like Nick, getting them to play games and watching them, making detailed notes, monitoring their brains and other signs of neurotransmitters. It was unlikely the Ethics Committee would have approved it, however valuable her results might be. Making addicts play games for prolonged periods can't be good for the volunteer. I suspected, although she never told me for certain, that she was also prescribing them drugs, to see if that helped.'

'Why would she embark on this secret and hazardous trial,

especially if she risked censure?'

'Like I said yesterday, she was so very dedicated. She wanted to keep the momentum going from other work, to build on it and allow patients to benefit from it. She always believed that medication was part of the solution too; medication plus therapy. I imagine she was putting her beliefs into action. And it sounds like it worked with Nick.'

'Ms Burton. We are now approaching the lunch break. How much longer will you have with this witness?' Judge Oliver's face was a closed book, but Judith knew better than to get between a judge and his sustenance.

She looked around her. Constance shook her head. She would rather press on with Dr Williams but, equally, she wanted to check in with Dawson and Greg, to get the latest on Eric Daniels and Liz's phone records.

'I think a break would be welcome now, My Lord, but I should finish well within time today,' Judith said.

***

Constance rushed into the break-out room Judith had booked for the duration of the trial, breathless and red in the face. She had picked up a call as soon as court adjourned and she needed to fill Judith in straight away.

'You've heard from Dawson?' Judith said.

'They pulled in this Eric Daniels guy.'

'Well?'

'He resisted arrest, thumped a police officer – not Dawson – so he's in big trouble, but they don't think he's our man.'

'Oh.'

'He has an alibi.'

'Really?'

'He was abroad for the weekend of 1st and 2nd of November; has a plane ticket to prove it.'

'Oh. The CCTV?'

'The wrong car, similar, but not his.'

'Damn. I thought it might be him.'

'So did I. But, while they were running all the CCTV again, to double-check, I asked them to check something else.'

'Something else, which is going to help us resolve this?'

'I think so. You haven't asked Dr Williams about the phone messages yet, have you?'

'I'd left it till next session. Weren't you listening?'

'OK, so perfect timing, then,' Constance said, ignoring Judith's slight. 'Here's what they found.'

***

After Constance had finished speaking, Judith took two bites from her sandwich, then lost interest and threw the remains at the bin in the corner, where it settled on top of a pile of plastic wrappers.

'What are you going to do?' Constance watched Judith, the cogs of her mind working furiously away. She never regretted being the solicitor, the one standing in the background, when Judith was up-front. She trusted Judith, implicitly, to perform, to find the right way of presenting the facts to the court, to tease the important parts of the story from the witnesses and to reveal their lies and prejudices when required.

True, you didn't take the glory for your successes in quite the same way as the person doing the talking, but Constance knew her own limitations, that her temperament did not suit the advocate's life. She was too cautious, too earnest, too sensitive. Judith could zone in and out, could shut off emotions and could formulate a plan in double-quick time. And she was also brave and that was what Constance felt was needed now. She waited for Judith's answer.

'Go for broke, I think. What do you say?'

Constance was not disappointed. 'I think so too,' she said.

Judith took a deep breath and then headed out of the room, down the stairs and back into court. As she entered, she saw Greg hovering by the door. He allowed her to enter first and remained outside. A minute later, Nathaniel arrived and Constance met him just outside the court. She whispered a few hurried words to Greg, to which he responded with a nod and a smile, then he and Nathaniel took their seats together at the back of the public gallery.

41

Sylvie Elliott was already in her place when Judith slid in beside her.

'I have some dream questions prepared for your client. Will we get to him today, do you think?' Although Sylvie's words were confident, that smug edge had disappeared from her delivery.

'I can't say for certain. But what I will say is that I don't think I will be too much longer with Dr Williams. Does that help?'

'Yes, thank you.'

Judge Oliver peered at both lawyers over the top of his glasses. Judith looked across at Jaden, then at Dr Williams, who was shifting his weight from side to side. Constance mouthed 'go for it' under her breath.

'Dr Williams. Just a few more questions for you. Why did you visit Dr Sullivan's flat on the night of her death?'

'Whaaaat?' Dr Williams' eyes appeared to grow to double their usual size and he raised himself halfway out of his seat.

'I have here the records from Dr Sullivan's mobile phone. I

am happy to go through them one by one, if necessary. But, to summarise, you arranged to visit her, at home, on the night she died, didn't you?'

Sylvie was out of her blocks in milliseconds, her champion running pedigree showing through.

'My Lord, we haven't seen these phone records.'

'The police located Dr Sullivan's phone last night. They were sent to your solicitor at the same time as mine.'

Sylvie's solicitor shrugged. She hadn't seen them and she didn't have her phone with her in court. The look Sylvie threw her would have frozen the sun.

'My Lord, given Dr Williams' time is so precious, and that both sides have had access to this material for the same period of time – albeit short – I should like to press on. I should be happy to allow a break for Miss Elliott to review the phone messages, once I have finished with Dr Williams, if you felt, then, that that was required.'

Dr Williams stared at the judge, who stared back. Jaden was now alert, head back, chin forward and his chest was beginning to move up and down, with the effort of his quickened breathing.

'I should like Dr Williams to answer the question. I don't see how we can all leave now, on this cliff-hanger,' Judge Oliver said.

'Thank you, My Lord. My feelings too. I will ask again. Dr Williams, what were you doing in Dr Sullivan's flat, on the night of her murder?'

'Do I have to answer that question?' Dr Williams was now very pale and his left hand, visible above the podium, was trembling.

'Yes, please.'

'Just because there are phone messages doesn't mean I went there.'

'Are you denying you visited Dr Sullivan at home that evening?'

Dr Williams remained silent. Now he folded his hands together and fiddled, again, with his wedding ring.

'You drive a Vauxhall Astra, with the 65 number plate, ending in "OPT",' Judith continued. 'A car matching that exact description was caught on CCTV 200 metres away, travelling in the direction of Dr Sullivan's flat at 9.02pm. Would you like me to put the footage up on the screen so we can see, for certain, if it's you behind the wheel?'

'No,' he waved his hands around. 'No, I don't need you to do that. I accept I went to visit Liz.'

He looked once at Jaden and then past Judith to Constance.

'When you arrived, was Dr Sullivan alone?'

Dr Williams seemed turned to stone. Judith waited.

'My Lord, can I ask for a short adjournment, in order to take instructions?' Sylvie was frowning for the first time.

'My Lord, this is not the time. The question needs to be answered. We have just had a break.'

'Dr Williams. Please answer the question.' Judge Oliver obliged.

Dr Williams remained motionless. Then, slowly, he smiled and nodded to himself. Then he turned his head to look across at Tom before returning his attention to Judith.

'Yes, she was alone,' he said.

'Did she tell you that anyone else had been there, that evening?'

'She didn't say, but she was clearing away some dishes to the sink and the dishwasher and I saw there were two plates and some wine open, so I did wonder, but I didn't ask. It wasn't my business. For all I knew, she might have had Tom home for a few days, although she hadn't said.'

'Why did you visit Liz that evening?'

'She wanted my help.'

'With her secret project?'

Dr Williams appealed to Judge Oliver one more time.

'Surely none of this is relevant. I shouldn't have to deal with these intrusions,' he said, but it was half-hearted and he knew the answer before the question had left his lips.

'My Lord, what Dr Williams was doing at Dr Sullivan's apartment, after Jaden Dodds left and shortly before she died, seems to me to be highly relevant, but clearly you must be the judge.'

'I couldn't agree more, Ms Burton. Dr Williams. Rest assured, I will ensure you are only asked to talk about facts of materiality to the events we are considering. Do please answer Ms Burton's question.'

'I was asking if the help Dr Sullivan required was for her secret project.'

'I remember, yes. One aspect of it. She was researching how the body behaved when you were gaming for long periods of time. She...' Dr Williams sought out Tom, in the gallery, again. Tom had folded his arms and legs and was staring back at Dr Williams. 'She had decided to be the guinea pig, herself,' he said. 'She didn't want to put her volunteers – people like Nick – through hours of gaming. Of course, it wasn't perfect, because she wasn't a problem gamer herself, but she could still monitor changes in her own physiology, the more she played.'

'Why did she need you?'

'I helped her set things up, put the sensors on her head, attached a heart monitor, blood pressure monitor. It wasn't the first time. It was, maybe, her fifth session. I would set things up and then leave her and come back a few hours later, to help her take everything off and save the data.'

Constance passed Judith a scribbled note. Judith read it and pocketed it.

'Why did you strap her to her chair?'

Dr Williams let out a sob and grabbed at the sides of the lectern.

'She was worried that she might want to stop, in the night, to give up, especially if she was tired,' he said. 'But the whole point was to keep going, until she was facing exhaustion, to examine how her body responded to being forced to play on and on and on. She had found, from the earlier sessions, that she didn't fit the mould of the addict; she would stop. I didn't want to do it, but she asked me to. She said it was key to making her research worthwhile.'

'You strapped her to the chair, you put sensors on her arm and head and chest, what time was that?'

'We set it up quickly. We were proficient after a few prior runs, probably no later than 9.45.'

'And then what?'

'Then I checked she had enough play in the straps, to be able to operate the keyboard and then I left.'

'And the plan was for you to return when?'

'I was to return at 5am. She thought seven hours would be enough this time, although she was planning longer and longer stints.'

'And when did you return?'

Dr Williams closed his eyes tight, as if he hoped that when he opened them again the court room and all its occupants would have disappeared.

'I set my alarm for 4am, but I slept through it. I had worked almost two full days, without a break. I woke up at eight and came straight over.'

'And what did you find?'

'I entered the flat and I experienced this strange sensation. Maybe because it was so quiet. And very hot. I knew there was something wrong straightaway.'

'You had a key?'

'I borrowed Liz's. She didn't need it, if she was playing. I called out her name and there was no reply. I knocked at the bedroom door and she didn't respond. So I went in and then I saw her.'

Judith waited before asking her next question. Everyone was transfixed. Tom was holding his breath, Greg was watching Judith closely, Jaden was gripping the sides of the bench.

'What did you see?' Judith asked.

'She was still sitting in the chair, but her head had fallen to one side, her eyes were closed and her mouth was open. I thought she was just asleep, but I called her again and she didn't move. The room smelled of urine. Her chair was wet with it. I rushed forward and opened the straps and she fell forwards into my arms and then I knew she was dead.'

'No!' Tom shouted from his seat. This time he buried his head in his aunt's chest and she hugged him tight.

'Why didn't you call the police, then?' Judith asked.

'I panicked, I suppose. I didn't want anyone to know about the work Liz had been doing. Although she had good intentions, a lot of people would have frowned at her methods. I didn't want her memory clouded by that.'

Constance coughed loudly behind Judith.

'And you would have had to reveal your own involvement?' Judith said, responding to her cue.

'Yes, that too.'

'So, instead, you moved her to the bed?'

'I lay her down and she looked so peaceful. Then I packed up all the sensors, switched off her laptop and I got the hell out of there.'

'I just want to be clear then, doctor. In your professional opinion, Elizabeth Sullivan died sometime between 9.45pm and, what, 8.30am, while she was tied to the chair?'

'I believe so.'

'And this was most likely as a result of her participating in an online gaming session, for a number of hours, without a break, including no possibility of going to the bathroom or even getting a drink of water?'

'Look, she could have stopped if she wanted, and the straps were fiddly, but she could have released herself too, in an emergency. She must have...decided to keep going, like I said, to push herself to the limits, to get the data. And, maybe the alcohol...impaired her judgment.'

'You mentioned that it was hot in her room.'

'It was; very warm. That probably contributed. She usually turned down the heat or opened the window. You get a lot of heat off the computer screen, but she must have forgotten this time.' Judith nodded. She had joined that dot last night, when her own flat had hit a stifling 26 degrees and she had checked the report on the temperature in Liz's room.

Constance looked across at Jaden. He hadn't spoken, but he had stood up in the dock and thrown his head back. Judge Oliver noticed him, clearly contemplated asking him to sit down, but then gestured to the ushers to allow him to stand. She nodded to acknowledge him, and her face was telling him to stay calm. It wasn't over yet.

'If I'd known about the HCM, I would never have let her do it,' Dr Williams began to lose control and his voice was trembling. 'And the Wellbutrin. I turned a blind eye, but I knew she prescribed it to Nick and the others. It's had fantastic results, but she should never have taken it herself – not on top of her other medication. I suppose she did it for parity, to ensure she was doing the same things the patients were doing, for the integrity of the trial. She could have suffered serotonin syndrome with the combination – essentially an overload of serotonin in the body.'

'And what happens then?'

'Three possible symptoms: neuromuscular hyperactivity – like spasms, or autonomic dysfunction, like blood pressure changes, or faster heart rate, and altered mental state, like agitation or confusion.'

'But she was a doctor, surely she would have known not to take these drugs together?'

'Not really. I mean, the risks are very low for a healthy person, which, we now know she wasn't. And I think the heat – so, dehydration and her alcohol consumption – they all contributed. Together, those factors must have pushed her over the edge. That's what killed her.'

Judith took a moment for Dr Williams' words to sink in. The jurors were all watching him closely; some were making notes. Tom was silent, his aunt's arm around his shoulder. Mr Jenkins was quiet too, a sad expression on his face. Nathaniel was seated at the back, with Greg and he was trying to make eye contact with Jaden, but Greg was whispering to him to sit still.

'Why didn't you say anything, when the defendant was accused of murdering Liz?' Judith's voice was cool now. She had Dr Williams completely in her power.

Dr Williams looked again at Jaden and, if looks could kill, Jaden would have been struck down in that moment, in the most brutal fashion.

'Lots of reasons. Anger mostly,' he said.

'Anger?'

'Liz was a wonderful, committed doctor. She helped hundreds of people directly, and thousands more, as a result of research and lobbying. She took on the WHO, the games manufacturers, the government itself. She never thought of herself, she sacrificed her personal happiness with her son, she jeopardised her own career and she paid the ultimate price. She lost her life. She's gone; dead. What a waste of her talent and energy. And it was all because of him.'

'Who?' Judith knew the answer, but she needed Dr Williams to complete his confession.

'Have you watched his show?' Now Dr Williams' voice began to increase in volume and strength once more.

'I have, yes.'

'Then you'll know why I feel anger towards him and everyone else who cashes in on this sordid business. "Gaming" they call it. "Gaming!". Games are supposed to be fun. OK, they don't all have to be about physical exercise, but in a game you learn a new skill, in a safe environment. This is no skill and it's certainly not safe. It's as dangerous as you can get. This isn't a game. It's all about profit and profiteering.'

He turned towards Jaden and pointed a quivering finger at him.

'You. You cause untold misery to people – people like Nick Marsh, people who are susceptible, suggestible, lonely. You do this just so you can make money from donations and subscriptions and build up your army of adoring fans, who write fatuous messages to each other on your website, send you gifts, like expensive trainers that cost more than an NHS nurse earns in a month. You can't be bothered to go and do a proper job – one where you have to work really hard at developing a skill of value, one which might help your fellow human beings or your community.

'We're all busy blaming the game manufacturers for people like Nick – and Marc Jones, *World of Warcraft* champion, nineteen years old. Hanged himself, he did; did Nick mention him? And Liz blamed herself for that. Were they all to be placed in a football stadium and blown into small pieces, that would be too honourable a death for them, parasites that they are, deliberately creating games that people want to play on and on and on. But without people like you, "JD", their hold wouldn't be so strong.

'You are a hero for these kids, they want to play like you, make money like you and you add the glitz and the glamour, you encourage them to spend more and more time online, to use money they don't have to buy expensive accessories, to enter competitions which involve playing more hours than there are in the working week. You are at the heart of the problem.'

He turned back towards Judith, shrank back into his seat and his voice returned to its normal level.

'So, when he walked into the picture, I thought it was poetic justice,' he said, with a narrow smile of recollection. 'That's what I thought. I kept my mouth shut and let the system run its course.'

PART THREE

42

JADEN AND NATHANIEL SAT with Constance outside court, a police officer next to them. Jaden's hands were cuffed, but the judge had instructed the officer to allow him to wait outside with his lawyers, rather than be forced to return to the basement.

'What's happening?' Jaden asked.

'He's deciding what to do next; the judge is.'

'Will he release me?'

'I hope so. Judith is speaking to him now, together with Sylvie. She'll be pushing for that.'

Tom Sullivan approached them and the police officer stood up to intervene, but Constance nodded that it was all right. At first, he just stood and stared at Jaden, but the fire of his earlier outburst had gone. Finally, he spoke.

'I was there too, that night,' he said.

'What? Tom, you don't need to say anything,' Constance warned him, searching for Aunt Eve or Mr Jenkins, but Tom appeared to have escaped them both.

'Dave was away,' Tom said. 'I'd been out for a cigarette. I just suddenly missed her, wanted to see her, thought I'd surprise her,' Tom went on. 'But when I arrived, I saw her through the bedroom window, sitting at her laptop, playing a game. I was very angry. Just like Dr Williams. Of course, I knew that it was her work, that it must have been for some *research* – always her research – but she was laughing at the game; really into it. It made me so angry that she was sitting there enjoying playing when she had said I mustn't play any more. So I didn't go in. I turned around and went back to school. I left her. If I'd been more…mature, then I would have gone inside and she would have stopped the game, we'd have had some food, watched some Netflix and she would still be alive now.'

'You heard what Dr Bailey said,' Constance said. 'Your mum had a serious heart condition. If it hadn't happened that night, it would have been the next occasion she pushed herself too far. Maybe even something as simple as running for the bus. You couldn't be with her all the time.'

'She only sent me away because of the gaming. She did it for me. And if I hadn't been so into gaming, she would probably never have got into any of this stuff in the first place.'

'It's not your fault.' This time it was Jaden who spoke and Tom took two steps nearer and sat down opposite him, their heads only centimetres apart. 'I lost my mum just over a year ago,' Jaden said. 'Not as quick as with your mum, so I did have time to say goodbye. My mum was a nurse, worked double shifts to help pay for stuff, got ill from too much work, doctors tried to save her, but she died anyway. There isn't one day goes past that I don't think of the times I did stuff that made her mad, stuff I shouldn't have done, stuff that might have changed our lives, so that, if I hadn't done it, she'd have never got sick in the first place.'

'I'm sorry,' Tom said.

'Yeah, me too. But I know she's watching me and I know that she would want me to take the life I have and do the things I want to do and do them well. And that she don't want me to feel like any of it was my fault. I'm sure it's the same with your mum. She did the stuff she did because she loved you so much and she was willing to make sacrifices for you, because that was what she wanted to do – and that's the important bit. What we have in common, bro, is that we were both lucky enough to have mothers who loved us so much they didn't always think about themselves enough, but they wouldn't have wanted it any other way, if they lived on this earth a thousand times over.'

Tom nodded first to himself, then at Jaden, then he stood up, turned around and walked slowly away. The court usher peered around the door and called them back inside.

***

'Jaden Dodds, please stand up.' Judge Oliver issued his order to Jaden sternly and Constance's heart leapt to her mouth. Judith returned to her position in front, but her face gave nothing away. Constance looked across at Sylvie, but she was also impenetrable. Constance thought she would burst if this wasn't over soon. She couldn't even imagine how Jaden was feeling.

'Your Counsel, Ms Burton, has submitted, on your behalf, a plea of no case to answer. In view of the evidence given by Dr Anthony Williams earlier today, I accept that plea. Members of the jury, that means that you will not be called upon to rule in this case, as I have decided that there is insufficient evidence that the defendant, Jaden Dodds, did anything wrong or was involved at all in the rape or murder of Dr Elizabeth Sullivan or the theft of her bag and unauthorised use of her credit card. Mr Dodds, the police officer will remove your handcuffs. You are free to go, without a stain on your character.'

Judge Oliver nodded to Jaden, then to each set of lawyers and then marched out of court, leaving his pencil rolling backwards and forwards on his desk. Nathaniel vaulted over each and every row of chairs and ran to embrace Jaden, making it a little tricky for the policeman to uncuff him, but it was managed after a few attempts. Sylvie turned her back and then insisted on watching the two young men from over her shoulder.

'It looks like you've broken your duck,' Judith said to her.

'What?'

'You said you never lose.'

'Oh that. I didn't mean it. Everyone loses some of the time.'

Judith opened her mouth to say something snide and then changed her mind. 'Will you prosecute Tony Williams?' she said, instead.

'If it was up to me, you bet ya.'

'He is a doctor.'

'No one is above the law and all that. But it isn't up to me, as you know.' Sylvie collected her books and piled them into a box. Then, she paused. 'I know you don't want to give away your trade secrets,' she said, 'but, well, wouldn't it have been easier to get Dr Bailey to admit all those things about the two drugs interacting? You started asking her, then you just let her off the hook. Granted she was happy you eased off, as you would have been challenging her professional judgment even more than you did. I just wondered?'

Judith stared at Sylvie. The truth was, now she thought about it, that she had got side-tracked with Dr Bailey. She had been focusing on disproving the rape allegations and she hadn't pressed as far as she might with the actual medical evidence.

'I suppose you'll just say that it had more impact to get Dr Williams himself to own up,' Sylvie said. 'And, you're right, of course. It was great theatre. But more risky too.'

'Do you really run marathons?' Judith asked.

Sylvie smiled. 'Yes, I do.'

'And do you enjoy them?'

'It's all relative. More than most other things, yes. You should try it.'

'No thanks. I think that running is definitely one activity I am too old to begin now.'

'It's wonderful thinking time.'

'I'm sure it is. But that's another reason why I'm not keen. Thinking is a bit overrated. If you'll excuse me, I'm going to see my client now.'

43

'DID SYLVIE OBJECT, when you were with the judge?' Constance asked, as she helped Judith pack up her books.

'No,' Judith said. 'She pretty much made my case for me, I'll give her that. She was gracious in defeat. Although Judge Oliver gave us both a lecture.'

'Really?'

'Said he couldn't understand the attraction of online games. Agreed with Dr Williams that this was a terrible waste. I think he was trying to show us that he was human, after all.'

'How funny.'

'You were right though.'

'What?'

'You said your money was on Tony Williams.'

'He didn't kill her.'

'Not directly.'

'And she knew the risks. She was a doctor too.'

'Now you're defending him?'

'Not really. It's just, after reading all those studies, their book, I can see why they both – him and Liz – why they hated the gaming industry so much, and why Dr Williams saw Jaden as part of it all.'

'I don't see Jaden as the problem,' Judith said, glancing at him over the crowds as she spoke. 'He's just a young man trying to find his way in the world, in the best way he can, who's exploited the zeitgeist.'

'I'll tell him that, then,' Constance giggled. 'Maybe he can use it in his marketing material.'

***

Constance approached Jaden, who was busy shaking hands with anyone nearby, including the police officer who had opened his handcuffs.

'How does it feel to be free?' Constance asked.

Jaden nodded slowly. 'I'm not sure yet,' he said. 'Bit of a surprise, even though you gave me the heads up. I kept it really calm, like you said. I had all my stuff ready for court tomorrow and it's still inside me, waiting to come out. But I think, instead, I'll take a long shower and stretch out on my bed. Ask me after that.'

'That sounds like a good idea. Listen, would you like to make a statement, to the press? They'll be waiting outside, I'm sure.'

'Do I have to?'

'No. You don't have to say or do anything. We can go quietly out the back, if you prefer. Or we can spend a few minutes writing something down and I can read it out for you. People usually prefer that, for us to agree something and I read it. It's not so easy to speak freely when cameras are flashing all around you, that's all.'

'I want to do it,' Jaden said.

'OK? Would you like to tell me what you want to say and I'll write it down for you?'

'What do you think, Nath?' Jaden was rolling his shoulders back and striding forwards toward the door.

'I think you can do it,' Nathaniel said.

Jaden stopped. 'That's what I think too. I didn't get to say my bit in court, so this is my chance now, and without being interrupted. I want to do it and I'm not writing nothing down,' Jaden had made his decision.

'All right. Do you need a few minutes?'

'I just want to get in that shower, so if we're gonna do it, let's do it now, then I can get going.'

***

It was only three hours since Eric had left but, during that time, Luke had aged three years. At first, he had justified his actions to himself, by his genuine belief that Eric was a murderer. He had had a lucky escape, he reasoned, on the many occasions they had been alone together. The man was a maniac, a terroriser, a devil. But niggling away at the back of his mind was the thought that if Eric had not asked him to change *Midas* again, had not ignored his obvious consternation, then he might have been willing to overlook Eric's deficiencies.

Even so, he had taken it upon himself to call the Olympic representative they were supposed to meet and explain, with appropriate gravitas, that Eric had been summoned to hospital with tremendous urgency, as a potential bone marrow donor for a very sick friend. He had run through many permutations of this excuse and this one had come out on top. The rep had been instantly accepting and had rearranged the session for the following week without turning a hair, sending good wishes to Eric. It always paid to keep your options open, Luke told himself.

Then, less than an hour ago, the breaking news revealed the real circumstances of Elizabeth Sullivan's death. Luke had scoured the online press, followed by Twitter, to discover as much as he could about the end of the trial. And then he had felt, first, relief and then trepidation. Relief that Eric was not guilty after all, but then lead in the pit of his stomach, spreading out through his torso to his limbs, until he was almost totally paralysed with fear, regarding what consequences Eric's return might bring for him.

But half an hour ago, he had rallied. He felt, in his heart, that he had done the right thing. That, if he hadn't spoken up and Eric had been the killer, he would never have forgiven himself. He was also proud that he had potentially sacrificed his own career ascendance, although, to be fair, this feeling had lessened by the second. This was particularly the case as the office gossiped, lamenting Eric's potential demise and what that might mean for all of them: redundancy, penury, starvation. Together with theories of who might have been responsible for 'grassing Eric up', to which the most disparaging comments were directed.

Luke felt sick and retired to the toilet for as long as he possibly could, without causing a stir. He wasn't to know that Eric had already been released from the police station, with a date to return to face charges of assaulting a police officer. Or that his lawyer was feeling optimistic that he could get him off with a fine. Eric had finally clicked who the 'Elizabeth' was he had been seeing and had put forward a defence that his despair at her death, exacerbated by the ongoing trial, had caused him to lash out at the officer, when her name was mentioned. Dawson had seen through this excuse for what it was, but accepted that, having already prosecuted the wrong person once in this case, it might be better for everyone to learn some life lessons and move on.

Luke also didn't know that Eric's call to Gerry, in his taxi departing the police station, had quickly revealed the most likely source of the intelligence leading to his arrest. Or that Eric's initial response had been to squeeze his stress ball so hard that it began to disintegrate in his hand, the crumbs littering the floor of his taxi. He didn't know, either, that Gerry, grateful to Luke for the update of the previous day and mindful of the fact that it was he who had identified Liz from her photo, had pointed out to Eric that, even if he claimed ownership of *Midas*, as he was entitled to do, given that it was produced on Valiant time, he probably needed Luke for the finishing touches. And, more importantly, a messy dismissal would almost certainly end their chances with the Olympic selectors.

And finally, he didn't know that, as Eric's fury was beginning to dissipate, although his nose continued to throb, the rearranged meeting invite, from the Olympic representative, pinged its way into Eric's calendar, together with some heartfelt good wishes and reference to how much he was looking forward to meeting both Eric and Luke in the flesh.

So when Gillian ran into the centre of the office and shouted 'They let him go. He's coming,' at the top of her voice and then the message came through that they should all gather for Eric's imminent arrival, Luke was still none the wiser. But more blather and rumour and surmise was prevailing among his colleagues, including the mundane: Eric had failed to pay child support, before Gillian confirmed knowledgeably that wasn't a criminal offence; Eric's unpaid speeding and parking fines (apparently there were many of these) had caught up with him; Eric was behind on the rent.

Of course, the staff, particularly given the substance of their day job, were also imagining, but not voicing, far more distasteful offences to match the speed at which Eric had been dispatched from them; importing automatic weapons from Angola, running a secret methamphetamine lab, diamond smuggling.

Then Eric marched through the door, wide smile on his face and high fived every one of them, making sure his eyes wandered long and searching over Luke's face.

'Team!' he shouted. 'I'm back. Did you miss me?'

'Yes,' they called, some loudly, some half-heartedly.

Eric climbed up onto a chair and then, as it began to spin around, he leaped nimbly onto a desk.

'I said, did you miss me?'

This time everyone roared out 'yes', including Luke, who found himself raising his arm aloft, with the rest of them.

Eric caught Luke's eye a second time and gave him a shallow nod, while simultaneously gritting his teeth and finally reducing his stress ball to dust, deep in his pocket.

Luke breathed again. He was in the clear, for now. '*Side show*', '*tiptoe*', '*touch and go*'.

***

Tom sat with Eve in Wagamama's on Fleet Street. He had, at first, insisted that he wasn't hungry, but then, as a customer at the neighbouring table received a bowl of noodles with a large piece of chargrilled salmon balanced elegantly on the top, he changed his mind and asked to see the menu.

'What did you say to him – to Jaden Dodds? I saw you two talking,' Eve asked, as Tom's glass of 'power juice' arrived.

Tom shrugged. 'Nothing,' he said. 'He just said he was sorry about Mum.'

He took a big gulp of juice and imagined it flowing through his body, like a river of nutrients, feeding his cells and sweeping away the backed-up sludgy residue from his cigarettes. He knew Eve wanted to ask him more – if he was OK, whether he wanted to go back to school, what she should do with him now. He had a pretty clear idea what he wanted himself, but he was going to make her sweat a little. It was nice to have power over someone else, even if only fleetingly.

'What are you thinking?' she asked, rather predictably, after he had ordered 'firecracker chicken'. He didn't tell her. He was thinking that he wanted food which would burn his tongue and scour his insides. Everything about the next twenty-four hours needed to be about purging, expelling, eradicating. Only then could he begin his life anew.

'I was just thinking how hungry I am,' he said, which was true, but only part of the story.

'Me too,' Eve said, reaching out and stroking his hair back from his face. And Tom swallowed hard and sniffed back the tears this time and sat back from her reach, after a polite interval, because, even though Eve looked and sounded nothing like his mum, her touch was almost exactly the same.

***

Jaden marched towards the door of the court, and Judith, who had missed most of his exchange with Constance, ran to keep up with the rest of his entourage. She caught sight of Greg, standing towards the back of the crowd. She lifted her hand to wave at him. She should really go over and thank him. Without his work to open Liz's phone, and then his making sense of her laptop use, they might not ever have found the real culprit. And all she'd done last night was cut him off and talk over him. She hadn't really shown her appreciation for all he had done. Then, suddenly, the crowd around her surged and, when she looked again, he had disappeared.

Judith took out her phone. She thought for a few seconds and then she typed in: 'Dinner tonight 7pm, Lemonia,' and sent her message. As she headed towards the fresh air, her phone vibrated to inform her she'd received a reply.

Jaden burst out through the main doors of the court building, flanked by Constance and Nathaniel. He stood, illuminated in the flashlights of a dozen cameras, amid calls of 'Mr Dodds, over here!', 'Jaden, Jaden, give us a wave!'

'Now?' he asked Constance.

'Yes,' she said, squeezing his elbow, for reassurance. 'Now.'

Jaden stepped forward and gave the press a broad smile. When they continued to pepper him with questions, Constance waved at them to quieten down.

'Ladies and gentlemen, my client would like to make a statement please. If you could do him the courtesy of allowing him to do so.'

The crowd ceased their chatter and Jaden stood tall and glorious. And then, in a deep and resonant voice, he started to speak.

'This has been a very difficult time for me,' he began, sneaking a sideways glance at Constance, who nodded to him to continue. 'I was wrongly accused of a terrible crime…well three terrible crimes. Sometimes, I closed my eyes at night and hoped that when I opened them in the morning, I would find it was all a bad dream.

'But I don't blame nobody. I was just one of those guys – in the wrong place at the wrong time. Nobody treated me bad. It's just that, being in jail, as I have been, since November 4th, it's not the greatest. You realise all the things you miss: your friends, your followers, pizza at midnight, the rain on your face.

'In fact, I think I've been lucky. Everyone says the justice system in this country is rubbish: delays, falling down buildings, that people like me can't get justice. Not for me. I had a fair trial and the truth came out. I have no complaints. I want to thank my lawyers for making it happen and my best friend, Nath, for being by my side always.

'The last thing I wanted to say was about Liz, the lady who died. I liked her the second I met her and, during the trial, I heard about all the good things she did in her work as a doctor, working so hard to help people, losing her life doing that good work. Sometimes, there's no way of explaining who gets to live till they're old and who gets taken away too young and I've learned there's no point complaining about that. But, if she's watching from up in heaven, I want to say "Liz, you made a mean chocolate cake. Rest in peace". Now I'm going home.'

'Jaden, over here. Will you continue with your show, after all that's happened?' A reporter from the *Mail* shouted at him.

Jaden thought for a moment. 'What day is it?' he asked.

'It's Friday.'

Jaden smiled to himself and looked at Nathaniel. Then he placed one arm through Nathaniel's and they began to walk away.

'Sure,' he called out, over his shoulder. 'We'll do a midnight special.'

Then he hailed a taxi and the two of them clambered in and drove away, photographers flashing as they left.

'Well,' Judith said to Constance. 'That's not quite what I expected.'

Constance laughed. 'Me neither.'

They began to walk away from the reporters and the courtroom, ignoring requests to say anything more.

'Will you be watching?' Constance asked Judith.

'What? The JD & Nath homecoming special. It's tempting, but I may just have a dinner date.'

'With Greg?'

'It might be.'

'I'm pleased to hear that.'

'But there could be time for you and me to have a tiny celebratory drink first. What do you think?'

'It's not even four o'clock!'

'Oh come on. Let's live dangerously. Just this once!'

And Constance and Judith linked arms themselves and walked up the street towards the Viaduct Tavern, where a very early happy hour was about to begin.

THE END

ACKNOWLEDGEMENTS

Without dwelling on the past 18 months too much, for obvious reasons, *The Midas Game*, my fifth Burton & Lamb novel, is my lockdown book; written in its entirety during 2020 and the coronavirus (COVID-19) pandemic. In some ways, the virus provided more opportunities to write – I had cut short a legal assignment to support two of my boys through exams which never happened – but in others more challenges. I was no longer permitted to spend hours at a time alone with my thoughts. I now had to go shopping in person for groceries, cook family meals at least twice a day and learn new skills, like hairdressing, basic plumbing and motivational speaking. Eventually, despite those distractions, I made it past the post, with thanks to the following people/organisations:

One of the main influences for this story was the work of COST Action CA 16207, *'European Network for Problematic Usage of the Internet', supported by COST (European Cooperation in Science and Technology)* www.cost.eu working in collaboration with:

the International College of Obsessive Compulsive Spectrum Disorders (ICOCS) and the Obsessive-Compulsive and Related Disorders Research Network (OCRN) of the European College of Neuropsychopharmacology (ECNP), and the Anxiety and Obsessive-Compulsive Disorders Scientific Section of the World Psychiatric Association (WPA).

This was a four-year long initiative, bringing international experts together to advance the understanding of 'problematic use of the internet' (or PUI), to clarify its causes and to develop effective interventions. My sister, Professor Naomi A Fineberg, Professor of Psychiatry at the University of Hertfordshire and Consultant Psychiatrist at Hertfordshire Partnership University NHS Foundation Trust, chairs this COST Action, and it was her sharing her interest with me, which led to my desire to learn more.

Thank you, then, to Professor Fineberg and your Network, for stimulating my interest in the first place and then, for providing me with links to numerous research papers, answering my questions regarding brain imaging, the impact of the World Health Organisation (WHO) classification of online gaming as a disorder and possible treatment for sufferers.

I am also grateful to Professor Marc N Potenza, Director, Division on Addictions Research at Yale University; Director, Yale Center of Excellence in Gambling Research; Director, Women and Addictions Core of Women's Health Research at Yale University and Professor of Psychiatry, Child Study and Neurobiology at the Yale University School of Medicine, USA, for providing me with considerable background on addiction to gaming and its impact, for directing me to various self-help websites, for providing an insight into competitive Esports and for explaining what features of online games tend to be the most problematic and why.

Thank you (again) to Dr Stuart J Hamilton, Home Office Registered Forensic Pathologist, for your clear and insightful advice regarding hypertrophic cardiomyopathy (or HCM), medical drug interactions and evidence of rape.

My thanks, as always, go to all the team at Lightning Books: to Dan Hiscocks for his continued support and belief in my abilities, to Scott Pack for his incredible editing skills and guidance, to Amber Choudhary at Midas PR for her superb marketing skills and Simon Edge for his novel and highly creative publicity strategies, to Hugh Brune for his enthusiastic sales campaign, to Nell Wood for the fabulous cover design, to Clio Mitchell for meticulous copyediting and typesetting and Rosemarie Malyon for attentive proofreading.

I must, of course, also acknowledge the enormous contribution of my parents, Jacqie and the late Sidney Fineberg, both inspirational teachers, who encouraged me and my sisters to spend all our waking hours reading.

Finally, a gigantic thank you goes to everyone who has reviewed this story or any of *The Rapunzel Act, The Cinderella Plan, The Aladdin Trial* and my first novel, *The Pinocchio Brief,* for taking the time to read my books and share their views in a variety of ways; including in radio broadcasts, space in some of our most prestigious national publications, for hosting me on their blogs and websites and for taking the time to post online reviews. Their support has provided me with the confidence to continue writing and, without their backing, I would not have been able to reach such a wide audience; I am forever indebted.

ABOUT THE AUTHOR

Yorkshire-bred, Abi Silver is a lawyer by profession. She lives in Hertfordshire with her husband and three sons. Her first courtroom thriller featuring the legal duo Judith Burton and Constance Lamb, *The Pinocchio Brief*, was published by Lightning Books in 2017 and was shortlisted for the Waverton Good Read Award. Her follow-up, *The Aladdin Trial*, featuring the same legal team, was published in 2018, with *The Cinderella Plan* following in 2019, and *The Rapunzel Act* in 2021.

If you have enjoyed *The Midas Game*, do please help us spread the word – by posting a review on Amazon (you don't need to have bought the book there) or Goodreads; by posting something on social media; or in the old-fashioned way by simply telling your friends or family about it.

Book publishing is a very competitive business these days, in a saturated market, and small independent publishers such as ourselves are often crowded out by the big houses. Support from readers like you can make all the difference to a book's success.

Many thanks.

Dan Hiscocks
Publisher
Lightning Books

'A first-rate
courtroom drama'
DAILY MAIL

ABI SILVER

A BURTON & LAMB CASE

THE PINOCCHIO
BRIEF

The Pinocchio Brief

A 15-year-old schoolboy is accused of the brutal murder of one of his teachers.

His lawyers – the guarded veteran, Judith, and the energetic young solicitor, Constance – begin a desperate pursuit of the truth, revealing uncomfortable secrets about the teacher and the school.

But Judith has her own secrets which she risks exposing when it is announced that a new lie-detecting device, nicknamed Pinocchio, will be used during the trial. And is the accused, a troubled boy who loves challenges, trying to help them or not?

The Pinocchio Brief is a gripping courtroom thriller which confronts our assumptions about truth and our increasing reliance on technology.

'An intense and
compelling legal drama
– quite wonderful'
GEOFFREY WANSELL

ABI SILVER
A BURTON & LAMB CASE
THE ALADDIN
TRIAL

The Aladdin Trial

When an elderly artist plunges one hundred feet to her death at a London hospital, the police sense foul play.

The hospital cleaner, a Syrian refugee, is arrested for her murder. He protests his innocence, but why has he given the woman the story of Aladdin to read, and why does he shake uncontrollably in times of stress?

Judith Burton and Constance Lamb reunite to defend a man the media has already convicted. In a spellbinding courtroom confrontation in which they once more grapple with all-too-possible developments in artificial intelligence, they uncover not only the cleaner's secrets, but also those of the artist's family, her lawyer and the hospital.

A new Burton and Lamb legal thriller with an AI twist from the author of the acclaimed *The Pinocchio Brief.*

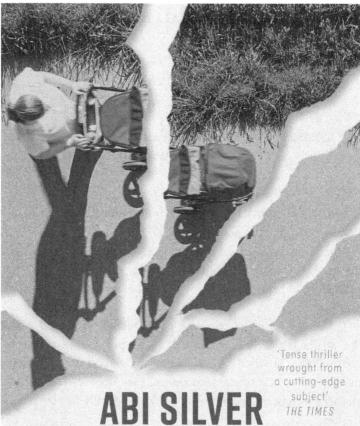

'Tense thriller
wrought from
a cutting-edge
subject'
THE TIMES

ABI SILVER

A BURTON & LAMB CASE

THE CINDERELLA
PLAN

The Cinderella Plan

Tense thriller wrought from a cutting-edge subject
– *The Times*

James Salisbury, the owner of a British car manufacturer, ploughs his 'self-drive' car into a young family, with deadly consequences. Will the car's 'black box' reveal what really happened or will the industry, poised to launch these products to an eager public, close ranks to cover things up?

James himself faces a personal dilemma. If it is proved that he was driving the car he may go to prison. But if he is found innocent, and the autonomous car is to blame, the business he has spent most of his life building, and his dream of safer transport for all, may collapse.

Lawyers Judith Burton and Constance Lamb team up once again, this time to defend a man who may not want to go free, in a case that asks difficult questions about the speed at which technology is taking over our lives.

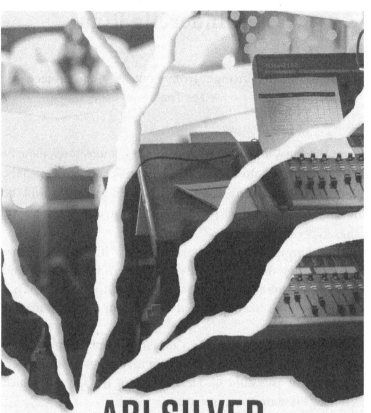

ABI SILVER
A BURTON & LAMB CASE
THE RAPUNZEL ACT

The Rapunzel Act

Can you find justice…when the world is watching?

When breakfast TV host and nation's darling, Rosie Harper, is found brutally murdered at home, suspicion falls on her spouse, formerly international football star, Danny 'walks on water' Mallard, now living out of the public eye as trans woman, Debbie.

Not only must Debbie challenge the hard evidence against her, including her blood-drenched glove at the scene of the crime, she must also contend with the nation's prejudices, as the trial is broadcast live, turning it into a public spectacle. For someone trying to live their life without judgment, it might just be too much to bear.

Legal duo Judith Burton and Constance Lamb are subjected to unyielding scrutiny as they strive to defend their most famous client yet.

Another thought-provoking courtroom drama from the acclaimed author of the Burton & Lamb series.